– Liverpool –
MMXXIII

LAMB

dead ink

First published in Great Britain in 2023 by Dead Ink,
an imprint of Cinder House Publishing Limited.

Print ISBN 9781915368041
eBook ISBN 9781915368058

Cover design by Luke Bird / lukebird.co.uk
Typeset by Laura Jones / lauraflojo.com
Editing by Gary Budden
Copy edit by Dan Coxon

Printed and bound in Great Britain by TJ Books Limited.

www.deadinkbooks.com

Supported using public funding by
ARTS COUNCIL
ENGLAND

Funded by
UK Government

LAMB

MATT HILL

dead ink

To Julia and Julia

PART ONE

DOUGIE

Dougie Alport was a lorry driver and proud, in that particular way northern men can be. He usually spoke to his son Boyd with indifference, his wife Maureen with his mouth full, or not at all. Lately he seemed glad to have fathered an only child; Maureen, at her most resentful, said he only liked being home when Boyd was asleep.

Dougie's lorry-cab was a modern hybrid, which he parked outside the house so he could keep an eye on it after hours. Boyd, an anxious sleeper, often woke to Dougie's pre-dawn alarm and went to the window to watch his father leave. He'd wonder where the day was taking his father, what he'd do there, and whether he'd come back any happier. Then, at night, when Dougie's cab returned with the unmistakable sound of airbrakes and cooling fans, Boyd would get up to watch his father emerge, that characteristic dark stripe of sweat where the seat belt had crossed his T-shirt. It wasn't that Boyd wanted to be noticed by his father, he told himself – it was that he wanted to understand him, find a way to reach him. Boyd would listen to Dougie hobble inside, take his dinner from the microwave, and watch the news until he fell asleep. In long-distance hauling you paid for your insurance and your tax, your fees, and your fuel card, but the real toll was paid with your body.

LAMB

On the day Dougie died, Boyd didn't hear his father's alarm, not knowing – not yet – that it had never been set. The morning was otherwise unremarkable. Maureen rinsed the soaked pots while Boyd filled Red the cat's saucer. Maureen made coffee while Boyd portioned out their cereal. Mother and son ate together, shared small talk, accepted their lot. Neither of them had seen Dougie since last night, but the cab was gone, and his phone was ringing out, so they agreed he must have gone on a longer run than usual. Cleaning up, however, Boyd noticed Dougie's job sheet face down on the table. It looked pristine, unread. Boyd turned it over. There were no oily finger marks, no coffee rings.

'Shouldn't he have that with him?' Maureen asked. Boyd leafed through it; his father was due up in Carlisle to collect EU pallets and assorted loose freight from a Scots-run customs facility. It sounded a simple enough contract – the warehouse crew had automatic jibs, built for quick loading – and, going by the route, getting there would need little thought or planning. Dougie's trailer would be empty from the depot, and motorway traffic was slight at five in the morning. He'd engage his tachometer and leave the auto-pilot running. 'Maybe the lads on site already know him,' Maureen said. Boyd nodded, half convinced, and pictured his father in the cab. He'd be well on his way now. Half an eye on his progress, flask of coffee between his thighs, swearing at having to take his mandated rest breaks. If Boyd's maths were right, Dougie would be home by nine. Boyd would come in from school, help his mother with chores, and turn in with a book. So he wouldn't fall asleep, so he wouldn't miss his father's return, he'd read on his belly until the cab pulled up.

The Alports lived in an ex-council house on the outskirts of Watford. There were four of them: Dougie, Maureen, Boyd and Red, the ginger tabby they'd inherited from a long-dead neighbour. They'd settled near Watford because Dougie's haulage firm had a yard up the road, itself situated for easy access to the M25 orbital and the rest of the country's motorway network. It was a decision, Maureen later told the police, they hoped might protect their scant family time. In fact, the yard was so close that Red sometimes followed Dougie on his short drive round there. Dougie swore she was cheating on them with another household, but indulged the mystery anyway. Red would loiter, make sure Dougie had spotted her, shift her head fractionally, teasingly, and make a distinctive squawk. Then she'd dart up the railway line towards London, mission unknown. Like Boyd at his bedroom window, Maureen at the sink, Red's movements were habitual, bound to Dougie. That she was also absent that morning made perfect sense.

Except Dougie was still in Watford. Having collected his trailer from the depot, Dougie had diverged from his marked route and peeled into Watford's oldest industrial estate, now mostly derelict and likely to stay so. Here, he'd driven to a mothballed factory unit he was subletting under a false name, paid for with cryptocurrency no one knew he owned, and nosed the lorry through its hangar-style doors.

Exactly what Dougie did inside the unit would later become a source of intense press speculation. But the best anybody could tell, he turned on a generator and a series of high-powered floodlamps, uncoupled the trailer from his cab with a mini-crane, and set about clearing his belongings from the dash and glovebox. Next, he pulled the dustsheet from a second lorry-cab, parked in the centre of the unit, and manoeuvred the mini-crane into position above it. According to the tabloids, he chose this moment to stand and admire his work. Because this second cab was Dougie's great and terrible secret, his months-long project: a pre-ban diesel whose bones he'd salvaged from local scrapyards, whose rust-eaten body panels he'd single-handedly scoured and refinished, and whose moving parts he'd carefully uprated. The cab now had an adapted tractor engine, performance filters, and a second, more powerful turbocharger. At each corner were heavier springs and dampers. And underneath, the chassis had been reinforced with welded steel braces. All these modifications were intended to cope with the unit's extra power and added weight; using a set of crude moulds, Dougie had also layered the cab's body, windows, fuel tanks and undercarriage with a composite of steel and concrete. The result was a fearsome protective shell he nicknamed 'road metal' in notes found during a warranted search of the unit. (Investigators later admitted their scepticism; none could bring themselves to write 'armoured' until some of the cab's panels were measured at four inches thick.)

At around six-thirty a.m., surrounded by staging lights, sling chains and a pulley system that spoke to Dougie's commitment, if not his inventiveness, he activated the twenty-ton winch and mini-crane and raised the armoured cab body away from the chassis. From the driver's seat, he used a remote control to reactivate the winch and slowly lowered the armoured shell around himself.

Half an hour later, he was on the motorway, northbound.

There were multiple audio recordings – Maureen and Boyd had to endure them on the second day of the inquest – of other truckers radioing Dougie to ask what he was driving. Their tone was friendly, intrigued, a long way from challenging. ('Having reviewed these tapes again,' the coroner said, 'it does sound like Alport's customised vehicle was regarded as a mild curiosity. Perhaps it was seen as a PR stunt, or a prop for a new film production?')

Dougie had fooled his employers, too. He drove the war-cab so carefully, so assuredly, that even the fleet operations team missed the signs in their data – the apparent drop in fuel efficiency, the lost time. It hardly mattered that Dougie had tampered with his tachometer and refitted his firm's black-box system to maintain the illusion that the original cab was moving. When everybody realised what was actually going on, it was already too late.

Dougie's wayfinder served him a stopover alert just after nine a.m. One of England's new regulations – litigation concern veneered with 'employee safety' – had it that truckers still had to take a break every few hours, as they had in the EU days. Dougie duly pulled in at the next available stop, Lorry Heaven, to maintain his cover; CCTV footage showed the war-cab circling the lot as he deliberated over where to park it. He settled on a far corner, facing a substation enclosure, where the standard trailer obscured the brazen cab and lengthened the odds of somebody asking questions. It did the trick. Despite wide-ranging interviews, not one staff member from Lorry Heaven's canteen, open-air dining area or adult shop recalled Dougie's vehicle being in the car park. And of the truckers already parked up, only two could make a statement. They, like the motorway truckers, had looked, snorted, and dismissed the war-cab as a joke.

The coroner thus saw it fit to send Maureen and Boyd to the scene themselves. Would they recognise something? Had Dougie spoken to them about Lorry Heaven before? Might they have intuited, even unconsciously, his plans? Despite Maureen's protests – how could they know exactly where Dougie went during work hours? – they travelled by police escort the same day. They were paraded through the canteen, the kitchen, the e-cigarette shop, and asked if they knew any of the staff, or if Dougie maintained relationships with any of them. Standing under forbidding clouds, they were made to review aerial maps and questioned on whether Dougie might have left or buried something – evidence – in the wasteland that bounded the site.

'No idea,' Maureen kept saying, exasperated. 'No,' Boyd said, dazed by the visit, by the act of being thrown into his father's professional world. Little wonder the trip affected Boyd profoundly. Over the following days, he complained to Maureen that part of him was still stuck in Lorry Heaven. He could smell the canteen in their own kitchen cupboards. He dreamed of its empty car park, haunted by the sad corrugated huts they'd seen on the other side of the fence – the fly-tipped loads left in wet piles, the abandoned ton-bags full of moss-covered shale – and he woke up sweating. In the dead of night, always Boyd's most restless hours, he questioned whether his father's war-cab had been designed to protect him from those very things. If, when Dougie climbed into that seat, lowered the cab body around himself, he did so because he didn't want to spend any more time alone in places like Lorry Heaven.

The inquest's reporting engineer called Dougie's modified cab a *sarcophagus* in his concluding remarks. On looking it up, Boyd realised he was wrong about his father's intentions. When the cab's stone-like bodyshell had settled over the chassis, there was no way for Dougie to get back out. And so it hit Boyd: he'd never again see his father park up outside the house and clamber down the cab's short steps. He'd never find his way to reach him.

Dougie had re-joined the motorway after Lorry Heaven and placed a twenty-five-second call to Maureen. The coroner asked what he'd said. 'That he loved me,' she replied, wincing in a way that suggested Dougie's words still felt abnormal. 'And that he loved our son.' She couldn't look at Boyd beside her.

'And even then,' the coroner said carefully, 'there were no hints at what he was about to do?'

Maureen scoffed. 'No. He's – he *was* – a quiet man. He was bone-tired all the time. You couldn't get through.' She touched Boyd's shoulder, as if seeking confirmation. Boyd, concentrating on his feet, sniffed and nodded.

The coroner stared at them.

'Don't you think I've gone over it?' Maureen asked. 'Over and over? What else do you want? He'd earned some spare miles, and when he'd picked up his load, he was heading for Barrow-in-Furness. He wanted to park up facing the sea. They have that big wind farm up there, off Walney Island. It goes right across the horizon. He likes things like that—' Her voice caught, and she paused. 'After,' she said, 'he phoned me again and repeated himself. He loves me. He loves us. And the worst thing was, I didn't even listen properly. I had the telly on; I think I was ironing. I even remember thinking he sounded surprised I'd answered. I said something like, "Okay, we love you too." And he went quiet and said, "It's about to rain here," and hung up. And that was that. That was it.'

Boyd glanced at Maureen. She'd welled up, and was squeezing something in her fist. He took her hand and stroked her tendons with his thumb. That she could stand at all was amazing. There was still such strength in her voice, enormous compared to the evening the police had arrived. (He hated thinking of that now. The way she'd knelt by the front door and wailed, 'What? What? What's he done that for?')

Maureen opened her palm to him; inside it was a damp penny. It passed, briefly, into Boyd's own hand, before she snatched it away and put it back her in pocket. He sniffed, confused, and let go. The coin's heat had been incredible.

LAMB

*

Despite his mother's testimony, and the inquest's cold analysis, Boyd blamed himself for what had happened. Not only had he brought in the letter that started the process, but he was convinced they'd all still be at home together if only he'd managed to wake up and knock on his bedroom window in time. He grew obsessed with an image of his father turning away from the cab, noticing, and smiling up at Boyd, suddenly aware of a reason to change course.

But Maureen wouldn't have it. She explained how silly, mundane things took on new meanings in the wake of death, and that it was natural to feel guilty.

'So you feel like I do?' Boyd asked in the hotel bar later.

Maureen's face softened above her glass of wine. She didn't answer.

'Mum, do you feel guilty?'

'I feel angry,' she said. 'That's what it is. I want to bring him back so I can wring his bloody neck.'

Still, Maureen's attempts to reassure Boyd kept failing. Boyd couldn't help himself. He always circled back to the night something broke; the night Dougie had come home earlier than usual and found Maureen and Boyd finishing their chores. The night Dougie, clearly irritated to have company, had sat down to eat a bowl of spaghetti hoops in front of the news. As ever, Boyd understood he should be seen, not heard; that sharing his father's evening time was a privilege. He made Dougie a drink, brought him a yoghurt, asked how his day had been. Dougie only grunted, so Boyd took the hint. He went back to washing up, finished it angrily. While it often stung that, unlike his classmates, he and his father had no football team to support together, no shared hobbies, it was always a wrench to accept that his parents' real conversations only started when he went to bed. He left the room, sharply aware of the distance between them.

Passing through the hall, Boyd found an envelope on the doormat. Bright white, cheap stock, addressed to Douglas Alport. Dougie had stepped on it coming in; Boyd wiped off the boot print and took it through.

'This came.'

Dougie glanced up from his bowl, sauce in his moustache. He was tired, road-blind – it was there in the creases, the lined whites of his eyes. 'What's the matter?' he asked.

Boyd waved the envelope. 'It looks important—'

'Bloody open it then!'

Boyd swallowed and opened it. Inside was a double-sided letter. Recognising his firm's logo, Dougie muted the television and leaned forward. 'What is it? Christ's sakes! Go on – your mother's lost my reading glasses again.'

Boyd cleared his throat and read: 'We regret to inform you that, owing to adverse trading and regulatory conditions, we have reached the difficult decision to make redundancies across the fleet.'

Dougie's mouth closed. He muted the television and settled the spoon in his bowl. Boyd read on. *Phased redistribution of critical workers. A result of long-term planned efficiencies. Increasingly prohibitive refuelling costs. The future.*

'The future,' Dougie hissed, 'can fuck off.'

Boyd waited, silent. Everything inside him felt wrong. He was seeing his father in a way he hadn't before – vulnerable, exposed – and with it came a sense of entering freefall. He wanted to comfort his father but didn't know where to start. Where, even, to put his arms. Maybe around the neck, or across the shoulders? He rubbed the back of his own neck instead. His hands were clammy.

'Get Maureen,' Dougie snapped. 'Fetch me your bloody mother.' And just like that he was calm again, all that fragility back under the skin.

But Maureen being Maureen had heard them already. She marched in and immediately asked Boyd what he'd done, a presumption that wounded him. He flashed her the letter. Maureen stood over Dougie, meek in his chair, as pathetic as Boyd. He'd spilled spaghetti hoops down his front. She saw that she had to take charge.

'Come on then,' she said.

Boyd passed Maureen the letter. After what seemed a long time, she said, 'We'll have to tell them, Doug. Tonight.' Her scowl suggested she was disappointed in them both. She leaned over Dougie, who was gaping at the silent television. The hems of her jogging bottoms caught on her heels, and Boyd was uncomfortable to see the pale flesh of her hips, her stretch marks.

'Doug?'

'I don't know,' Dougie replied.

Maureen nodded to herself, mind already working. 'Yeah, we'll have to tell them,' she said. 'We won't be able to afford the rent on this place.' She pointed to a section of the letter, incredulous. 'Are you *listening*, Doug? It says it right here, black and white: "Your circumstances have changed. Consultations will begin next week. By signing this letter, you accept these terms."'

'They've already wiped out our pensions,' Dougie replied feebly. 'Does this mean they'll not pay owed holiday, either? None of it, Maur? We've got two months' cash, tops, in the building society. That's it.'

'Then don't be so bloody proud,' Maureen said. 'We'll move, and you'll find something else. Another firm.'

'They'll only do the same to me there!' he shouted. 'What good am I going to be when everything's gone full auto?'

'You'll find something else. You'll be *good* at something else.'

'Like what! Factory inspections? Making sure some chirpy fucking robot's painted its lines on straight?' Dougie grimaced at her, or else at the changing world, and slumped back with his eyes closed. Boyd, watching, wondered if his father might be trying to stop himself from breathing.

'Shall I go?' he asked his mother quietly.

Maureen nodded once.

Boyd went up to his room. Reading didn't work – the words were a jumble. He thought about going to the window, looking out on the cab. To see if it was really there, or if this was all a dream he'd wake from, and soon. But he couldn't find the energy to move. He wrapped his pillow round his head and listened to his parents' muffled arguing for hours.

Afterwards – after what Dougie did next – but before the inquest and the reparations, the flattening grief, Maureen reminisced with Boyd about the fact Dougie had wanted to drive trucks ever since she'd met him. She spoke with a new fondness for her husband, an affection Boyd had rarely seen or heard before. It was as if Dougie's death had reminded her how she truly felt about him, or that she'd only weather his loss if she escaped to happier memories. Either way, she didn't stop. Dougie had caught the bug because he liked driving cars, always had. Yes, she'd some-times worried it was old-fashioned to let Dougie drive her everywhere – but how could she not enjoy his enthusiasm? He loved long journeys under big skies. He was a sucker for quiet stretches, country or motorway, where he could plant his foot. There was one section of the M6, she said, which channelled you into the Lake District, where the fells rolled up on either side. It wasn't *that* picturesque. But it had a feeling. You knew you were about to get there when Dougie started grinning.

Boyd believed her, even if he found their romance hard to see. The thought of them together, alone. 'We did have something,' Maureen assured him. 'What you don't understand is that growing up really gets in the way.'

She continued. The young Alports had bought a modest second-hand caravan just after Boyd's third birthday, which they towed all over the Western Isles of Scotland, along the raw Northumbrian coast, into deepest Devon, between touring sites along the Jurassic Coast. ('You don't remember *any* of that?' she asked, almost insecurely.) All of which was why lorry driving came naturally to Dougie; it was the logical next step. It was driving and caravanning in one, and as a bonus you were paid for it. The cab even had Wi-Fi built in, and before an American corporation absorbed the firm for tax relief, you could buy yourself a games console through a salary sacrifice scheme.

Boyd listened intently, beginning to understand the things he'd always wanted to understand about his father's job, and in turn his father. Soon they moved to Dougie's stories, the characters Boyd heard snippets about from his bedroom, from the top of the stairs, from behind a book. It was true, Maureen admitted, that Dougie kept strange friends. Certainly in the early days, before the weariness, he'd been on some adventures. Dougie was known for the sparseness of his cab, his unusually practical choices. He never went in for the Christmas tree lights, the personalised number plate in the window, the football scarf. He used a fridge, a custom-made cup holder, and a pedal bin he cleaned fastidiously. He wasn't picky about his acquaintances, either – there were even traffic officers he knew by name. (One officer, the inquest revealed, used to let Dougie fly her reconnaissance drone from a roadside café on the A1M, and was genuinely distressed to hear what he'd done.)

'And what do you think of all that?' she asked.

While Boyd couldn't match Maureen's stories, was still too young to fathom the depths and layered intimacies of a long marriage, he did have one of his own. It was the only story Dougie ever told him directly, and it mattered to Boyd that Maureen made the space for him to share it.

It was about the time Dougie had met another haulier in the toilets of a Clitheroe service station. The haulier was a Yorkshireman, a road veteran who liked you to know it. He wore a mesh cap like an American trucker. He had thick sideburns, tattoos of wounded seraphim up each forearm, and no sense of discretion – he engaged Dougie mid-flow at the urinals. He asked if Dougie's cab was the green-wrapped hybrid out the front, so that straight away Dougie knew where the conversation was going. (Trying to signal progressivism to an increasingly cynical public, haulage firms were wrapping their hybrids in neon greens and twee messaging about sustainability, a fad which made their drivers a target of derision for the old guard.) Dougie ignored the Yorkshireman, finished his business. But the Yorkshireman was persistent. 'How many miles? What's the range on that pussy-wagon?' He followed Dougie to the washbasins, the driers, out to the canteen.

When Dougie bought soup and a sausage roll to dip in it, the Yorkshireman sat opposite and watched him eat. ('I couldn't shake him,' Dougie told Boyd. 'He had this intensity, like a smell.') When Dougie finished eating, the Yorkshireman followed Dougie out to his cab. There he shared some of his own tales, detailed in lurid ways the wants and needs that cab life, road life, could never fulfil. And at this point in the story, Dougie had taken out his wallet and passed to Boyd a yellowed newspaper clipping from the rear sleeve. 'You like to read, don't you?' he asked. And Boyd smiled, because he did, and felt understood. The article was about a lorry driver who'd been found guilty of murdering a young cleaner in his cab. Being imaginative, Boyd pictured it all, spinning out the hinted-at descriptions of what the Yorkshireman had done with the body. It made him feel homesick, even though he was sitting with Dougie in their kitchen. 'Exact same bloke I met in the bogs,' Dougie said. 'And I'll tell you, son: a lorry cab is a tiny place to do all that to someone.'

'Do you think he'd have—' Boyd started.

Dougie shushed him. 'The trick,' he said, 'is never noticing how close you've been.'

Maureen smiled when Boyd was done. She seemed unperturbed by the story; if anything, she was proud he'd told it so well. She wiped her eyes, blew her nose, and said, 'You know, for a minute, he was sitting right here.'

The inquest concluded that Dougie was inspired to armour his cab by old combat videos from Iraq. Records showed he'd watched hundreds of hours of footage over a three-month period, and had searched extensively around makeshift tanks, improvised explosive devices, and ballistics. The inquest heard that US troops had their own term for it: hillbilly armour. To counter new threats in a fast-changing theatre, troops used to bond extra materials to their vehicles. Dougie, seeing a crisis overtaking him, had set out to do the same.

These revelations were hardest on Maureen, who began to grasp how well-planned Dougie's mission was. The body of evidence spoke to a kind of warped emotional affair, whose reminders kept turning up long after they returned to the Watford house. They'd find scraps of paper in Dougie's pockets, stuffed in old boots, secreted in drawers between receipts Maureen never checked or threw out. There were contact details for metal fabricators, panel-beaters, mechanics, welders, labourers – people who might in their own way have contributed to the whole – as well as lists of the passwords that secured his crypto wallets. Dougie had even used some of Boyd's old exercise books to scrawl notes about people willing to give him a crash-course in wiring, plate-setting, or contribute a few hours' work for cash.

Bereavement was a weak word for what Dougie left behind. But the worst pain came from his actions making so little sense. Any angle you came at it, any room you went in, you found a new betrayal, and each discovery added to Maureen and Boyd's guilt, their shame, and a growing burden they shared: even with their love, they hadn't done enough to save him.

Boyd, meanwhile, took comfort from his mother's stories. He had to trust his father had still loved being on the road as the end approached. That while the industry was moving against him – cameras, speed limiters, ever-stricter parameters on rest time – and redundancy loomed, Dougie had still taken pleasure from driving, from being out there, untouchable in his war-cab.

Boyd also had to trust that Dougie would miss them. Had he thought of Maureen, of Boyd, of Red the cat? His two fleeting phone calls to Maureen suggested so, which helped. But had it pained him to make his decision? Were there any second thoughts? Or had he allowed himself to close over, callus up, become that bit too used to being isolated, alienated, just as many older drivers warned?

Under a bright sun, Dougie's hillbilly-armoured lorry approached the Bolton-based headquarters of the firm he judged to have robbed his future. By then the police had been following him for seventy miles, themselves trailed by drones, news helicopters and fire service support vehicles. None knew that inside the cab, Dougie was using a home-made periscope and live cameras to track them. Nor did they know he'd planned for interventions.

Boyd never saw the chase live, being at school on the day, but he watched every recorded minute from the itchy beige seat in the inquest room. For him the footage took on a filmic quality, an otherness, and as with Lorry Heaven, he carried certain images into his dreams. The convoy was a funeral procession; it had its own iconography. Sometimes he sat beside his father in the cab, suffocating. On the roof of the trailer, Dougie had neatly stencilled the words AUTOMATION IS ANGLOCIDE, so that everyone streaming could derive a motive. Here was a man who'd received a vision, saw the wolves circling, and had made ready. Here was a man trying to say: 'Sometimes you have to draw a line.'

Though they had friendly colleagues call him, Dougie never responded – he'd sewn a basic Faraday cage into the cab's liner, which, when turned on, rendered the cab mute. Though the police tried spike-strips to slow him, Dougie had fitted run-flat tyres. And though several vehicles, including police horse trucks, attempted tactical contact, the armoured lorry was far too heavy to stop. When marksmen took turns shooting at the cab, the fuel tanks, the wheels, their rounds scuffed his armour at best.

Dougie arrived at Native Innovation business park close to one p.m., ran his truck straight through the parking barrier, and breached the lobby at fifty-three miles per hour. The impact destroyed the building's façade and reception area, before the cab laboured on through multiple stud walls, bringing down large sections of the first floor. The cab was finally arrested by a reinforced pillar two metres shy of the chief executive's office, where falling debris crushed its roof. A small electrical fire broke out and was doused by the building's automatic sprinkler system. The truck fell silent.

Nobody in the building was injured. By sheer coincidence, the monthly fire test had started ten minutes before, and the entire staff was gathered around a smoking shelter in the car park. Witness accounts spoke of people standing silently as multiple sirens approached, as Dougie's lorry burst onto the site. It was deemed unlikely that he even saw the crowd. Police officers declared Dougie dead five hours later, when firefighters with sonar and specialist cutting equipment peeled open the hull, and a bomb disposal team cleared the vehicle. Beside Dougie's partially clothed body was a two-litre lemonade bottle part-filled with urine, a three-season sleeping bag, half a flask of tea, and an unopened pack of chocolate biscuits. Two desk fans had been rigged to a leisure battery. In the sleeping compartment were several canisters of oxygen with masks, an air purifier, and a cheap phone containing a pay-as-you-go SIM card. There were no offensive weapons in the cab. Dougie had placed his fuel card and driver's licence on the passenger seat. Alcohol and talcum powder on the steering wheel and console, and on door handles and crane controls at the Watford lock-up, were later linked to four sanitising wipes and surgical gloves found in Dougie's pockets.

The pathologist recorded trace alcohol and no other stimulants in Dougie's bloodstream. Of some interest was a wrap of sheet moss taped to Dougie's left palm, rolled up and secured like a napkin by his wedding ring. The moss was later matched to a sample taken from the Alport family's rear patio. Maureen gave no comment. Boyd took from the brevity of discussion, and the coroner's sympathetic tone, that his father had simply wanted to take a piece of home with him.

But no, there was no note. There were no messages on Dougie's burner phone. Dougie had died of asphyxiation, hanged from the cab's rear-view mirror with his company lanyard.

Boyd, Dougie's only son, was fifteen years old.

DAMP

Maureen sent Boyd to school on the morning of Dougie's cremation. Boyd went alone, sat in the common room with toast from the canteen, and played truant in the toilets till the bell went for first break. His second lesson was biology, during which Mrs Heywood noticed yet tolerated his detachment. The other kids swerved him, avoiding eye contact. Since news of Boyd's father had broken, they hadn't been able to find the right words, found his sadness too vast to broach. Which Boyd accepted – it wasn't much different for him.

It was Mr Williams, a solemn but gentle maths teacher, who walked Boyd out to the gates during lunch. 'You know you can call me Eddie?' he said, offering a hand. It was warm in the sun, and dozens of children were playing with clumps of freshly mown grass on the football field. Most of them noticed Boyd as he passed, slowly stopped to watch. Boyd, sweating, felt as if he should be standing over there with them, watching himself from a distance, from outside himself. None of it – the sun, the grass, the shoes on his feet – seemed fully real.

'Are you all right?' Eddie said.

Boyd squinted at the teacher and turned back to the field. An older boy waved awkwardly from the hip. Boyd didn't know what to say. He was forever separated from his peers, now. And what would he even call the feeling? A numbness, a heaviness, a constant churning. But there was also a thread of relief: the idea of his father being stuck in a freezer drawer, like a murder victim in one of those programmes his mother often watched, had been troubling him for weeks.

He said to Eddie, 'Do you think I should be all right?'

Eddie gave Boyd a strange, thin smile. A lot of adults had been doing this since the inquest. Boyd lived in a more candid, colder world now, yet lacked the means to keep up with its rules.

'It's all right to feel whatever you feel,' Eddie said.

'Then I hate it,' Boyd replied.

Eddie straightened Boyd's tie for him. 'It'll feel better after the service,' he said. And he went to add more, clearly wanted to, but stopped himself. He settled for a platitude: 'We think you're doing very well.'

Boyd nodded politely. He'd heard this sentiment, too. 'I haven't been to a cremation before,' he said. 'Does it smell?'

Eddie blinked at him. 'It's… quiet. It's peaceful.'

'And you don't hear the fire, or anything like that?'

'I don't think so, no—'

'Zara swears she heard her uncle crackling.'

Eddie shook his head. 'She's mistaken, there—'

'She said your ashes get mixed up with dogs'. And they steal your jewellery.'

'I don't think that's true, either, Boyd. It's a delicate job.'

Boyd sniffed. 'And it won't take longer cos he's been frozen? Cos that's what Krish told me. He said if you're too cold to start with, it costs your family more. The gas bill.'

Eddie pulled his tight smile again. 'I'm disappointed they've spoken to you like that. They're old enough to know better.'

The two of them stood there a while longer. There was a helicopter going over, and Boyd wished he were on it. Then he thought of his father's convoy, all the helicopters that had followed it, and wished instead that he could crawl out of himself. He wanted to stop and be asleep, except without the dreams. Or to be somewhere else, *someone* else. Finally, the taxi arrived. The rear windows were tinted, so Boyd couldn't see his mother properly. All the same, he knew from her faint outline that she was facing the other way.

'That's you,' Eddie said, and gave Boyd a chummy clap on the back.

The taxi door slid open. Boyd saw his mother's heels, her bobbled winter tights, the tails of her long overcoat. She didn't lean to greet him. He sat next to her on the rear bench. She didn't speak, either. Beneath her perfume, the soapy scent of her make-up, there was a sharp, musty smell.

Boyd put on his seat belt.

'Ready?' the driver said.

Outside, Eddie the teacher raised a hand. The same awkward wave the older boy had offered from the field.

After the funeral, where Boyd kept his head low and his eyes mostly closed, Maureen and Boyd returned to Watford and entered a weird limbo, waiting on paperwork, for answers, for whatever came next. The problem was, the outside was beginning to push back in. Every morning, packages of unhinged, admiring letters, supposedly screened by their caseworker, were being delivered to the door, while Dougie and Maureen's joint account was still being frozen and unfrozen as investigators continued to analyse Dougie's transactions. And the creditors were starting to call.

In response, Maureen turned inwards, away from any accountability. She divided up their chores as she always had, but did so like a robot, as if she were trying to perform her life using faulty memories as cues. She'd say things like, 'Your father loved that,' and, 'Be a love and check if he wants one,' without specifying anything. She'd appear in the doorway with, 'Turn down the telly so you don't wake him.' And she regularly served three plates before putting the third in the microwave, explaining herself with, 'Late one for him tonight.'

Boyd did what he could to cope with the starkness of their situation, Maureen's pain, and tried to get his head around her grief as a force. Without Dougie, they were shipwrecked and adrift, but if they only stayed together, they could be an island. So, aware of her new scent – the must, a dampness on her clothes – he reminded her to shower. Noticing she was spending too much time in bed, he brought her simple things to eat, took sole responsibility for Red. And desperate above all else, he hoped that by being a better son, he might just prove to be enough.

He made a ritual of shredding and burning Dougie's fan letters without reading them. Maureen let him hold her. And when he found Maureen's night-time crying intolerable, he took Dougie's side of his parents' bed, settling into Dougie's impressions in the memory foam. This way they could at least cry together and try to accept their newly shrunken life.

Sometimes they woke with their fingers linked. Other times Boyd would wait for Maureen to fall asleep, then kiss her clammy forehead. But every night without fail he'd lie on his back and watch with grim fascination a patch of damp that was slowly developing on the ceiling above them.

They were going to the post office to withdraw money when Maureen's shakes started. She was trying to hide it from him, pocketing her hands and slowing her pace, but then the tremors reached her voice as well. Eventually she gasped and fell against him in the queue.

'What is it?' Boyd said, straining to keep her upright, feeling her whole body lock and spasm. Frantically he used one hand to search her bag for water, found only used tissues and receipts. She couldn't even speak, her teeth bared and eyes wide, as though she were trapped inside herself. 'Mum?'

'Don't,' she hissed, as people around them began to notice. 'Don't!'

'She's fine,' Boyd told them, though clearly she wasn't. Back outside, pale and clammy, her symptoms abated. She was adamant they'd been trailed by two masked women in an unmarked car. 'They get off on it,' she insisted. 'They sneak about, block our payments. They want us to know they *can*.' But when Boyd scanned and couldn't see anyone, and tried to reassure her, she snarled at him. 'And what do you know about the real world?' she asked. 'Or do *you* blame me, too?'

The same week, they were doing the big shop when Maureen seized up again at the checkout, apparently unable to remember which card to pay with. As her panic rose, sweat came through the headscarf she was using to hide herself, and a smell of turned earth plumed around her. Her hands shook violently as she went through her purse, until there were cards and receipts all over the floor. Boyd, trying not to be humiliated on her behalf, had to guide her outside before taking her purse to pay. Next time, he suggested, they'd use cash. Or he'd start doing the shopping alone.

'Next time,' she said, hissing, 'you'll just *believe* me.'

Then Boyd would hear Maureen on their home phone, placing calls to unknown numbers, begging for something, a terrible pleading in her voice, as if she were being held against her will – only to find the landline socket torn from the wall.

And he found her, one night, with her mouth and nose inside a brown envelope, a terrible heat coming from her body.

'They sent it to me,' she told him, pulling out the contents. 'They were going to throw it.' A sealed polythene bag, labelled EVIDENCE, containing a knot of vegetation and a plain gold band. Dougie's moss wrap and wedding ring. Maureen put the moss back in the envelope and gave Boyd a certain look and said, 'It was his gift to us. But it has nothing, nothing, to do with you.'

Maureen and Boyd learned that, despite the inquest's conclusions, Dougie was being investigated for links to organised terrorism. Dougie was variously part of a nativist dissident group, a climate activist, a member of a neo-Luddite cell, an anarchist radical, a day-zero cultist, and an ultra-nationalist militia leader (their legal counsel said Dougie's naïve use of 'Anglocide' hadn't helped). The charges did Maureen's paranoia no favours; in retaliation, she cancelled Boyd's imminent counselling sessions lest they be used to see whether Dougie might have indoctrinated him.

'They reckon the apple doesn't fall far from the tree,' she said. 'But what do they think you'll do? You're barely ten stone dripping wet.'

Boyd was also at a loss. 'I didn't know what they were on about,' he said, rolling his eyes and affecting a kind of solidarity with her. But given the situation at home, he was disappointed to forgo an outlet. Because the truth of Dougie's motives was harder to carry: he'd acted alone, hadn't told anyone about his project, much less conspired with anybody. As he'd built up his war-cab, he'd also stripped out his internal life. There had been no ripples, none of the telltale signs that Boyd read about in his mother's lurid supermarket magazines. They could try to remake normality all they liked, but the facts were immutable.

She challenged him: 'Do you think we were never happy? Is that it? Do you think we never had fun?'

the bed, as though to plead for help. Boyd followed Maureen only to find her attacking the kitchen wall with a hammer. The whole house stank – heat and mud and metal – as if Maureen, acting on her fever, had drawn it all out. When he found the courage to confront her, she faced him down. The coin was forgotten; apparently, she was now committed to undoing Dougie's handiwork, his mark on their lives. Boyd wanted to placate her, to stop this, so he pulled away the hammer and simply agreed to help. In turn, all their memories, their family photos, his grandmother's art, were soon heaped on the large rug. A new presence in the living room, something made from absence. Boyd wasn't sure what they'd done together, never mind if it would help. But for all the guilt and fear, she was calm again, more like the Maureen he knew. He went to the east-facing window, where dawn light stretched over the motorway and the tiled roofs of their estate.

'You'll need sun cream on today,' Maureen said quietly.

Boyd turned to her.

'You're so precious,' she added.

Maureen let Boyd hold her. He promised himself that he'd try and hug the shame off her, every day. 'We should just move,' he said, as she broke off. 'Get out of Watford, this house. It's hurting you to stay.'

Maureen smiled tenderly.

'I mean it,' he said. 'We could move nearer Nan's care home. I've been thinking about her. That book I wanted to read you – she used to read it to me.'

Maureen sniffed, turned to the light. Boyd saw through her: the face every parent makes when they lack a decent excuse.

'Your nan's too old to have to worry about us,' Maureen said. 'If she'd even recognise us. And it's not a care home – it's a retirement village.'

'It's Nan, Mum. She's—'

'And I'm telling you there's enough on her plate. She won't want the fuss.'

Boyd stared at his feet. Something else he hadn't been told. Was it that Joan was ashamed of them? Did she even know about Dougie?

His mouth was so dry. He said, 'Nan knows about Dad, doesn't she?'

Maureen didn't answer.

She hadn't been at the cremation service, either…

'Get ready for school,' Maureen said coldly.

'I want to know what's going on—'

'Now!'

Boyd sloped upstairs. It was all unspooling, and he couldn't keep up. Maureen's outbursts and shifting temperament. Last night. The idea his mother and grandmother could abandon their closeness. Before Dougie's incident, at least, they'd talked semi-regularly over the landline, always with meaning and laughter. Now their lack of contact was glaring. He sat on the bed, frustrated that, even at his age, Maureen still forbade him from having a mobile, and refused to own one herself. And wouldn't a fresh start do them good? It wasn't like he'd miss anything – he'd hardly been to school the last few months, was unlikely to pass his mock exams. He repaired their pillow wall and pulled the bedcovers around him and thought of other kids whispering about him. The bolder ones with their questions: 'I heard your dad's a murderer. Was he?'

Boyd had always shaken his head, tried his best to explain, but none of them had ever bought it. It wasn't how gossip worked.

After school, Boyd came home to a pair of sports holdalls and a tatty suitcase in the hallway. He shouted for Maureen, who appeared on the landing. 'You were right,' she said, coming down the stairs.

Boyd was dumbfounded. Maureen was lucid, invigorated. Her hair was clean.

'To Nan's?'

'No, no. Up north. And yes, your nan knows.'

He pointed at the bags, puzzled. 'You packed?'

'Essentials.'

'You packed my stuff?'

'Plus a new toothbrush. What's the face for?'

'I didn't—'

She shushed him.

'How, though?' he asked.

'Taxi's on its way – that's a start. There's a house. Somewhere new. You're not as daft as you look, are you?'

'But how will we afford it? What about the landlord for this place? We can't just leave, can we? What about Nan?'

'Beggars can't be choosers, Boyd.'

'I don't—'

Maureen's face had hardened. She coughed thickly. 'It's all sorted.'

Boyd went past her, into the living room. The windows were open. Fresh air, for the first time in a long time. Pale shapes where the picture frames had been. And the pile on the rug had grown: Dougie's clothes and shoes were now on top of the broken picture frames and porcelain.

He tried to ignore the tracery of black mould growing in the far corner. The scent of damp.

Maureen came in behind him. She said, 'He doesn't need it, does he?' And by her face, Boyd could believe she was about to set the pile on fire. When she went upstairs to grab the rest of their toiletries, he retrieved his father's outdoor jacket from the pile and went to the kitchen. The jacket was too big, smelled like old dog, but he didn't care. He ran the sleeve under the tap, like Dougie used to, to check its water-proofing. It was still beading up.

Upstairs, Maureen was banging about again. It sounded like the bathroom shelves were being cleared into a binbag. Boyd took his chance and searched the kitchen drawers for lighters and matches, then threw them all over the back fence.

Maureen returned with an open paper bag from the chemist. It was filled with tablet boxes. These she stuffed in the suitcase before asking Boyd to sit on it while she zipped it closed. She was still smiling, but an awful animal smell rose from her neck.

'Are you sure you're—'

'Ten minutes,' she said.

'*Ten?* What about Red?' Boyd jumped up and darted for the stairs.

'Boyd! Hang *on.*'

He searched his room. His mother's room. Both had been turned over, as if Maureen had been hunting for her coin again. More mould was growing across the landing, and there were balls of dirty newspaper on the carpet where Maureen had obviously tried to clean it off.

'She's down here!' Maureen called.

Boyd hovered on the landing. Red was at the bottom of the stairs, close to Maureen. Boyd went down and knelt and brought Red into him, closing his father's jacket around her. She sank her claws into his shoulder, trying to get out. He held on till she relaxed.

'Did you find it?' he asked Maureen.

A car horn pipped outside.

'That's us,' she said, ignoring him.

Boyd found he had nothing to say. A door closing, like that, on his childhood.

The driver, a severe older woman, waited by the cab's open boot. She helped Maureen load their bags while Boyd put Red in the footwell and strapped himself in. Red coiled up and preened between his feet. Maureen sat in the front. No one spoke. Later, Boyd wondered if Maureen and the driver knew each other; he swore he recognised her. Or was it that when she looked in her rear-view mirror, she recognised him?

Without asking, Boyd opened his window a crack – the damp smell still with them. Red, as though put out by this, hopped between the seats, into Maureen's lap.

The taxi driver dropped Maureen and Boyd in Sile, an old Pennine market town. Their new house was a fully furnished red-brick terrace on a road off the high street. In their first week there, they moved the furniture around until they agreed they'd had their say. Red, meanwhile, conquered the flagstone yard in the back, hunting insects and parading along the wall. It was always overcast. Warnings for unpaid bills arrived, were discarded. Boyd asked Maureen if she wanted him to register them at the local doctor's surgery and dentist, sort their utilities, but she took it personally – as if that were something he only needed to worry about in the old house – and told him to concentrate on settling in.

And yes, Maureen seemed better, generally more together. Her illness, if it could be called that, appeared to have receded. Or at the very least she pretended to smile more. 'Better to have less sun,' she said of Sile's grey climate. To get fresher air than 'all that badness washing off the M25'. And wasn't the water cleaner-tasting, in your tea? It certainly felt different in your hair. Boyd agreed, mainly for a lack of options. He was wary of her brighter mood, but wasn't ungrateful. And he was distracted anyway, adjusting to life as an outsider in Sile. When he tried to orient himself – running small errands, shopping for cat food – he felt too obvious, painfully conscious of his light southern accent.

LAMB

Then it was decided that he should go back to school, to try and prep for his mocks. Boyd said he could just as easily learn from home. Maureen smiled wanly and disagreed. She said, 'I remember being your age. Too self-absorbed to ever think your mum might want her own life.'

They continued to share a bed, but Maureen's new pillow wall was noticeably wider. At least, Boyd thought, there was no damp.

Sile was drab: broken pavements and potholed tarmac, a lattice of speed-limited roads, car parks and one-way streets that converged to feed the busier trunk road out towards the motorway. Boyd's school was three miles away, a community academy whose core specialism was sports science. Boyd, neither sporty nor science-y, a late bloomer physically, dreaded to think what going there might involve. But soon he discovered a peace in solitude. While local kids caught the bus, he walked in beside low fields and overgrown hedgerows, uncovering what felt like a deep and powerful secret. He watched birds and squirrels, foxes and badgers crossing the road ahead. He went in all weathers, and did so happily, calmer in his own company. Even Red left their yard occasionally to escort him to the edges, perhaps recognising Dougie's waterproof jacket. Sometimes, two or three miles out, Sile well behind him, Boyd would stop and marvel as the clouds broke to reveal blue sky, warm light, and imagine he was living in another world, one where Dougie was still around.

And school was fine. While Boyd made no friends – felt no compulsion to – the other kids left him alone, and the teachers treated him indifferently. He learned to use his outsider status, to be a nobody, to have no past. None of these kids seemed to know his story. He was new to them, new to himself.

At home, though, Maureen's paranoia – no longer suppressed by the novelty of their new surroundings – was leaking again. One afternoon, Boyd came in to find her crouched beside a rotten toddler buggy. He recognised the teddy bear swaddled in the seat, and a peaty smell that turned his stomach.

'Turned up,' she said. 'The new tenants in Watford pulled it out of the attic.'

'Why?' he asked. 'Why didn't they throw it?'

'A message? Their way of saying they know where we are.'

'Whose way? The new tenants?'

Maureen rubbed her eyes. She stared at him. 'Not *them*,' she said.

'Who, then?'

Maureen shook her head. Her eyes turned glassy; she kicked the buggy so hard it tipped into the wall. Boyd flinched, moved back. She pointed at him. 'This'd all be easier if *you* were gone as well.'

Her harshness could still take Boyd by surprise. His face burned, but he made a clumsy attempt to hug her. She pushed through his arms and ran up the stairs, started screaming in the bathroom. He went into the lounge and covered his head with cushions. His school trousers were itchy. His mind was full and racing. By way of distraction, he fed Red, and washed up, looked in the cupboards for what he could scrape together for supper.

When Maureen eventually came down, her make-up was gone. There was a clump of hair missing from her temple. 'I'm sorry,' she said, drawing Red between her knees. 'But what your father did nearly gave us away.'

Boyd tried his best to ignore her appearance. The dread acceptance she was relapsing. 'Are we in trouble?' he asked her. 'Is it debt? Are you ill again? You don't tell me anything.' This constant sense his mother was trying to confess what she also needed to hide.

Maureen swerved his questions, went on playing with Red's collar. There were *adult* things in play that she wasn't saying. Some things he couldn't begin to understand.

He reminded her it wasn't their fault. That nobody but Dougie had been hurt.

Maureen simply laughed. Red stared up at him. 'Look at you,' Maureen said softly. 'You've grown up far too fast.'

'But nobody here knows us yet, and never has to. Not if we don't want them to.'

'That's not enough,' Maureen said, standing up. Then, with more purpose, 'Come with me.'

Boyd followed his mother into the yard. She squatted by the downspout from the roof, where rainwater ran over smooth stone. 'We have to believe he's still protecting us,' she said. And she leaned back to let him see the way she'd carefully weaved Dougie's moss into the drain cover.

Boyd worried about what Maureen did while he was out at school. Most days he could leave her sitting on her bed and come back to find her in the exact same place, often with Red's chin on her thigh. As far as he could tell, she liked to nap, to watch TV, to arrange things into piles, and occasionally go to the supermarket. But even when there were other signs of activity, she was furtive. The days when Boyd found takeaway tubs full of greasy brown residue that smelled strongly of fertiliser, along with sachets of rehydration treatment and anti-emetics. Nights he'd find her missing from the bed, the back door open and a draught coming up the stairs. Soil and fragments of vegetation under her nails, gone before he could ask.

Trying to keep her level, Boyd redoubled his efforts to care for her. He continued to feed Red, changed her litter without complaining. He did the weekly shop without seeking

Maureen's approval of the list, weathering comments from a few older lads on the grocery aisle ('Where's your weirdo mam today? Why's Mummy's Boy out on his tod?'). He weeded the yard flagstones, watered Dougie's moss alongside the previous tenant's abandoned plants – rose bush, raspberry, a tragic little cherry tree. In bed, he stroked Maureen's arm when he was sure she was asleep, hoping to smooth out her dreams. And before she roused, he methodically cleaned away the fresh mould on the exterior-facing walls, algae on the window frames.

When this strategy flopped – there were days she barely noticed him – Boyd resolved to take more radical action, and set out to irritate her, to force her back into her personality, or maybe even her role as his mother. He kept his shoes on, brought mud through the lounge and all over the kitchen lino. He left tissues from masturbating in obvious places. He turned on the hot water when she washed, and left Red's litter tray untouched. He played the obnoxious teen to a tee, modelling the surliness of some of his new classmates.

But this, too, was futile, as if Maureen had somehow allowed for it. And on the Friday evening when he purposely burned their pizzas, she brought his charred meal through and set it on his knee, then smiled knowingly and watched as he tried to eat. She said nothing, because there was no need to: she had made herself unreachable.

Boyd started sleeping in his own bedroom after that, and Maureen started drinking. A nightly nip became a glass, which became a bottle. Blind drunk on cheap whisky, she announced to Boyd that she'd miscarried twice before he was conceived. Both babies, she said, had come away from her. He watched her, heartbroken, as she shrugged. 'They were just bad copies,' she said, and left it at that.

*

Maureen had always been striking. In their Watford house, Dougie had kept a picture from their wedding day in his beside cabinet, which Boyd had secretly inherited. Now it lived in his wallet, a neatly folded reminder that there was a time before heartache; a time before him.

In the photo, Maureen wore bronze and cream, gold thread. Her hair glowed red in the light – an autumn wedding, cheaper for it – and behind her a chill-blue sky contrasted red-gold oak leaves. Dougie, gazing at Maureen, wore brown and navy, his hair fashionably longer. Boyd liked the photo because in it his parents were invincible, iconic. If it was them versus the world, then they'd won.

One afternoon, Maureen caught Boyd sitting at the top of the stairs, staring at this photo. She sat down and tapped it. Her breath was sour. She said, 'You wish we were still like that, don't you? Let me tell you: I took four diazepam that morning.' Numb, she wanted to insinuate, was her way into life with Dougie. Boyd said nothing, saw Maureen was being cruel because the good memories pained her as well. She wanted to make it sound as if the two of them getting married and having Boyd was simply a way to meet expectations. Most of all, she wanted to deny the woman in the picture.

'Don't,' Boyd said.

Maureen cocked her head innocently. 'Don't what?'

'A while ago you asked me if I remembered you being happy.'

Maureen pursed her lips. 'And?'

'I'm trying,' he said.

Then it was too late for trying.

The day before his sixteenth birthday, Boyd came home to find the living room floor lined with clingfilm and flattened cardboard boxes. The lights were off, the house was cold, and there was mud on the kitchen lino. Boyd shouted for Maureen, heard fear in his voice. His throat closed up, and he had to lean on the sofa to gather himself. She was definitely home, because the door had been locked and her keys were on their peg, and her coat was in a heap at the bottom of the stairs. He called again. This time a response – a muffled groan. Had she fallen? Was she hurt? Running upstairs, he noticed the bright smells of body odour and sun cream. The bathroom door was closed, but the light was on. He pushed. It wouldn't give.

'It's me,' he said.

'Go away,' someone said. A moment to recognise her voice.

Boyd kicked the door open. A sheet of filthy tarpaulin was hanging from the shower curtain rail. Maureen was crouching naked in the bath, her hair and face slick with grease.

Her eyes fell slowly to him. 'No,' she said. And with uncanny speed, she dragged the tarp down from the rail and wrapped herself in it. 'Don't you *dare*,' she said.

Boyd stood frozen in the doorway, ears keening. 'Were you sick again?' he managed. He could see her arms and chest were covered with sun cream; there were empty bottles all over the floor. The smell of decay was overpowering.

'I can tell it's on you too,' Maureen jeered. 'Growing all over you.'

'What is?'

'Oh, little light. It's *all* coming off you.'

Boyd massaged his throat. It hurt to swallow. 'Let me get you a towel,' he said.

'Fuck off!' she yelled.

'Mum! I'm—'

'Go on! You're all the same!'

'I'm your son!'

And Maureen reared out of the bath, covered in sores and swollen under the cream, her face crimson with rage. 'I'm my own woman! I don't answer to that selfish bastard anymore, and I won't answer to his son!'

Boyd closed the bathroom door and went downstairs. His legs trembled uncontrollably. He considered calling an ambulance, but worried they might take her away; that he'd be just as bad as all the people she'd been paranoid about. Instead, he stood at the sink for a long time, trying to ignore his reflection, the mess on the floor, trying not to cry. Red sauntered through, saw him there, and continued straight to the yard.

The bathroom door stayed shut all evening. Boyd went to bed without cleaning his teeth. He came down the following morning to a birthday card, a bowl of dry cereal, and an engraved spoon from his childhood laid out for him. There was a note under his mug:

Hello love. Happy birthday. I've gone for eggs x

Like nothing had happened. Like none of it had happened.

Maureen began to blank Boyd, far more attentive to the spaces around him. Boyd, out of his depth, kept out of her way, retreating to his room after school, after supper, until she withdrew to her own. In a way, it was better: he was terrified that discussing the bathroom incident might set her against him forever. He'd already lost one parent, and when he thought too hard about what was going on – Maureen giving in to whatever internal battle was consuming her – he could see the beginnings of losing another.

Fresh mould flourished in Maureen's bedroom, and she coughed relentlessly. Their milk soured quickly, and sometimes fresh vegetables turned overnight. Boyd found trails of vomit up the staircase, dark smears on his door jamb, and several times he caught Maureen snacking on still-frozen oven chips, apparently unaware. She'd terrorise Boyd in the early hours, demanding to know where he'd hidden her 'suppressants', then say he was 'working against her' when he protested; that even sun cream would fail him if he 'lay there and allowed himself to be taken over'. And every time, Boyd would cry himself back to sleep, questioning if she was right; if he was somebody else; if he was an imposter living in her house.

So it followed that Boyd fantasised about escaping with Red. Just keep walking, or catch a bus and ride to its last stop, and catch another, and another, until he was lost. Some days, only his fear of Maureen dying brought him home. He'd surely find her turned to broth in a too-hot bath, drunk in her bed, hanging from the coat rail…

Which was around the time that Boyd's school decided to intervene. A report, in which he was noted as an intelligent young man who was increasingly refusing to apply himself, had gone unanswered. There were complaints from other pupils about his clothes, which often smelled sour. His shoes were visibly worn through.

Social workers started visiting the house. Maureen clearly loathed it, begrudged them all, but went along with it. Soon a well-dressed counsellor arrived to see Boyd without prior appointment, and opened with, 'I want to stress that it's fine to feel rubbish,' and, 'You've been through a lot. Some people might call what happened with your dad a huge disturbance.'

Boyd felt himself prickling. He wished he had Red on his lap, to hide behind. 'How do you know about him?' he asked.

'We have a duty of care—'

'I'm not ill,' Boyd said. 'She is. And I've seen stuff like this on the TV. You can't take me away from her.'

'Do you watch a lot of TV?'

Boyd blinked at the counsellor. 'If Mum goes to bed early.'

'And would you like to talk to me about your mum, Boyd?'

Boyd immediately closed up. Because Maureen was, for better or worse, his world. Because, despite her lapses, he had to protect her in all the ways he could.

'It's fine,' the counsellor insisted.

It wasn't fine, and Boyd clutched his throat. Talking to the counsellor – like coming home after school, like watching his mother's maladjustment – put a lump there. He didn't want to give any more away.

The counsellor nodded. 'If it's all right with you, Boyd, I'd like to stay in touch. Do you think we could talk again?'

The counsellor had a reassuring smile, but Boyd wouldn't allow himself to be hoodwinked. The man put on his blazer and asked if he could use the toilet. Boyd cringed to think of a stranger in their bathroom, with all their bottles of sun cream on the windowsill. Still, he directed the counsellor up the stairs. When the counsellor returned, he said, 'Your mum knows there's some quite heavy damp on the landing, doesn't she?'

Boyd nodded. A rancid black-green fungus had been creeping from his mother's room into the corners, just like in Watford.

'It's not the healthiest,' the counsellor added.

Which Boyd knew all too well. Which was why, since Maureen wouldn't acknowledge it, he'd been trying to clean it away. Which was why it upset him that no matter how hard he scrubbed, the mould always returned.

MOSS

One dull Tuesday morning, Boyd woke coughing from a vivid dream of moss: star moss, sheet moss, emerald and purple, dying brown and deathly grey. His father's moss on the drain outside had grown all through the house, matted and purposeful, powered by its own weird energy. Then it had come to Boyd's bed, across his body, wet and heavy, to enter his mouth. He remembered feeling a damp heat, half-stirring to throw off his covers, and a sensation he could only liken to drowning.

On his side, shivering, Boyd was aware of his room's smallness, its thick smell. He cracked an eye at the clock – nearly six in the morning, still dark – and shut it again. He couldn't shake the idea that the dream had been a vision, albeit one that held the uncanny weight of a memory. It was a memory that made him cough again, clutch his chest. The dream's lingering image was of a damp patch on the ceiling, like the patch that had spread across his mother's bedroom ceiling in Watford. But this time, the patch had darkened and stretched down to meet him.

He listened. Muffled coughing from Maureen's room. A dog barking in the middle distance. Early traffic washed along the high street. And under it all, inside him, his pulse raging. Swallowing was painful, and a faint wheeze passed his lips with each breath. It was a school day, but he wasn't up to it. There were also chores to do.

Behind his curtains, the glazing was misted with new mould, a spray of brown-green fractals. It extended down to the sill, which was dotted with dead flies. More coughing seized him as he wiped the mould away – a run of sharp, wet barks. He thought he saw spores, suspended near his head. He opened the window as fast as he could.

The bathroom was little better. The curtain was rotting where it hung, and the tile grout was steadily blackening. He braved the shower; squatted in the bath with the showerhead against his face, hoping the steam would clear his sinuses. The water sputtered, hissed, and ran a muddy colour. He got out, dried and dressed on the landing, went downstairs. There was some out-of-date paracetamol under the sink, but the tap water had developed an appalling vegetable taste. When he cleaned his teeth over the dirty dishes, there was something fibrous in his spit.

Again, he pictured the damp on the ceiling. As though, in dreams or by illness, the house was working its way inside him.

The fridge was empty and the cupboards were bare. He ate a folded crust of bread, moistened with the dregs from a ketchup bottle, and used the last tin of Red's food to fill her bowl. They needed to go shopping but his whole body ached and the idea of going to the supermarket was overwhelming. He didn't want to wake Maureen for cash.

The cat flap sounded, and Red sauntered over to her meal.

'We've forgotten you again,' Boyd told her.

Almost in reply, there was a crash on the ceiling above his head. Boyd, concerned, ran straight upstairs to Maureen's door.

'Mum?'

Maureen grunted, which Boyd took as permission. Far from hurt, though, she was sitting up on her bed, wearing a thin beige camisole. There was a suitcase on the floor. The windows were closed, and the room was humid, ripe, like Boyd's own. A fruity smell. Every wall an awful tapestry of mould. Maureen moved languidly: she looked to Boyd and then into her lap. She was reading the pink-covered fantasy novel from Watford. He was confused by this, and equally by how young she appeared. Her delicacy against the sun-bleached curtains. And then her hair: much darker than its usual ashy blonde.

'Did your own coughing wake you?' she asked. Her face was serene, her posture perfectly straight. She hadn't spoken to him so softly in months.

Boyd stared at the book, then at her hair. That was it, wasn't it? A new fringe. Maureen turned and put the book down beside her.

'You've not barked like that since you were a toddler,' she said.

'I was already downstairs,' Boyd explained. 'There was a bang.'

'Oh,' she said. She pointed absently at the suitcase. 'I'm having a clear-out. It's not a problem. You know you were mumbling in the night? I came in to check on you – you were running a temperature. Do you need to go in today? I wondered if we could… No, actually. Probably better you give it a go.'

He wanted to say, 'It's this house'; instead, they watched each other in the pallid light. The idea of her standing over him made Boyd itchy. Flashes from his dream, moisture and heat. The moss in his throat. A wariness that kept him alert. Maureen broke eye contact and picked up her book. When Boyd coughed again, she sighed.

'What's the matter?' she asked.

'We've run out of food,' he told her. 'Red hasn't got any, either.'

'Can't you go before school? Are you well enough?'

Boyd nodded once, seeing no alternative.

'Good,' Maureen said. And this time she smiled for real.

Boyd carefully backed out of the room. As he eased the door shut, he swore he heard her say, 'I do love you, you know.'

Red was by the shoe rack, staring accusingly.

'I'm going now,' Boyd told her, coughing into his sleeve. The cat watched as he put on his father's jacket and school shoes, wiped a dusting of mould from their uppers. She'd disappeared again when he opened the door.

Outside, Boyd struggled to process his conversation with Maureen. Why did it make him suspicious? Was it that she'd been so considerate? Present? He felt almost as if a veil had been lifted; that, for a minute or so, he'd been with a younger, more tactile version of her. He went along the high street rubbing his head, glad for the fresh air. His skin was still clammy, and a secondary pressure was building – rain soon. As he passed the hair salon, the unease coalesced: it *was* Maureen's hair that had got to him. And there was more to it than a fringe, or dye. Her face was sharper, or her scalp had moved. She'd looked noticeably younger, yet frailer. He could believe she'd tried to revive herself, made progress, then given in. And when he thought of it all together – the mould on his window, his dreams, his mother – he saw that their morning had been different, and altogether new.

A queue had formed beside a recycling lorry in the super-market car park. Approaching, Boyd noticed a team of work-ers wheeling crates of food into the trolley bays. Another worker came forward, took a crate, and paraded it for the people queuing, who picked out what they wanted before the remainder went in the lorry's waste hatch. Boyd couldn't see what was being dumped, but sweet rot thickened the air. He went inside.

The fresh produce shelves were bare. More queuing, and a febrile atmosphere – somewhere on the far side of the building, people were arguing. 'I'll lose customers!' a man was shouting. 'Where the hell's the meat?' Closer, a young worker, red-faced and sweaty, was trying to mop up a yellow puddle. There were maggots flailing under the units.

Boyd swallowed hard and aimed for the tinned goods aisle. Again, the shelves were all but stripped. His head throbbed; he couldn't tell if it was his illness or the supermarket itself. He scanned himself: there was still a funny taste in his mouth, but at least the coughing had eased. 'It's like a blight,' a woman said into her phone, almost in awe. Another man, passing, shook his head at Boyd. Was it panic? Or rage? It didn't matter: Boyd felt it all in his chest, filling up the gaps in him. If there was sickness here, some sort of outbreak, then he surely knew the source. He pictured their fridge, their own rotten vegetables. He couldn't outrun the thought; it was like an avalanche – this could be Maureen, and it could be him. The Alports together. For a few frightening moments, he stopped still. The damp on the walls he couldn't wipe away. The slime in the bathroom. The mould on his windows, on his shoes, on his chest—

'They'll have to burn it,' the woman said grimly into her phone.

Boyd knitted his hands and regretted coming. It was a big feeling, a bad feeling – like being exposed. And all these ways he'd watched his mother turn…

'Here he is,' somebody said. 'All right, pal?'

It was one of the workers who'd previously picked on Boyd about Maureen as he shopped. Taller, maybe a year or two older than Boyd, with a scrappy beard and greyish skin. The edge of his cap was frayed and unwashed. For his age, he had horribly receded gums.

Boyd turned away.

'Oi,' the boy said. 'What's up with you?'

Boyd shook his head. He didn't need it. But the boy wasn't done.

'What's she up to this morning?'

'She's in bed,' Boyd said.

The boy smirked.

'Colour nighty's she wearing? Eh, why don't you stop and chat? Am only messing mate. Only messing. It's—'

Boyd kept walking. He knew the run of this, and how he'd feel afterwards if he wasn't firm enough.

'I said hang about,' the boy said, keeping his voice low.

Boyd rounded the aisle and accelerated down the next. The boy was waiting at the other end.

'Got eyes on your mam,' he told Boyd. 'All of us do.' He nodded, letting it go in, but Boyd wouldn't be drawn. 'Reckon you're better than us? Is that it?'

Boyd tried to move on. This time the boy stepped in front of him.

'What's up with you, pal?'

'I've got school,' Boyd said.

'I've got *school*,' the boy said, mocking. And he came right into Boyd's face, so close Boyd could smell his breath, and touched his forehead against his.

'Bit early for that, isn't it?' came another voice.

Both of them turned to a girl, also a little older than Boyd. She frowned till she was sure they'd noticed, then smiled. She had a lot of freckles.

'He giving you shit?' she asked Boyd.

Boyd shook his head unsurely. The boy had already stepped back.

The freckled girl angled her head, glanced between them. She looked as if she knew her way around. Or was so at ease with herself she didn't care which way she went. 'Go on, dickhead,' she whispered to the boy. 'Piss off.'

The boy smirked again, sloped away. 'In a bit,' he said.

Boyd stood there, flushed. For want of something useful to say, he said, 'Thanks.'

The girl smiled, measuring him. She had an edge to her, and Boyd was suddenly conscious of his school uniform. She said, 'Not the first time, that, was it?'

'I don't know what it's about.'

She shrugged. 'They're harmless enough – they just get bored. Maybe you're an easy target.'

'Maybe. Sorry you had to do that.'

The girl sniggered. 'Southerner? Apologetic southerner?'

Boyd nodded tentatively. Then, trying to justify himself, he added: 'But my dad wasn't.'

The girl thought about that. Now Boyd could smell *her*: burnt wood and vanilla. When she rubbed her hairline, her forearm was very toned.

'Sure you're okay?'

'Yeah,' he said. 'Better crack on, though. Get these bits.'

'Cool,' she said. And the girl tipped her own basket towards Boyd and added, 'They've got fuck-all that I need, mind.'

He watched her go. Three aisles over, the boy was watching. He gave Boyd a thumbs-up, mouthed an insult. That same confident smirk. Boyd went back up the aisle and took the long way around the shop to the pet food section. He grabbed a few tins of Red's favourite meat and joined the checkout queue. It was close to eight-thirty. He didn't have long enough before school.

*

The freckled girl was out by the taxi rank, observing the exchanges still happening in the car park. Boyd gave her a half-smile as he went by, polite if not embarrassed, and realised she was waving him over.

'What's even going on?' she asked him. 'Checkout girl said the garden centre's closed, too. Everything's turning nasty.'

'Weird,' Boyd said, clearing his throat.

'Weird,' she agreed, before a hesitation. 'You get your stuff?'

He nodded.

The girl laughed through her nose. 'I don't bite, mate,' she said.

'I'm not—'

'Nervous?'

The girl had a gappy smile. Spit glistened between her two front teeth. He told himself not to stare, pivoted a certain way to signal he needed to leave.

She wouldn't blink. 'What's your name?'

He told her.

'Boyd,' she said, before nodding approvingly. 'Boyd the southerner. My name's Leigh. Like Lee, but with an *e* and an *i*, and a *gh* to finish. Leigh.'

'Right,' Boyd said. 'I've got to—'

'Which school you go to?'

'St Mary's—'

'Oh, Catholic? You little perv!'

Boyd shook his head, baffled, until Leigh laughed. 'I'm not – ha. It's all right. Don't be thinking I'm like that knobhead in there.'

'It's fine,' he said.

'I quit school after my exams,' she went on. 'Boss sent me down for supplies. Thinks I'd have the change for a taxi back – they don't think right, the blokes round here. Do they?'

Boyd searched himself and wasn't sure what to say. He settled for, 'I need to get back.'

Leigh frowned. Maybe she was getting bored, or he'd annoyed her. Her mischievousness had given way to a flinty look, as if she'd been reaching for something only to realise Boyd couldn't give it to her.

From nowhere she said, 'You after any pocket money, at all?'

'You mean a job?' He shook his head. 'Don't think I can.'

'You already got one?'

'No.'

Her grin was back. 'What do they call you at school? Captain Charisma?'

Boyd didn't reply.

Leigh chuckled and hugged herself.

'I'd better—'

'Yeah, course, no worries,' Leigh said. 'Keep keeping you, don't I? Here, though – just in case.' She gave him a business card that read A+F RECYCLING LTD.

'Up the road,' she explained. 'Edge of Neighton Prangle. If you ever need the cash, text me.' And she wrote her own number on the card.

Boyd blinked at her. He wasn't sure how to take the offer.

'Or just keep walking towards Neighton. Can't miss it.'

He pocketed the card. 'Okay,' he said.

'You've never worked before, have you?'

'It's been hard…' He trailed off. There wasn't anywhere good to start from.

'Lazy bastard,' Leigh said, grinning. Then, more animatedly, she waved down a cab and left him to it.

Boyd's encounter with Leigh had thrown him. He was anxious about going home with nothing but the cat food, was unsettled by what had happened at the supermarket, but mostly he found himself dissecting how he'd spoken to her. His awkwardness had been a reminder that, even at sixteen, he lived within a small circle: his mother and Red and Joan, and Sile. A circle that, pressured by his father's death, his mother's deterioration, had only tightened. He brought the shopping bag close to his chest, as if that might protect his smallness. Craving security, he cleaved to what had made him, his childhood before now. There was no doubting that his happiest memories came from their old caravan trips, in the other place, that other world, where they were safe together as a family. Motorway services, fields of yellow rapeseed, low-lying campsites, weeks at his grandmother's bungalow on a harsh coast to the east, a home where everything was purposely quiet, purposely insignificant against the headland, the massive sky. The call of cuckoos and the smell of rain. He relaxed his shoulders – it was working – but God, he grieved his younger self, and those times. His parents playing cards and drinking boxed wine while Boyd read books, or played Ludo alone, or watched cartoons. Never with them, per se, but still *of* them. There'd been so much laughter, even if sometimes it was directed at him, his naivety, or his misuse of adult idioms. And how many nights had he lain on boards over the caravan seats, falling asleep to the sound of rain, to drunken giggles, to a gentle but rhythmic knocking on the bedroom wall, and never once minded?

Boyd stopped by the chip shop to retie his shoelaces. When he stood up, a woman wearing a long yellow anorak and walking boots was watching from the other side of the road.

'Maureen's son?' she called over.

Boyd tensed right away. He felt he knew her yet couldn't place her. The anorak's hood was tight over her head, which emphasised her wrinkles and made her blue-grey eyes especially keen. He told her he was going to be late for school. She touched his shoulder. 'I know your mum,' she told him. 'Where does it hurt?'

Boyd didn't understand the question. The woman flashed a *doesn't matter* expression, then asked for his name.

'What?' he asked.

'I can help you,' she said. 'But you have to tell me.'

He shook his head. 'Nothing hurts,' he said.

At this, the woman took him by his right bicep.

'She's not well, is she? Your mum. She's getting worse.'

Boyd didn't know what to say. The woman's scent – warm, like butter pastry – was dizzying.

'You have to tell me,' she went on.

Someone went past using their phone, and the woman glanced round. Boyd saw his moment. He planted a foot and used it to lever himself out to the side, put distance between them. The woman glared after him, then shook her head.

'I want to help you,' she said.

Boyd broke into a panicked run. He felt smothered and faint. Most of all, he needed to tell Maureen that he loved her, too.

At the corner of his road, Boyd nearly went over the bonnet of a small electric hatchback as it moved silently across the junction. He waved an apology without making eye contact and walked straight into a puddle.

'Oi!' someone shouted behind him.

Boyd glanced over his shoulder but didn't stop. The hatchback had pulled up on the pavement, and the driver was out and leaning over his door. It was the boy from the supermarket, still wearing his green and beige uniform, his cap.

'I'm talking to you!' the boy shouted. 'What's that all about?'

Boyd stopped. Cold water seeped through his socks as he turned.

'Where you off?' the boy asked, adjusting his cap against the rain.

'Home?' Boyd said.

And he continued, but in fear had slowed to a jog. A few doors from the house, the hatchback appeared next to him. The boy had turned the car around, had his window down. 'We'll give you a lift,' he said, gesturing for Boyd to get in.

'I'm all right,' Boyd said, trying to keep his eyes forward. 'Cheers.'

But the boy was persistent. 'Thought you had school today?'

'I forgot something,' Boyd told him.

'We can help with that,' said someone else. The car's passenger was leaning over the boy's lap. He was a larger man, middle-aged, wearing a waxed jacket and a sarcastic grin. He said, 'Only looking out for you.'

Boyd kept going. The pavement was empty. He was aware of his breathing and the heat of his skin. The heaviness of his feet. In his peripheral vision, he saw the car crawling along the road beside him.

'Is your mam home?' the boy asked.

Boyd didn't answer. This time the car jolted to a stop. Boyd considered running again, but couldn't see where he'd go.

'Got to look out for each other!' the passenger shouted.

Boyd passed his front door and looked towards the end of the road, where the kerb rose into a disused recreation ground, gravelled tennis courts turned over to dandelions and tough grass. Cross the rec ground fast enough, and he'd make it to the path by the brook, where the boy's car wouldn't be able to fit.

There was a scraping sound. The hatchback was still creeping after him, but now the door was open, and the boy was driving one-handed while using the other to drag a hammer along the pavement. Boyd's skin was electrified. He kept his head forward and broke into a run.

It was futile. The car followed him up the kerb and pulled across him. The boy climbed out, casual as you like. Boyd, level with the driver's door, pushed hard, but the boy was stronger.

'Don't be a fanny,' the boy said, hammer against his chest. 'And don't worry about that stuff before. We're all pals.'

The man nodded. 'She make a nice cuppa, your mam?'

'I'm nearly home,' Boyd said uselessly.

'Most accidents happen close to home,' the boy said.

'Can never be too careful,' the passenger added, sliding his chair forward to expose the rear seats.

There was no one back there – only a bag of wet clothes, a toolbox, a wrap of binbags from the supermarket. A point of light played on the hammer. Boyd understood his position. He went around the bonnet. Before he got in, he took a breath and held it for as long as he could.

Maureen wasn't downstairs when Boyd unlocked the front door. The house was arranged so you came straight into the living room and onto a ridged plastic mat which crackled loudly. Usually you heard movement at this point: a shuffling upstairs, a utensil placed down in the kitchen. Red hopping down from the sofa. But the house was still, the curtains drawn and lights off, and there was a new smell – resinous, sharp, like rotting pine. Boyd chose to assume Maureen had tried to disinfect something. All the same, he was grateful she wasn't in. It validated his excuse, gave him more time to think of a way out.

The boy was first in behind him. The man in the waxed jacket waited by the open door. Boyd tried the switches, but the lights wouldn't come on. The living room was gloomy, soft-edged. Red wasn't in her bed, nor on the sofa.

The man said, 'Power cut?' and flicked on his phone torch. Boyd didn't answer.

'Bloody starving, me,' the boy said. He took off his cap to reveal a shaved head that shone with sebum.

'What's for brekkie, then?' the man said, poking about in the corner before taking the landline handset from its cradle and listening for a tone. 'That's weird,' he said, frowning. 'Phone's dead as well.' He gestured to the boy.

The boy snatched Boyd's shopping bag and pushed past him into the kitchen, where the blinds were closed but it was a touch lighter. The man took Boyd's collar and marched him through. Here the boy shook out the tins of cat food, looked at Boyd in disgust, then rifled the cupboards. He was careless and a bag of flour popped on the counter, showering the floor. Boyd could only watch. What really rattled him was the shape of his mother's coat lying in a heap at the bottom of the stairs. It was exactly where it ended up whenever she came in through the back door, shrugged it off. Which told him she could be home, after all.

'What does she feed you?' the boy asked. 'What do you eat?'

Boyd barely registered the question. He told the boy he needed to get his school bag from his bedroom. He said if they found anything, they were welcome to it. And he meant it. He hoped that if he was accommodating enough, they might just move on.

'He wants to go upstairs,' the boy said, wiping dust from a jar of pickled onions.

'What for?' the man said.

'A wank?'

The man and boy laughed together.

'Mum'll be back soon,' Boyd tried.

They ignored him. 'A wank!' the man roared. 'But he can't even wank, can he? Can he! What colour's your cum, pal? What colour? You're funny, you. I bet you've never seen cum.'

Boyd went round the dining table towards the stairs. His legs were heavy. At the bottom of the staircase, the man barred his way. 'It doesn't work for us,' he said, shaking his head.

'I can't—'

'Can't what? Come off it, bud. We're having a laugh. We're only messing. You pair got off on the wrong foot, before. So let's just put it right. No mither.'

'But what do you want?'

The boy and the man looked at each other. 'What do you *want*?' the boy said, repeating Boyd in falsetto.

'What's your name?' the man asked.

Boyd told them. The boy sniggered. 'Boy? He's called Boy?'

'*Course* he is,' the man said.

'And Boy wants to go upstairs for a wank.'

'How old's Boy, do we reckon?'

'Eighteen, easily. Or nineteen.'

'I'm sixteen—'

'Sixteen! No wonder he wants a wank. And here, we're just two decent fellas who've made sure you got home safe.'

At this, the man leaned across the sink and opened the blinds. His face was lit up: jowly and sallow, small pink eyes. He smiled with only his mouth and said, 'See if we can't check out your mam's pants drawer as a reward.'

The boy sniggered. 'Oh aye, that's the one.'

Boyd shook his head. 'Can't you just go?'

The man licked his lips. 'Ah, now, don't be like that.'

The hairs on Boyd's arms rose. The boy drew closer to him, the hammer cradled in both hands. It seemed rehearsed. It was obvious they were enjoying it.

'There's nothing up there,' Boyd said. But they saw he was cornered, and it was getting harder for him to disguise his fear.

'How come you're so nervous?' the man asked, snorting.

'How come you want us to go? We're only having a sniff.'
Again, the dirty laughter.

In a way, Boyd hoped Maureen really was home. That she
was hidden and safe, having read the situation and called the
police. But even if the landline was working, she'd never do
that. After Dougie, through Dougie, she'd lost all faith in the
authorities. What was to say, in her mind, that the man and
boy weren't officers themselves? Boyd rocked on his heels.
His laces were too tight.

The man winked at the boy and said to Boyd, 'You rest
up, there, son.' And Boyd was pushed into the corner of the
kitchen units, all but smothered, so that he could smell the
boy's breath again, feel the hammer against his ribs.

'We don't have any stuff worth taking,' Boyd said, trying
not to sound pleading.

'Oh?' the boy said. A frostiness now, as if the play-acting
had finished. 'You saying we're up to no good?'

'There's nothing worth taking—'

'Then shut your *fucking* mouth.'

The man was about halfway up the stairs. 'Reeks of piss
up here,' he called down.

'You think we're on the rob?' the boy asked again. 'Nah
mate, nah. We know what your mam is. We know *exactly*.
And your little girlfriend isn't here now, is she?'

Boyd's blood roared in his ears. He was confused – what
did they think his mother was? He thought back to the
woman in the yellow anorak. What was it she'd said about
Maureen being ill? He worried that he'd squandered something, and simultaneously saw that he and Maureen could
never live the anonymous life they'd wanted. That, in some
way, the house had been leaking into the ground…

Helpless, Boyd tried to bolt. The boy swept his legs and
drove a fist into his stomach. Boyd collapsed and lay grunting
on the lino.

'Nah,' the boy said, tutting. 'You don't have it in you. Where will you go?'

From this angle, the boy's face gleamed horribly. There were pale, hairless patches under his chin, and his teeth and tongue were yellow.

Boyd tried to speak and found he couldn't.

Just then a clipped scream came from upstairs. Boyd glanced to the stairwell. It hadn't been his mother – it was too animal, hurt. But it wasn't Red, either. The boy sprang away from him and peered round the stairwell. He cleared his throat.

'Tone?'

Next came a rumble, not unlike footsteps, though much too fast. It travelled from one side of the house, over the landing, and into the bathroom. Boyd stayed very still. Then a bump, and another, as something heavy came to the top of the stairs, paused, and started down.

The boy strained, angling his torch. 'Tone?'

Another cry, this one sharper. The boy's eyes widened before he fell against the stairs, his expression a mix of surprise and pain. With strange understatement, an object rolled into the kitchen, shedding bits of dirt and twig-like debris, and came to rest in the spilled flour. Boyd knelt up, still wheezing. The object resembled a bale of purple moss, breezeblock sized. Neither Boyd nor the boy spoke. Behind it came the man's limp body with a terrible clattering. He came to rest at the bottom of the staircase, his head in Maureen's coat.

'Tone?' the boy said, plaintively.

The boy gripped the end of the stairwell wall and stood up. He dropped the hammer and glared at Boyd, who simply stared back. The walls, the ceiling, the air – everything had contracted. The boy mumbled something indistinct – an excuse, Boyd thought, more than a threat – and squatted by his friend. 'Tone!'

Boyd staggered towards them both, clutching his belly.

'Tone!' the boy was shouting. 'Tone!' And when he clocked Boyd: 'Stay over there! Over there, you prick!'

Boyd waited. Tone's body was slack, face turned away. There was a soil-like material stuck to his neck. A deep laceration behind his ear, like a whip mark.

'Wake up!' the boy was screaming now, voice breaking. He was trying to lift the man, but he was too limp, too heavy. 'Tony! Tone! Tone!'

'Is he dead?' Boyd said.

The boy turned to him. 'Call the ambulance,' he said.

Boyd shook his head without a second thought. He had no mobile and the landline was down, so he couldn't. But he knew he wouldn't anyway. If Maureen had taught him anything, it was to expect the worst of people. The police, the ambulance service, whoever – one or both of them would be taken away, and that would be that.

The boy swore. His balled fists. His eyes full of tears. He took out his own phone and shrieked. The handset appeared to have melted; the rear panel was running like hot wax down the boy's hand.

'What the fuck is this?' the boy shouted, trying to flick it off. 'What the fuck have you done to us?'

Boyd stayed where he was. Tone's chest gently rose and fell.

'Tone!' the boy screamed. 'Tone!'

The older man was too still, crooked, his legs straight and his arms bent, and his head turned away—

'Fucking hell,' the boy said. 'Prick! Stay here with him. Stay with him. I'm getting the boys. I'm getting the boys over, and you're done. You hear me? You're *fucked*, you prick!'

And he ran out of the house.

We know what your mam is.

RED

Boyd stood numbly between a supine Tony and the bale of moss. It felt physically impossible to even glance at the man, who was whining thinly through his nostrils, so instead he regarded the moss, alert to an immediate danger passing, a kind of relief, everything in flux. He had some sense that an unfixable crack had opened in the world, and that he was falling through it. The acid fear had receded, but a dull pain radiated from his stomach, down his legs and up around his temples. Behind this thrummed a voice, soft yet insistent, that kept telling him to kill himself. Dissociation: an image of his own body, puffy and grey. Who'd even notice? Who'd ever know?

He waited there, like that, for a long time. Eventually he gave in to curiosity and poked the block with his foot. It was definitely moss – it had the texture, that anxious, springy movement. And it had begun to ooze a thick liquid. He experienced both a strange compulsion to eat it, and a powerful disgust, as if staying so close might poison him.

At last he found his voice and called out for Maureen, even as his gut told him she was gone. It was a deep knowing, in fact, which came with its own lightness – a faint recognition that, untethered from her, he could at least drift on. The house was too quiet, and slowly his perspective shifted.

This wasn't his fault. He went to the staircase and knelt by Tony's head. There were grubby marks in the carpet where Tony and the moss-block had come down.

'Tony,' he said in a halting voice. 'Can you hear me?'

If Tony could, he wasn't in a state to reply. The blood behind his ear was congealing, and the sticky brown material on his neck, which up close had a texture like old wallpaper, was also in his hair. Boyd touched the man's cheek. The skin was warm. His ribcage rose and fell. There was a string of saliva from the corner of Tony's mouth, in which Boyd saw movement, particle life. A hot wave of nausea passed over him. He remembered to breathe. He remembered he shouldn't move the man, lest he worsen an injury. If nothing else, he could see that Tony, despite his position – the feet and legs still partway up the stairs – was comfortable enough, head cushioned by Maureen's coat.

Before he went upstairs, Boyd barricaded the front and back doors with kitchen chairs. He'd already lost any sense of how long he might have until the boy returned with friends.

'Gnnngh,' Tony said, as Boyd stepped over him. 'Gnn-nngh…'

Boyd took the stairs slowly, as though each were rotten. Pain flashed in the cartilage between his ribs, and his legs felt like someone else's. Tony had been right: the smell of the house changed halfway up. Sharp pine gave way to mud and leather, a rich, bitumen stench; on the top landing, a foul sweetness. The damp had spread quickly; now the entire landing wall crawled with it, and it was making a start down the stairs. In one corner, the wallpaper had peeled away to expose slimy plasterboard. There were fibres of moss all over the carpet.

We know what your mam is—

Boyd went to his room first. It was empty, exactly as he'd left it that morning. Duvet in a pile, yesterday's socks in a ball. In Maureen's bedroom, there were clothes neatly folded on the bed. The suitcase was still on the floor, but it was open. The main compartment was packed with comfy sweatshirts and bottles of sun cream. The netted pocket held a pair of compression socks, and several of the plain pharmacy boxes he'd seen Maureen with before. To one side of the suitcase – placed, rather than discarded – was the pink fantasy novel, a sheaf of paper tucked inside its cover. Boyd stooped to pick it up, cradling his belly. A list of partial phone numbers, a receipt for rent, and a bank statement showing weekly deposits from an anonymised account.

Boyd pulled back Maureen's bedcovers. A sheen of sweat and moisturising oil, Red's moulted fur. Scattered on the far side were various used tissues, some bloody, the rest blackened by Maureen's efforts to clean the walls.

She wasn't in the cupboards, or behind the curtains, or under the bed. But when he turned to leave again, there were three severed heads hanging from the back of the door.

Brunette. Silver. Crimson.

Boyd rubbed his face. The fear again. He caught himself. They weren't heads – they were wigs on hooks. He went to them, wiping his nose down his sleeve. Each wig was a simple shoulder-length bob, shorter than Maureen's natural style. He touched the brunette wig, knowing it was the same one she'd been wearing that morning. The hair felt real, expensive. He took the wig from its peg and sat on the stool by his mother's dresser. All those times he'd watched her getting ready in the Watford house. This same stool. The same mirror. The same orange-backed brush, whose collected hair he occasionally found in the toilet bowl. He could see her, if he really looked: casually dressing and doing her make-up. And when he held the wig to his forehead, he almost became her. The same brow, the downturned mouth, the dimpled cheek. He put the wig on the dresser and opened the middle drawer. A collection of make-up pens, pads and brushes. Exactly the same products in the right-hand drawer, and again in the left.

The same items, arranged in the same way. A make-up set for each of the wigs. A way to lighten or darken her features to suit.

Guilt rose, now. He was intruding, betraying what remained of their bond. At the same time, a mystery had unlocked itself. Maureen had created a way to become three other people, each a stranger to him. More of a stranger, that is, than she'd already become.

Which led Boyd to another, bigger question: who knew these other Maureens?

He thought of the woman in the anorak.

The boy who'd been downstairs.

This time he knew he was going to be sick for real. He rushed to the bathroom. The tarpaulin curtain was back, bundled into the tub. A starchy substance – possibly sun cream – had clotted in its folds. The tiles were slick with condensation. He went to his knees and noticed a mark on the toilet cistern, impressions of unnaturally long fingers. Even the toilet contained threads of the moss. His throat tightened. He retched. The wave passed once more.

He rested his head on the toilet lid. When he was sure he was okay, he got up and sat on it. A breeze blew through the window. Had Maureen jumped out? He checked through the gap between pane and sill. Below, the greening concrete flags of the yard, cheap flat-pack garden furniture. No chance. Not without breaking her legs.

He pushed the window fully open and leaned on the sill, trying to gather himself. Trying to find reality. The draught and drizzle were welcome, and stayed his urge to cough. He pulled up his top and studied his bruising torso. His knowing was still there, right behind his ribs. The deep knowing she'd gone, which overrode any urge to reassure himself, as he'd so often had to reassure her.

What else could explain Maureen's behaviour that morning? The clarity of hindsight: he'd mistaken her serenity for detachment, when really it had been resolve.

Or, worse, she'd known what she was about to do, and had tried, in her way, to apologise.

I do love you, you know.

Time passed. Rain thrashed the windows, eased again. Part of him didn't care what Tony's boys might do. He was tired and cold and sore from the blow to his stomach. And he was angry. That he and Maureen had never had mobiles was more than frustrating – it felt like neglect. With the landline broken, he couldn't call her, he couldn't check in, he couldn't call anyone else for help. Hindsight again: this had always been always a risk. His mother had put far too much stock in the bounds of their relationship.

He circled back.

She's gone.

I'm on my own.

Boyd went downstairs, stepping over Tony, and used the gas stove and a saucepan to make a cup of tea the way Maureen liked it: milk and one sugar, except there was no milk, so he took the teabag out sooner. The block of purple moss was unchanged, though its leaked fluid had thinned and spread by another foot or so, its colour leaching into the spilled flour, creating a pinkish paste. From some angles, the liquid was iridescent. Boyd set the mug on the table, as if that alone would bring Maureen through the door. Then he had to look away. From sink to fridge, toaster to oven, he could so easily picture her there.

But he knew, didn't he? In the bones of him. So, he'd have to be logical, to retrench and consolidate. Since Dougie, their circumstances had at least taught him to rationalise. When had

Maureen gone? After he left for the supermarket, but before he came home. Why had she gone with nothing? Because she expected to come back. Unless, of course, Boyd and Tony and the boy had disturbed her, forced her hand... Yet there was no way out that didn't involve coming downstairs. No loft access, nor basement, and only their small back yard.

He glared at the moss. It meant something. He knew this, too, as real as the dream, as a premonition, some future memory. Which was when he came back to Maureen's intent and spiralled again. She'd obviously planned to leave. Why else pack a suitcase? The wigs, the make-up, the phone numbers, the bank statement; the fact she'd made no effort to hide any of it.

And she'd *wanted* Boyd to know she'd gone.

To say nothing of the woman in the yellow anorak, who'd collared him, who also knew...

She's not well, your mum, is she?

A rustling sound. Boyd turned to Tony and saw Red coming through the cat flap. The cat immediately went to sniff the moss on the floor. 'Don't do that,' he said, shooing her away. Red lapped at the liquid anyway, then nuzzled into him. He scooped her up and sat on the armchair he'd dragged in from the lounge. She smelled like vinegar. He told her he was sorry, and meant it, and took the blanket from the chair to pull around them. 'Only for a minute,' he said, because he knew a point of decision was approaching. The blanket smelled of Maureen. He felt abandoned, cheated, hollow. Red, curled into him, mewled bleakly. As if she knew just as well.

'We've got to leave today,' he told the cat.

Red drew away from him.

'I know,' he said. 'But it's what we've got to do.'

Red angled her narrow head. She went to Tony's body. She sniffed along him and paused at his jeans pocket, looked back at Boyd. Boyd said, unquestioning, 'Oh.' And with a rush of hope, he saw through fear to opportunity. Red waited by the man until Boyd came forward, then sauntered away, back to her own business. Tony's mobile phone. Forty-six missed calls.

Boyd took Tony by the chin and waved the phone over his face. Owing to the sticky matter on Tony's cheek, it wouldn't unlock. So, Boyd peeled back the material, drier than its appearance, and was alarmed to see it squirm at its edges, a living thing. He swallowed, prised open Tony's eyes, and tried again. The phone unlocked. He went to the settings and changed it to keypad unlock, set a new PIN, and pocketed it.

Some of Boyd's fogginess was lifting. Heavy dread, yes, but a fuel. With new resolve, he sprinted upstairs, changed from his school uniform into weekend clothes, packed a rucksack with underwear, layers, toothbrush, sun cream and wallet, and went downstairs. There he balled his mother's blanket into his bag, shrugged on his father's rain jacket and pulled the chair away from the back door.

'Red,' he shouted back into the house. 'We've got to go.'

She was nowhere obvious. He didn't have time, but hoped she'd heard him. He opened the back door and saw the lawn pulsing with a clean, clear green. There were shapes in it, shifting lazily from one side to the other. A breeze, or something more. The longer he looked, the more he was convinced that the shapes were directing him. Towards the sheet moss his mother had sown beneath the downspout. The moss from Dougie's inquest sample.

The previous night's dream gathered into a single, silver-bright fact, irresistible. Boyd was back in the inquest room, that itchy beige chair, being asked a question. The heat of his mother's penny, pressed into his palm. A still of the moss-wrap and wedding ring taped inside Dougie's dead fist...

Boyd went to the corner of the yard. He knelt, prodded

the moss. Cold, saturated. He tore off a chunk as big as his hand. It was heavier yet softer than he expected. Rainwater coursed down his forearm. The green of the moss shifted, another climate, its own world-system in miniature. He put one chunk in his pocket and the rest on top of the block in the kitchen. The link seemed clear: if the bundle of moss in Dougie's hand had been a message for Maureen, a love letter, some private explanation, then the block in the kitchen was Maureen's own message to Boyd. He stood up with the satisfied feeling that his dream had been resolved. Immediately the moss from outside started to lose its colour. He understood – not through any rational process – that soon it would be gone. By a tenuous but compelling logic, he felt he should accept Maureen being gone too.

'Red!' he shouted. 'We've got to—'

Car doors were slamming on the street. Banging on the front windows shook the kitchen cabinets. Cries of 'Tone! Tony!' came through the house.

Tony's boys were back.

And Red the cat had vanished.

Boyd balled his fist around the moss in his pocket. More shouting, and a crash. He closed his eyes and exhaled and trusted his instinct to go.

Sile was quiet as Boyd ran down the high street. It was gone ten, a fine rain in the air. Diseased trees leaned in cages along the high street, dripping honeydew onto parked cars. The shops' roller-shuttered doors creaked. Out by Sile's last sign – THANK YOU FOR DRIVING CAREFULLY – where the town gave way to green belt, there was still a low mist glowing in the fields. Boyd entered an area of woodland and unzipped his father's jacket, holding up his top to get the breeze over his stomach, wiping sweat from his face. He stood and pissed over soft ground: leaf litter, tawny moss, fern and nettle. Then he went deeper, until the light changed and the air cooled, and he pulled on more layers. Finally, he sheltered under the fraying canopy of a dying ash tree, and caught up with himself, his breath, both hands tucked under his armpits. Again the fear receded, but he didn't know how long he had. Only dull pain remained, with the promise of more tomorrow. He thought of the time Dougie had come in from the pub, livid after being mugged by kids for a tenner, and wanted someone else to blame. Boyd had worked out fast enough that you had to stay stock still, shrink yourself. You had to be there, but not.

He'd got himself there – the safety of the woods – and now he'd try to be *not*, to hide himself. He wrapped Maureen's blanket around his shoulders and took Tony's phone from his pocket. Fourteen more missed calls. It was low on battery, but it did have signal. He toggled the dialling pad and tapped in his grandmother's number.

Joan's landline was the only number Boyd had ever memorised, though it'd been ages since he last used it. Certainly it was before Dougie's incident, or maybe even the Christmas before that. He hadn't seen Joan in person for at least two years – not since he and Maureen had moved her from Northumbria back to the Cotswolds after Ted, Joan's partner, died of stomach cancer. Finding their cottage too big to clean, its garden too wild, its stairs increasingly testing, Joan had asked to return to her hearth, a tiny village whose name Boyd never remembered. Dougie – working shifts – had at least sorted a Luton van for the job. Maureen and Boyd were to drive up, pack and load, and hand over management to a local estate agent, who'd finalise the sale. Arriving, they'd found Joan reclining in the garden, tending a thick-smoking fire.

'I've been productive,' she told them. By which she meant she'd burned all of Ted's clothes except his favourite blazer – a green Harris tweed which hung from the hosepipe reel like a trophy pelt. Boyd remembered feeling upset: there were pieces of Ted's life all over the garden. Charred books, shredded magazines for kindling, still-boxed tin cars, ancient certificates, and photos of him in RAF uniform. Boyd had spent the afternoon bagging up the detritus, criss-crossing the garden while Joan mocked him from her deckchair, and Maureen saw to paperwork inside. Later there'd been a song and dance about turning off the stopcock. When they were finished, the sun was going down, and Joan was drunk. Boyd had helped her into the van, taken the keys round to a neighbour, and pulled the wheely bins onto the front lawn. Then Maureen had driven them south too quickly, as if she were trying to force the day out of her system. Joan had enjoyed the journey, whooping and clapping as the heavy van leaned through corners. She didn't care what happened to her, Boyd had decided; this was already an escape, freedom from the task of grieving Ted, perhaps even from living. He remembered thinking she might throw up on him. The heady smell of sweet woodruff drying in Tupperware on the dashboard – Joan's last thing to pack.

They'd arrived at the retirement complex six hours and four toilet stops later. 'Can you *believe* they're putting me in a home?' Joan had asked Boyd, as Maureen went to the security desk. And, as Maureen returned, 'Do you remember that *terrible* night?'

If Boyd still had it right, Maureen hadn't replied, hadn't even looked at her mother. A tension he was too young to grasp, or perhaps care about. Maureen, apparently distracted, had spent ages trying to park, and Boyd hadn't minded, too mesmerised by this village where Joan had once lived, where his own mother had grown up. Its old stone and meandering streets. A series of low-walled gardens whose paths were being gently dismantled by an invasive orange-flowering plant. They'd unloaded Joan and her essentials and guided her into what would be her new flat. A single-floor maisonette with lots of considered features, like handrails in the bathroom. 'I do rate the kettle,' Joan later told Boyd during one of their brief, stilted weekend calls. (Maureen used to supervise, in case he said anything insensitive.) 'But the other residents don't know their arses from their elbows, and the water isn't how I remember it – it's got all these bits in.' And another time: 'I'm going to escape, you know. Just like your mother expects,' before she'd added, conspiratorially, 'Will you visit me – by yourself? When you're old enough to drive? I'd like that. I'd like to have you all to myself.'

Two years on, Boyd still pictured her sitting in that deckchair, surrounded by boxes and smoke, telling him to do something. They'd always be about to leave, and she'd always be smiling at him with her curious gaze, equal parts perplexed and impressed. A sadness in him as he replayed the moments when Joan had been all too aware of Ted's absence. A silence in which she might have been taking an inventory of herself, her life, and how little of it she had left. Dandelion seeds drifting through low sunlight.

The call to Joan's flat wasn't connecting. There was an error tone, every time. He checked the number, saw no mistakes, and kept trying. Nothing. Either Tony's phone was broken, or Joan's phone had been disconnected.

His heart hurt.

He tried one last time, in case he had it wrong. But as he recited the number from the screen – it had a song as much as a sequence – he knew it was useless. There was no way to reach her, not like this. In frustration, he found a large stone and smashed up the phone, spread its parts around him. It was hard not to think about death again, and defeat.

He closed his eyes, exhausted, and resorted to a technique he'd found useful during his estrangement from Maureen. You had to roll inwards, towards numbness, away from the past, from care and togetherness, to concentrate only on what you felt around you. The moss in his pocket. The cotton on his legs. The trunk and damp bark at his back and elbow. Soon enough, he was floating, his breath slowing. The trance came in. He drew everything down into the knotty ball in his gut, and tensed his stomach, held it there. Eventually, even the cold fell away, and he went into the blankness of sleep.

Boyd found unexpected peace in his dreams. The setting was familiar: his parents' old caravan. They were playing cards together – rummy, hearts – though nobody was winning. Their pitch was coastal; beyond grubby windows lay the sea, cast in a weird orange light. Waves rolled up but never came in. Tiny glowing flies kept sticking to the window, as if the caravan were moving through the landscape at speed. He was listening to his mother and father, but couldn't tell what they were saying. He talked back anyway, and they smiled sincerely. Even the caravan tablecloth, wipe-clean and spongy, put him at ease. Simple connection. Hands touching. Closer to consciousness, he found he wanted to stay.

When he did wake, his surroundings didn't shock him, and it took a while for his dread to pool. Fully conscious, he felt more pragmatic. Dusk in Sile, a whole afternoon lost, but something else gained. Inspired by the dream, he took his parents' wedding photograph from his wallet. It was such a pure capture of them, even if Maureen had once tried to pass it off as a performance; even if his impression of them was probably more like a false memory, a story he'd inherited, badly wished were true. But no: you could *see* them. Happy for real, their eyes blazing. The picture remained his best answer to Maureen's denials of love for Dougie; the best argument against her attempts to convince Boyd she'd always been in pain. She'd wanted him to believe they came together naively, lived together through convenience, were married by default, and that Boyd had appeared between them, a mistake. But the longer he looked at their photo, the more Boyd saw victory. And he saw that while his mother's deterioration might have owed itself to something more than heartbreak, the loss of Dougie, it was still likely catalysed by it.

So, what needled him? He wondered if he might have betrayed his parents by letting himself be pushed into this corner by Tony and the boy. Or that, in his abandonment of the house, he'd also missed a vital point. The moss, the mould, Maureen's disguises... These hidden lives of his parents, all their cryptic conversations, the suggestion of some complexity that Boyd wasn't to be trusted with.

But it was much simpler, in truth. It was Red – Boyd's link to both his parents.

Boyd stood up. He owed it to all of them – in the face of every slander, every threat – to fetch their cat.

Boyd took the back way into Sile. He skirted the overgrown cricket pitch, the abandoned BMX track, and followed the old branch line's overgrown rails past the industrial units on the fringes of the town. There he reached a footbridge over a disused service road and came in through the sixties housing estate. Oily puddles scattered the dwindling light. Before him was a row of shops and the top end of the high street. There were a few people walking, but the curtains of every house were drawn. He kept his chin high and eyes forward and walked with confidence, believing he could contain his motives if anyone challenged him.

Under a mauve-grey sky, Sile had a strange, muted atmosphere. Once or twice, Boyd heard an engine start and fade, while four streets over he saw a confident fox dart between binbags with a slice of pizza in its maw. The gritstone in every building looked darker than ever.

The church bells sounded on the hour, just as Boyd reached the turn for his road. It was there he noticed a flash of yellow disappearing into an alley between two shops.

'Wait!' he called, realising what he'd seen.

Net curtains twitched. Boyd buried his chin. The woman was waiting around the corner, hood down. She was even older than she'd appeared the day before. Her hair was gunmetal grey, and her blue eyes cut right through him. He knew at last: it was the woman who'd driven their taxi from Watford to Sile.

'Did anyone see you?' she said, panickily scanning the space behind him.

'Like who?' Boyd said.

She took hold of his jacket, tapped his pockets. 'Are you leaving?'

'Who are you?'

'A family friend. Where are you going?'

'Home.'

She shook her head rapidly, grip tightening. 'Can't.'

'What? Let go a second—'

'You can't go in there.'

Boyd stepped away. The woman held on, reconsidered, and released him. Boyd's stomach was turning. His bruises throbbed.

'I saw you with that girl,' the woman said. 'At the supermarket. Who was she?'

'I… you saw me? She just—'

'Can't trust her.'

'I don't even know her—'

'And don't go home. Understand?'

'You can't just—'

'I can advise you. While it's easier.'

'Easier? We live there! What am I meant to do?'

'She's gone, Boyd.'

A cold wire spread along Boyd's spine. He wanted to lash out. He pressed his hand on the wall. Cool and damp, like the moss in the kitchen, the moss in the garden. The moss in his pocket. He let his rage pass; he imagined it spreading through his hand and into the wall. The moment flipped.

'It *was* you,' Boyd said.

The woman didn't react.

'You drove us here, from Watford. The taxi. Mum and Dad talked about there being someone else – I remember it. Who are you?'

'Boyd,' the old woman said. 'I won't do this here.'

We know what your mam is.

'Did they find her?'

The old woman closed her eyes. Her head moved fractionally. It wasn't a yes, but it wasn't a no. Boyd took another step back, eyes stinging.

'I can only help if you ask me to,' she said. She gestured with her chin. 'The car's up here. We don't have to wait. There's another place for you. You'll be safe. You shouldn't see what's in there.'

Boyd sniffed. He was thinking of the police, Eddie the teacher, the counsellor, Tony and the boy. His parents themselves, and all their evasions. 'You all start off like that,' he told her.

The woman kept her face straight, her head very still. 'Chip off the old block,' she said. 'Aren't you?'

Boyd turned back to his road, both rows of terraces gently tapering away. When he looked back, the woman was marching up the alley.

On his first pass, Boyd actually missed the house. It was as if his internal map was there, and working, but the road itself had been altered. He went back and forth counting houses until he stood, stupefied, at theirs. The door bulged slightly from its frame. Roots or rhizomes, slick brown, ran out from under the threshold, across the pavement, and down into a drainage grid. The ground-floor windowpanes had cracked in their frames, themselves warped and splitting. Inside, the curtains were drawn and pushed up against the glazing, which was streaming with condensation. The faint suggestion of a force pushing outwards.

Absurdly, Boyd pressed the doorbell – some reach for normalcy, or confirmation of how badly his relationship with Maureen had dissolved. They were like two divided friends, each wondering if the other still thought of them, each too scared to check. No answer. He stood back, searching the wall. His skin was tight, and his feet were wet and cold. There were scorch marks above the doorframe, which spread into the roof of their shallow porch canopy. Either Tony's boys had tried to light a fire here, or there'd been a fire on the other side. He reached up and touched the paint. His finger came away sooty. He tried his house key, but the lock barrel slid straight through. He winced, waiting for the bang, but there was no sound. He put his eye to the hole. The living room was dark and hazy. A smell – bitter, herbal. He wasn't getting in from here.

He went round the back through the ginnel between the terraces, ducked the washing line and entered the yard. He couldn't see Red anywhere. His father's moss was blackened, dead. As with the front, the UPVC frame of the back door bowed outwards. But here, at least, there was a gap in the seal. He tried his luck, grazing his knuckles on the lock mechanism, and found he could touch the latch. It moved, but the door was stuck in its damaged frame. He applied his bodyweight with no luck. Then he charged with his shoulder and fell straight into the house. The door crashed onto the lino. Boyd rolled over, held himself, and froze.

Tony was gone. The kitchen was muggy. A powerful smell of cucumber and something else – acrid, burnt. The purple moss had spread and bloomed with unbelievable speed. It was up across the cabinet doors, over the work surfaces, in places as high as the tile splashback, which appeared to be crumbling. It had filled the cupboards and drawers, the oven, the microwave. Boyd was amazed, appalled. The whole floor was now matted with a fibrous material, less moss than mulch. Soft undulations where the lino had deformed and blistered up, or disappeared completely.

'Red,' he said, urgent. '*Red.*'

He went through the kitchen, the ground spongy underfoot. The moss, unable to pass under the door to the living room, had instead mounted it, forced it open. Boyd tasted metal. There was a sound, internal, way up in the high range, which intensified as he moved. He questioned whether he'd lost his hearing, but could hear his own jaw working.

What he found in the living room made him retch.

The sofas were covered with thick ropes of vegetation, coiled like entrails. Tendrils, delicate as veins, had spooled away from the floor covering and penetrated the plug sockets. Moss had displaced the mantelpiece porcelain, which had been caught by a thick polyp-like growth beneath. The television had come apart, its components suspended in the air as if frozen mid-explosion. And a centrepiece: a large, pale column, which had formed on the rug. It best resembled a hay bale standing on one end, only smooth, with the colour and finish of a tooth. It was being fed umbilically by a network of filaments that entered its body through invisible seams. As Boyd moved closer, the column began to pulse with lustrous, near-indefinable hues. Some were close to purples and pinks, neon orange and blood red, but the greater effect was one of blinking and glimpsing something on the inside of your eyelids, unrepeatable the moment you're conscious of it.

Boyd held his face in dumb shock. His whole body was trembling. And he saw her, then. Red was lying on top of the column.

'Red?'

Their cat was fully extended on her side, resting in what looked like a velveteen bed: plump, soft tissue which outlined her perfectly. She didn't stir at his voice. He couldn't see if she was breathing. He touched her neck, which was warm. One of her ears twitched.

'Red—'

Red chirruped, a contented or relieved sound, and her one visible eye twitched and rotated. Her fur was knotty with a slimy residue. Boyd ran his hand across her whiskers. No response. He tugged her collar in an attempt to lift her away from the column, afraid to touch it himself. There was a sucking sound: her other flank was clearly stuck down, and she couldn't move her tail. He relented in fear of hurting her. By way of apology, he stroked the fur around her chin. Then, as if she'd recognised him, Red raised her free paw, a deliberate if drunk-looking movement, and put it on the back of Boyd's hand. He held it there, shaking away the thought she was being absorbed. 'Red,' he said, more desperate. 'Get up. Please.'

Red tried to roll. It was clearly uncomfortable, but she managed to expose most of her belly. Boyd ruffled the fur around her ribs. She purred and whinnied, and he smiled at her through tears. 'It doesn't hurt, does it?' he said. But it didn't look to. If anything, she was being sedated, or –

kinder – settled by the process. She might even have been pleased with herself. Boyd cleared his throat and wiped his arm across his eyes and said, 'I have to go upstairs. I'll come back, okay? I'll come back.' And he tore himself away and checked the front door, whose entire face was charred. What remained of the lock barrel had been raised up on a thicket of moss, presented to him as though apologetic. This was why there'd been no sound when it fell in. Still, he wondered if the scorch marks on the ceiling meant that Tony's men had also pushed fuel through the letterbox, tried to burn down the house; and if the moss had smothered the flames...

He left the room with a leaden stomach, stumbling on the uneven lino. New smells came in waves, dizzying. Fruiting bodies covered the roof. Bright motes, spores, churned freely in the kitchen. The whole house seemed to be flexing around him. Oddest of all was the sense it was still *lived-in*. Full and welcoming.

At the staircase, the bitter smell turned sweet. Boyd started up the stairs like a toddler trying to walk. The moss ended on the first step, where the carpet fibres were eaten away, corroded right down through the underlay. To balance himself, he had to touch the step in front of him; it was singed and rough, and left a tarry substance on his hands. To one side were a number of pale, gristly-looking wires running up the wall. They were stretched taut from top to bottom, parallel with the handrail, and thickened near the top into something more like tendons. Boyd emerged on the landing to a second pale column, fed by the same wires. This one was smaller, or at least less established, than the one in the lounge, and it was more tubular in structure. He looked inside. A kind of raw, bloody gullet ran directly into a flat base, where the light *just* picked out wet movement, something sheened and slippery, and churning. As Boyd watched, things emerged from this sludge, as if the column was deliberately showing them to him. First a yellow, mercury-filled molar, then a tangle of dark hair, then a noduled, cracked piece of meat, powdery yellow – exactly like Tony's tongue. Terrified, Boyd reared back and nearly fell down the stairs. He gagged and looked again with a terrible curiosity. This time he saw shoelaces, a filthy branded cap, and a hammer.

The boy had been back. Tony had moved – or *been* moved – up here. The ligaments, on the walls. The house had dealt with them both. *Digested* them. Now it was displaying its trophies.

There were three more rooms to check. He had to leave, but he had to know. Every wall was saturated with damp and mould, and the remaining wallpaper had sloughed away to reveal venous cracks in the brickwork. Intricate, ribbed forms spanned the ceiling – organic waves that might have been shaped by the fumes that were filling the house. He went into his bedroom. His clothes were piled on his bed, the way Maureen had piled his father's clothes in the Watford house, the way Joan had piled Ted's belongings in her garden. The mattress was wet with mould. He sat on one end, trying to see a way forward, and saw he'd be waiting a long time. In the mirror he was older, haunted. He was conscious of taking things detail by detail to protect himself from the whole. He stood up and walked, eyes closed, to his mother's room.

Of course she wasn't there. Of course she'd gone. The house had filled the void with dank life. Yes: a third column was thickening by her dressing table. He could see her wigs near the top of it, partly melted. A more vibrantly purple moss had twined and stiffened around the furniture, and almost consumed the mattress. The walls were covered with dirty handprints, though, again, the finger marks were much too long. The curtains were almost translucent. They could have been made from skin. The suitcase was buried.

The pink fantasy novel had been torn up. Sheafs of its pages, still bound by glue, lay in a rough path around the room. He closed what was left of the door.

Then the bathroom. On pushing, something heavy fell against the other side of the door. Boyd was struck by the image of a giant swollen tongue lapping at the frame. In desperation he kicked and clawed and shoved. But his efforts only caused a golden liquid like rendered fat to run onto the landing. The remains of the carpet began to smoke. There was a hissing sound, as if a pressure had been released, and then the stench of vomit. Tony's boys are in there, too, he thought. And, as if to reply, the column on the landing glowed hot. Rasps and trickles and a deep, timorous groaning, a shuddering from the footings to the roof timbers.

Panic got the better of him. He ran downstairs. Back through the kitchen, towards Red. He thought the house was about to collapse, or, improbably, turn into something else. The moss had weakened everything. Red was still in the front room, suckling on a nubbin of material that had emerged from the column. She was placid, eyes flickering with a lucent blue glow. Her neat, dextrous tongue had taken on the colour of the column. Her fur rippled as if she were being stroked. Boyd tried to grab her, but was thrown against the wall by a precise, directed heat. He checked himself, surprised enough to believe he'd been stabbed. He pawed at his chest. Again the heat, hard against his knees. He sprawled. He was the intruder, now. When he said, 'Red, can't you just come with me?' his voice sounded like somebody else's. He had a vague memory, an idea of a response he should make, a claim or bargain; but he couldn't even reach himself. He wanted to be certain, and he wanted to forget.

He said, 'Mum?' and there was another blast of heat, this time to his face, and with it a conviction: the house would make him part of itself, as it had Tony and the boy. And the walls shuddered again, as if he'd spoken and the house had heard. A clean, undiluted thought. A *correction*. The house was warning him, protecting him, pushing him away. The doors and windows bulging outwards weren't signs of the house trying to spread, but fighting to hold something in.

And if Boyd stayed, the roof would slide off, the joists would buckle, the walls would collapse, and he'd be buried with it.

He told Red he was sorry and ran to the flattened back door, which was already being lifted back into place by the moss in the kitchen. He fought past it, back into the yard, where the carpet of blackened moss visibly recoiled at his presence. The moon was rising, pink-tinged. He left Sile by the long road towards Neighton Prangle.

LANDFILL

Herring gulls clouded the boundary of Neighton Prangle, underlit by floodlamps and misshapen by dusk. Approaching, Boyd watched the birds scavenge a mound of earth that rose behind a concrete wall ahead, uneasy at their number and the way they phased in and out of the shadows. A torch beam swept towards him, lingered on his face, and snapped off. Boyd squinted, dazzled. When the floaters cleared, he could only stare. Standing there – one foot pushed insouciantly against the wall – was Leigh.

She watched Boyd shuffling up the hill, but didn't speak or gesture to him. Boyd, embarrassed and surprised to see her, stopped a short distance away.

'Why didn't you call?' Leigh said.

Boyd stood there, sweating, as the gulls' shadows harried the ground between them. 'I lost your card,' he croaked, patting his pocket. 'And I don't have a phone.'

Leigh spat on the road and came towards him. She looked dirtier than he remembered.

'Getting late,' she said.

He wasn't sure what to tell her. Where he'd even start.

But Leigh seemed to read him anyway. She smiled, tilted her head back towards the mound. 'See for miles on a clear day. Right out to the power station if you're lucky. You cut a sad figure, coming up.'

Boyd gazed up at the birds, trying to imagine their view. He came back to the dirty wall, its graffiti tags. The litter in the dank puddles beside it. 'You live here?'

Leigh chuckled with the smallest hint of superiority. 'Kind of.' She came forward and touched Boyd's shoulder, pinched the heavy fabric of his father's coat, then squeezed all the layers beneath. 'Have you run away?'

Again, Boyd didn't answer. He was staring at the mound, then at her. Is that what he'd call this? Running away?

'You want a brew?' Leigh asked. 'I've got the heating on.' And Boyd realised this wasn't even aloofness – it was confidence. He was in Leigh's territory now; he was on her terms.

Boyd nodded, too exhausted to be polite, and wiped the sweat from his nose. There was still a faint scent of Red's fur on his hand. It was hard not to feel infected, that he was shedding spores.

'Christ,' she said, grinning. 'I'd almost forgotten how awkward you are.'

He tried to smile but didn't quite manage it. There were lots of things in his mind at once. Then Leigh rolled her eyes, led him towards the gap in the wall, lifted a section of rusted chicken wire, and ushered him through.

'The kennel's just over here,' she said.

Leigh's kennel, it turned out, was a rusty panel van at the base of the mound. It was lashed down with luminous tent ropes, each carefully fastened to the chassis mounts and tyreless rims, with one doubling as a clothesline for overalls, boots and socks. Somebody had graffitied the van's dirty sides with yellow happy faces. All around it lay piles of scrap metal, plastic, and wood salvage, neatly sorted.

Leigh stood Boyd near the van's rear barn doors while she

unlocked the side, grinning to herself. He looked alternately between the birds, his hands, and the looming mound itself, a great dark hillock of wild grasses, weeds and part-buried waste. An ageing bulldozer was parked halfway up it.

'I see what you're thinking,' Leigh said, sliding the door open. 'She *actually* lives here?' She opened the rear barn doors from inside, emerged with a grin. 'But she does.'

The van's interior was decorated with fairy lights and bright rag streamers. A single mattress was propped on a wooden box frame, and a pair of heavy woollen blankets hung from a length of fishing line strung through the roof. The van's bulkhead had been torn out, and a shower curtain hung from a rail above the space where the front passenger seat had been. Everything smelled of burned candlewax and toast.

'Cosy enough,' Leigh said, kicking off her boots.

Boyd stepped inside. There were pictures of loved ones behind the dangling fabrics, unframed and stapled into ply lining. A saucepan set. A cool box. Leigh, with practised ease, was already lighting a jet-stove on the kickstep.

'Hot milk all right? Out of teabags till I've done another shop. Got some mad herbal shit somewhere, but I won't force that on you.'

Boyd shrugged. 'It's fine,' he said.

'Even better with honey,' Leigh said. 'Try the trunk for me?' She meant the wooden crate by Boyd's feet. He opened it: cardboard dividers separating recycled jars. He tried a few – marmalade, pickle, chutney – until he found it.

'And take that frigging coat off,' Leigh added. 'Making me uncomfortable just being near you.'

Boyd squatted to unzip his father's jacket. He kept it on, though. The trials of the day had reached his knees. The urge came to tell Leigh everything – unload and collapse, let it out, let someone else carry it. But what he'd seen in the house, the exposure of his mother's second life, also held him back. He'd entered a parallel reality, and was nowhere close to processing it.

'I left,' Boyd said at last. 'I've got no money, and I need to get to my nan's.'

Leigh glanced up from the pan, a flash of worry across her brow. She took two mugs and poured the milk. 'Right,' she said.

'You said there might be some work.'

Leigh nodded thoughtfully. She stirred in the honey with the blade of a Swiss Army knife. 'I'd have to check with Gaff.'

'Gaff?'

'Bossman. Site's his – I only look after it. A caretaker.' Leigh passed Boyd a mug. He held it with both hands, enjoying the warmth. Leigh settled herself on the floor with him. She clinked his mug with hers and said, 'You're lanky, so you'll probably fit lengthways down here. If we can find you some squashy stuff to lie on.'

'Are you sure?'

'Can't turn away a waif, can I? We'll chat work in the morning. The only condition, mind, is that you actually say something. With actual words, I mean, and not this puppy-dog face you keep pulling. Cos, serious talk, your chat's pretty shite.'

Boyd nodded, as if to prove her point, and sipped his milk. It went down like syrup, coating the inside of him. Rich and soothing around his ribs. He exhaled, letting some of the tension go. Outside, wind rattled the scraps with a surprising musicality. The gulls moved tidally, up and down the mound, though it was much harder to see them individually now the light was gone.

Leigh sipped from her mug, too. Just studying him.

*

Later, Boyd lay on the floor while Leigh brushed her teeth and used the compost toilet without closing the shower curtain. She didn't seem to care that Boyd was there, or perhaps actively revelled in his discomfort. She settled on her own mattress and rolled away from him. He stared at all the crudely filled boltholes in the roof and thought he heard her say, 'It'll be better soon,' before she dozed off. He lay extremely still, scared of sleep, of dreams taking him back to the house. Cloying dusklight had turned every surface a bruisy, infected colour. That old tightness in his chest, spreading upwards and settling behind his eyes. He resisted as long as he could, motionless but drifting, taking inventory. Penniless, homeless, motherless. The gulls' cries on the cold draught.

But even the gulls stilled, in the end.

When Boyd woke up, it was to a series of loud bangs down the length of the van. A man's muffled voice, low and rough. Leigh reached over and flicked Boyd on the cheek.

'Gaff's in,' she whispered, swinging her legs off her bunk. 'Tell him you'd like some hours, and don't be gobby.'

She opened the barn doors. Watery light filtered through. The smell of plastic burning. Boyd couldn't see Gaff yet, but the man's presence was thick.

'Now then,' Gaff said.

'All right?' Leigh said.

Gaff laughed. 'I am, girl – are you? Only I was reviewing our CCTV this morning... You've not got some little rentboy in there, have you?'

Leigh snorted and shifted so Gaff could see behind her. He and Boyd came face to face. He was older than Boyd had imagined: a horseshoe of self-shaved white hair above a prominent brow, a broad red nose, a wrinkled but still powerful neck. On seeing Boyd, he grinned a set of nubbin teeth. It was a cruel mouth.

'Good Christ, Leigh!' he said, chuckling. 'Stone me! Tell me he's not a keeper. The bloody state of him!'

Boyd stared at Gaff. Inadequacy slid through him.

'He's over from Sile,' Leigh said.

'Well, that explains about half of it. And what are you doing here, son? What d'you want with our Leigh?'

'He's no trouble,' Leigh went on. 'After some work.'

Gaff chuckled. 'And you've got Leigh talking for you already, is that right? We gonna have to get union-busting round here?' He turned back to Leigh, incredulous. '*Does* he speak, or what?'

'Hi,' Boyd managed.

Gaff shook his head. 'Oh, he says, "Hi!" Anything else in there? Or are you always a fucking salad?'

'I didn't want to interrupt,' Boyd said.

Gaff laughed. 'And he's a bleeding southerner an' all! Come *on*, Leigh. We can't help them, not round here.'

'Gaff,' Leigh said. 'He's—'

'It wouldn't be for long,' Boyd said. 'A couple of weeks. So I can buy a train ticket.'

'Train?'

'To go south.'

'*Gaff*,' Leigh said.

'Show me your hands, kid,' Gaff said. 'Come on.'

Boyd shuffled towards the rear doors, palms out. Gaff peered at them, then reared back, shaking his head. 'See, girl, you've purely bad taste, simple. It's all soft. Lad his age ought to have roughed-enough hands already. I'd want these clothes smutted and dirt under the nails. That's how you earn your food on a big bloody plate each night.'

'He's good for it,' Leigh insisted.

'So you keep saying. But are you, son?'

Boyd said he was.

'And you get it, do you? You get what I'm about?'

Boyd nodded cautiously.

'So come right out here, will you? My back's no good in there, blasted van. I want to see these arms of yours. Come out and let me have a go.'

Boyd was mindful of being in his underwear. He stepped, barefoot and blinking, onto the wet earth. Gaff looked him up and down. Boyd was roughly the same height, though Gaff was twice his width. Gaff touched Boyd's neck first, pressing his way round it. Boyd stayed still. Then Gaff threw a full hand around Boyd's nape, so that Boyd stumbled forward. Gaff caught him and braced his shoulders, shook him. Next, he squeezed Boyd's arms from tricep to elbow, right down to the wrists.

'Mole arms,' Gaff announced, self-satisfied. 'A racing snake, Leigh – a real streak of piss. Which is right enough for tight holes, eh? Eh? Tight holes! We'll have to call you pipe cleaner, lad – get you dipping. Eh? No trouble, and no lube, neither!'

With that, Gaff released Boyd and laughed until he was spluttering. He turned to Leigh, face swollen. She was visibly conflicted. 'And you still want us to hire him?' he asked her.

Leigh hesitated for effect, then nodded. 'More the merrier,' she said. 'Could do with the help. So long as our deal still stands. He needs some cash, that's all it is. Isn't it?'

Boyd nodded to Gaff. 'To get down to my nan's.'

Gaff glanced up to his right, calculating. 'Can you drive?'

Boyd nodded again, though this time he was more unsure. Dougie, in one of his more present moments, had taught him the basics in a supermarket car park, though it hardly qualified him. 'Yes,' he said.

'Then maybe you'll squeeze a week's trial out of me. But you have to give me something for insurance. What's in there with you? Shoes? Decent watch? That jacket of yours looks smart, actually. I'll take any deposit, me. And you, Leigh –

you'll feed him, sleep him. So long as he sticks to the plan. Call it sub-contracting. He's your side-hustle, now.'

'Fine,' Leigh said. 'But no deposits. It's on my word.'

Boyd felt bewildered. He couldn't see why Leigh was so keen to see him right. He also had the feeling that if he asked, she wouldn't say.

Gaff pursed his lips in appreciation.

'And you're how old, again?' he asked Boyd.

'Sixteen,' Boyd said.

'Sixteen! Sixteen! Them were the days. Runty sixteen with noodles for arms. You got any pubes down them pants, or what? I say it like I even know your name. Face like a twenty-one-year-old's, body like a girl's…'

Boyd nodded. He started, 'My name's—'

'No!' Gaff snapped. 'Don't just *say* it, you daft bloody apeth. Don't tell me. You're better off me calling you nowt. Taxman rocks up here, I don't want to know who you are from Adam.' He turned back to Leigh. 'Go on then, love. Give him a whirl. You get any crap off him, though, and he's gull feed.' Then, to Boyd: 'Lot of places round here to bury someone. Cute, isn't she?'

'Piss off,' Leigh said.

Gaff smirked and went to turn away. As he did, he slapped Boyd across the seat of his boxer shorts. Boyd's obvious shock made Gaff snigger again. 'The plan is the plan,' Gaff said. 'But do us all a favour while you're at it, will you, son? Pack that pecker away.'

Leigh looked across. Boyd looked down, mortified. He was hanging out of the slit of his boxer shorts.

After breakfast – half a bowl of porridge with water and butter, Leigh's 'proper way' – she gave Boyd clothes for his first day up the mound. A set of greasy, oversized overalls;

a pair of battered work boots whose steel toecaps were visible through the leather; and a shovel, which he could only carry awkwardly across his chest using both hands. Leigh, meanwhile, had taken up a small but lethal-looking pickaxe, slung over one shoulder; a trowel; and a bunch of faded plastic shopping bags for her back pocket.

'What were you dreaming about last night?' she asked.

Boyd couldn't remember. If anything, he'd woken up feeling safer, even more detached. Convinced, by some wild process, that what had happened to Tony and the boy had been their own fault. Or that none of it had happened at all.

'You watched me?' he asked.

'Couldn't bloody help it,' she said. 'You were twitching like mad. I'd have lit more candles to help you relax, but it would've been too hot with two of us. Next thing, mind, your eyes are wide open. You were staring at me, except you weren't awake.'

He didn't know what to say, and was glad when they reached the base of the mound, where her focus shifted upwards.

'Doesn't matter, anyway,' she said. 'Let's crack on.'

The mound was steeper than it looked, and Boyd kept tripping in divots and deep holes concealed by rubble and chunks of plastic. Height brought a different perspective: the mound was more like a dune, where refuse was added to the base and pushed upwards, pushed deeper in, layered over and gradually compacted. In places, Boyd could detect a heat being generated inside it, vented from holes. Settlement, compression, matter breaking down. Pale, feeble weeds sprung from the gaps, their leaves coated in a sticky brown film that rubbed off on Boyd's boots. He thought of his mother and saw his own roots as equally friable. He thought of a word: *orphan*. And he thought of the moss, the front room, his deep knowing, and, nauseated again, began to avoid the weeds as much as he could. Not like Leigh, who went so lightly, with all the self-assurance of a Sherpa.

Further up, away from the most rancid mulch, it was easier to recognise individual items in the junk. Remnants of other lives: toys and appliances, broken discs and smashed electronics, chain-link fencing and pieces of garden furniture. A legless doll whose hands were outstretched, pleading.

Nearer the summit of the mount, where the herring gulls were congregated, Leigh said, 'There you are.'

The view was of bleak hills and fallow fields, the old roads he'd once walked to school and back. The town of Neighton Prangle, with its prettier semi-detached houses and their brick chimneys. And the terraces of Sile, far enough away to feel neutered. Boyd leaned on the shovel and allowed himself a moment of respite.

'This is all we'll leave behind,' Leigh said, kicking at the mound. 'Some species. And it won't even look so bad, will it. Another bump in a field, green as grass. Like we never happened at all. Don't you wish you could see it? The ending?'

Boyd turned his back on Sile. The waste tapered away down the mound, multicoloured, a sum of impossible angles. He wiped his forehead with his sleeve and nodded. Further up, the gulls billowed and resettled to carry on sifting the cover-fill. He wanted to ask Leigh if he'd imagined it all; if his mother had been imaginary, a fake from the start.

'Maybe,' he replied.

Leigh rolled her eyes and sat on a slab of sofa foam, feet crossed in front of her. She'd brought a small notepad and was now writing in it. The gulls cawed and jostled. Sometimes, Boyd thought, their cries sounded too human.

'It's nice for remembering,' Leigh explained. 'Even a half-page'll do. Just one a day. I saw this thing once – if you don't record it, it'll stop existing. You know how time runs so much faster when every day's the same? This – this helps you pin it down. It helps you remember.'

Boyd tried to take that on board. He asked if her family lived nearby. She gave no verbal answer – just a tell, a sheepish twitch in her nose. He tried a different tack: how *long* had she been here?

'Eight months, six days,' she replied, her voice glassier. She turned the page, used her wrist to break the spine. Then she pointed her pen at Boyd. 'You know what,' she said, 'I think I liked you more when you kept your mouth shut.'

Boyd bristled, defensive. 'So what am I meant to do?'

Leigh tutted into her notepad. Their age difference – unconfirmed, though blatant – felt clearest in moments like these, when she asserted herself sharply enough to remind him.

'Are we trying to find stuff?' he asked.

'Obviously,' Leigh said. She stabbed her journal with the pen, over-emphasising a full stop, then closed it. 'I wanted to give you a quick tour first,' she said. 'Okay? And now—' she pointed to the bulldozer '—you can stay up here while I get us started.'

Leigh skipped down the mound like a dancer, climbed into the dozer with no loss of grace. The thing choked on in a cloud of black smoke and made the whole mound vibrate, the topmost layers shifting beneath Boyd's feet, scattering the gulls. Then Leigh lowered the dozer's plough and powered downhill, pushing a swathe of waste towards her van. Churned up, the mound released thick new smells, and the gulls rushed in for fresh pickings.

Leigh stopped the dozer near the base of the mound. 'Never gets old!' she shouted. The birds roiled at the wound; Leigh's face was bright with sweat and pleasure. She climbed onto the dozer's engine cowl, beckoning him. Just then he saw an orange animal move between the fence and her van. For a moment, he thought it might have been Red. He shook his head, struck by a sense of intrusion, a pang of fear. A fox, he told himself. Had to be.

Leigh met him at the bottom with pair of gardening gloves and walked him along the stripe of waste pushed from the mound. The gulls were manic around them. 'This is the inbox,' she said. 'Now we have to work out what's junk.'

Boyd nodded, but he was distracted. He was thinking of Red, the way he'd left her. The smell and taste, that terrible heat on his face.

'Seriously,' Leigh said. 'Are you listening?'

'Sorry,' he said.

'Look.'

He looked. Wet items like spilled organs, knotted plastic bags bloating with decay. Rolls of sodden carpet and wadded paper; baled plastics and green polystyrene; torn, mouldering fabrics. Crushed hardcore held together by broken roots. Swollen, blackened nappies. And so many new things growing in the squalor.

But Leigh wasn't bothered by any of that. She took up a lump of charred wood, launched it over her shoulder. Undeterred, almost perversely calm, even as things split and dripped and smeared her overalls. Yet when she found something with wires attached, her expression changed. She wiped the object down her legs, held it out at arm's length, furrowed her brow.

'Electrical stuff?' Boyd asked. 'Is that what you're after?'

Leigh smiled cynically. 'Mostly.'

'Does any of it work?'

'Nah. But metals have weighbridge value. We clean up the good stuff. Split the cash when Gaff pawns it. Like tips, yeah? And it's all right by me. It does work out. You won't believe how many wedding rings you turn out. Necklaces, bracelets, wallets… dildos.' She scratched her cheek thoughtfully. 'Some fucking *massive* dildos. And then there's this.' She unzipped her overalls and took a tatty piece of paper from an inside pocket. It was a photocopied image of multiple hard drive models, annotated with a marker pen. 'Real gold.'

'Hard drives?'

She laughed. 'Crypto. Like, some kid in Manchester binned her dad's wallet-drive last year. Two million in Britcoin, and trackable. Came right through the system and wound up here for processing. Owner rocks up with his maps, promising a big cut if they can excavate. Except Gaff won't have it – says the tracking app isn't accurate enough. He palms the guy off and brings me in to help, just in case. You wanna see the decryption gear he's running in his caravan.'

Boyd was amazed. 'Does this guy know you're after it?'

'Course he does,' Leigh said. 'Keeps popping up with new deals, better terms. But Gaff just mugs him off.'

'Why wouldn't he just let the owner search?'

Leigh snorted. 'Principle? When your stuff winds up here, Gaff owns it. You let one sad-sack in, there'll be queues of them wanting all the sentimental shit they've chucked on impulse. He'd have no business left.'

'And if you somehow find it, you get a bit of what's on it?'

Leigh shrugged and blew out her cheeks. 'Truth is,' she said, 'you're asking the wrong person.'

Boyd went to speak again, but Leigh had turned away.

'Crack on, yeah?' she said. 'You'll get into it.'

So Boyd pulled on the gardening gloves, took up the shovel, and did his best. Offcuts and metal strips, rotten wood, nothing much committed. Nothing like as nonchalant as Leigh. A short while later, growing in confidence, he removed a polythene bag filled with rags. The bag was heavier than it looked and snagged as he tugged it out, spraying his legs with a stinking liquid.

He coughed into his sleeve.

'Beginner's luck,' Leigh said, trying to keep a straight face. 'Doubt you'll need a tetanus.' She came over, patted him on the back, and dangled a handkerchief in front of his face. 'Rub it under your nose,' she said. 'Does the job till the stink's burned through your most sensitive bits, anyway. Which is to say: oh mate, I promise it gets easier.'

Boyd pulled the rag into his face and inhaled. Warm vanilla, sharp menthol, then burning citrus. The mixture caught in his throat. Astringent, like the air fresheners that had failed to mask the smells back home.

INGRESS

It was punishing work. Leigh and Boyd broke only for treated rainwater, long-life milk and tinned food, to plaster cuts and scrapes, compress bruises and tape ankles, and, beyond sunset, to sugar-soap grime from their skin. Boyd was clearing a metre every ten minutes or so, faster if the items were big enough, though he especially hated the white goods and wet mattresses. His body ached from bending and twisting, and his feet were blistered at the toebox and solid heels of the boots. When Gaff came by to check on their progress – assessing the sifted junk behind them, inspecting items of note – he suggested Boyd do some squats and lunges. 'Like you're having a dump in the wild,' he said. 'Speed you up, get those glutes nice and pert.'

Yet despite the pain, Boyd took some relief from the job. Its repetitiveness was intense enough to numb some of what had come before. Instead of being haunted by what he'd seen, by the existential shock of Maureen's disappearance, he found he could partition himself; believe those things had happened to another person, that they were merely bad dreams, half recalled. An idea that Maureen wasn't gone, only temporarily absent. And when he did lose himself to dread, he found it useful to focus on the fact he was now earning the money he needed to escape the situation. Acting was better than not. He'd do this, find Joan, and with her try to make sense of the world again.

Leigh, meanwhile, rarely spoke as she worked. When a thought came to her, she preferred to take out her notebook and jot it down. Similarly, she continued to duck Boyd's questions, openly cringing when he attempted small talk, or tried to find out more about her, like how she'd come to live on the site. 'Not now, dickhead,' she'd say. 'Not when there's this much to sort.' Something had happened along the way, he judged, and she was hiding her scars. All the same, she maintained a self-reliance he admired. She dressed his grazes, made their tea, spoke persuasively about alcohol. And no matter how much she sweated, how long she went without a shower, she never seemed to smell as bad as him.

So their days rolled together, and his first week passed. It was all forgettable, which felt like the point, until one afternoon Boyd dug out a hard drive. 'Leigh,' he said, scraping mud from its ports. 'Leigh!'

She'd already stopped. One hand on her hip, beaming at him. 'Spicy,' she said. 'What we saying? Six out of ten? What's the make?'

Boyd rubbed the case and squinted at the debossed logo. 'Think it says Blapfort?'

'Oh, that's an easy seven,' Leigh said. 'Hardcore encryption on those. Might've seen a few quid in its time.' She looked away, as if to double-check Gaff wasn't near. 'Maybe let's keep that one back,' she said. 'Try and crack it ourselves.'

Boyd felt pleased with himself, worthy of something, and pocketed the drive. But he was careful to hide a smile, because Leigh's scoring of the Blapfort had also betrayed her: she was playing her own games to cope.

He said, 'And he'll definitely give us a cut?'

'Sure,' Leigh said sharply. 'It's…' She trailed off. Her expression had changed – another flicker of remorse, or even shame. She checked the horizon for sundown, the gathering night, and dropped the child's car seat she had in her hands. 'Shall we call it a day? My hands are shagged.'

Back at the van, Leigh lit candles, rinsed nettles for tea and threw a blanket over Boyd's legs, tucking him in without irony. He liked it when she brushed against him, even accidentally. He also liked listening to her faint singing as she pottered around the van. Was a kind of comfort or contentment growing between them? There was definitely a straightforwardness they could both draw from.

Then Leigh stopped singing, and Boyd swivelled to see her fiddling with the rear doors. Licking her lips, pressing down with her fingers. Concentrating.

'What's up?' he asked.

She glanced over.

'Leigh?'

'Nothing,' she said, but her neck had reddened.

'Is it broken?'

'It's nothing!' she snapped. 'Wait!' Then, catching herself: 'It's maintenance. It hasn't happened for ages.'

Boyd threw off the blanket and joined her. She'd stuck a piece of used chewing gum to the inside of the door.

'What's that do?'

She wouldn't look at him. 'Please,' she said.

'Was that a hole?'

She sighed and rubbed her eyes. 'It's...' She went to her bunk, sat down. 'He just wants to wind me up. Show off in front of you. He'll have been at the pub last night, that's all, and I didn't spot it. I've covered a few this last couple of months. No big deal.'

Boyd's stomach had curdled. 'Gaff? He watches you?'

'I don't know. I don't think so. He has this little metal

punch. You only have to tell him to piss off, pack it in. He can act like a nonce, sure, but it's more like a power thing. When I get mad, he'll say I shouldn't have such a mouth on me, shouldn't bloody run it at my elders. He's always different in the daytime. My old man was the same. You just have to manage him.'

Boyd wasn't biting. He could tell Leigh was downplaying something, or didn't want to scare him. And equally, that saying it out loud was making it real for her.

He pointed to the hole she'd filled. 'You're all right with him doing this?'

Leigh shrugged ruefully. Her confidence had drained, exposing a vulnerability.

'Have to keep him sweet,' Leigh said. 'Especially when you need your spends. Like, I'm due on my period next week, and I'm running out of towels.'

'That's a crap excuse.'

'Maybe,' she admitted. 'But it's the deal.'

Boyd stared at her.

'I owe him. My family does. It's—'

'You don't have to tell me.'

'Well I will, if you can shut up for five minutes.'

Boyd sat down again, pulled her blanket round his shoulders.

'Dad worked here, once,' Leigh explained. 'Him and Gaff were partners. But Dad fucked up, big time. Screwed Gaff for a few grand and did a runner with his fancy-piece. Left me and Mam, too. Gaff and some of his lads turn up at our house, threats and all of it. I had to take the flak for Mam, because what was she gonna do? She was already broken, Dad was gone. I said I'd cover it. I said I'd level things out. So now I'm here till Dad's debt is settled. And that's how I know it's a good thing I found you, even if I do feel shitty for pushing my luck.'

Boyd blinked at her. 'You thought I'd help find more stuff to sell?'

'Maybe.' She coughed. 'I wanted to spread my bets. You help me, I help you. But I'm not a user, Boyd. I swear on Mam's life, I'm not. I saw you in that supermarket. Like, *saw* you. It takes a stray to know a stray.'

Boyd took a deep breath.

'We just have to find the right stuff to flog,' Leigh went on. 'Earn our cut. And anyway...' She moved away from the doors. 'I wanted to give you this. I found it yesterday.'

She went to her bunk, under her pillowcase, and told Boyd to close his eyes. She pressed an object into his hands – a spiral-bound notepad. There were stains on its cover, but she'd done her best to clean it up. He turned it over.

Leigh grinned. 'Open it, knobhead.'

The first page was a calendar. There were harshly drawn circles around a few dates, as if somebody had resented having to remember them. The next page had BOYD written at the top.

'Better this than the pile of jazz mags Gaff's about to give you,' Leigh said. 'I told him you're better off learning to remember. Write your stuff in here, all of your shit, and you'll remember. And you won't go blind, either.'

Boyd leafed through the notebook. He felt awkward. He didn't *want* to remember.

'Plus,' Leigh said, 'we're taking tomorrow off. Gaff's cleared it – there's something I've been meaning to do.'

She knelt by the trunk and pulled out a rusty tobacco tin with a Queen of Spades etched on its lid. It contained a sheaf of brown envelopes, which she spread on her bed.

'Seeds,' she said. 'From back home. I know a place with the right kind of shade. We'll make it a project.'

Boyd looked at them, then at her.

'Okay,' he said.

LAMB

*

A sharp draught woke Boyd early. Leigh was dressed and sitting by the open side door, lacing her boots. Steam from the kettle was curling through the van. He stretched and coughed drily. Leigh had been coughing through the night, too.

'Morning,' he said, trying not to overthink it.

'Hi,' she said grimly, as if she'd been waiting.

'What's up?'

'Uh, there's been a thing.'

Some of the gulls had died on the mound overnight, was the news. Gaff had been up early, brought their carcasses down with him. 'Had them by their necks,' Leigh added, with fascination. 'Eight or nine. They were so *pale*.' And sure enough, there were white feathers blowing around outside, collecting against the inbox like slush after a hailstorm. Boyd, still in his boxers, pointed as if they'd turned up by magic. One feather blew against Leigh's boot. 'Blood and all,' she said, picking it up, wiping it on her overalls. 'Never really think birds have blood in them, do you?'

Boyd didn't know what to tell her, and couldn't face the mound. The closer he looked, the more rot he saw.

'He took them, anyway,' Leigh went on. 'Or at least the ones that wouldn't fit in the burn barrel. If he brings stew round later, just pretend you've already eaten. I know what he's bloody like.'

Boyd asked, 'What killed them?'

'I dunno.'

'Gaff didn't say?'

She coughed. 'Fox? Or maybe they ate something? It's toxic as, some of this stuff.'

'Yeah,' Boyd said, thinking guiltily of the animal he'd seen on his first trip up the mound.

'Yeah,' she agreed, and gestured to the kettle. 'Isn't it your turn to brew up?'

'Okay,' he said.

Leigh went outside and slid the side door closed. She started pacing, apparently struggling to clear her throat. Despite her nonchalance, he could tell she was uneasy.

'Are you having one?' he asked through the door.

'For my flask,' she said, nodding. Then: 'I'm nipping into town after.'

'Sile?'

'Neighton.'

'To see your mum?'

She shook her head. 'Painkillers and throat syrup. My head's banging. Isn't yours?'

That afternoon, they went to plant Leigh's seeds near a bank of tall nettles at the site's far wall, hidden from view by the bulk of the mound. Leigh had already cleared flagstones and aerated a patch of soil. 'I'll give Gaff "side-hustle",' she said, ordering and reordering her seed packets by some mysterious criteria. 'Dog rose, daisy, bluebell, wood anemone,' she whispered, sowing them in turn. She marked the plot with a pair of criss-crossed car aerials. Boyd watched in a reverie, as though suddenly aware of her complexity. This, he saw, was Leigh at her most sincere. The careful way she turned the soil, tipped in the seeds, patted it back. It was in her face when she spaced the seeds to give them their best chance. A sense it mattered enormously.

'I do miss Mam,' she told him, as if to confirm or concede to what she'd revealed about Gaff and her father the night before. They squatted in silence for a while, as the gulls wheeled overhead.

Then Leigh stood up. 'Come on,' she said. 'No point moping about. It's going to hammer it down.'

Leigh's introspection lasted as they stood eating pastries under a plastic sheet rigged to the van. Sure enough, the rain fell hard; Boyd wondered again if there was a deeper affection between them, a bond he couldn't name or wouldn't dare to. Part of him wanted to settle it, to ask her if she felt the same. Another part of him yearned for the kind of attention he'd been losing ever since Dougie had died. The rest of him, however, was well trained in rejection, and he managed to keep the lid on.

'Tell me more about your mum?' he said.

Leigh stopped chewing. 'Oh?'

'I didn't always get on with mine.'

'And you want to know what that's like, do you?'

Boyd shrugged, then smiled, and Leigh laughed. Her mother had trained as a florist at night college, brought home a new bouquet each night. 'The house,' she told him, 'smelled different every morning.'

They used to hike together, too – walked most weekends till arthritis blunted her mother's toes. Even then, her mother worshipped the hills, her beloved trig pillars, heather bashing. Soil and orange clay and the darkness of bare peat, tricky to get out from under your toenails, along with what would – or should – grow where. How her moors might still be forested, if humans hadn't been around. Sphagnum moss and bracken and lichen, and bogs, and deergrass, and mountain hares in their winter coats – and all the rest of it. Unzip your jacket to dump some heat. Reproof the thing when it starts wetting out. Then Leigh's dad had started drinking, and money got tight. Her mum took a second job, at a textiles factory. Leigh worked weekends with her dad at the site, got to know Gaff, under-stood the job. Leigh became a runner for her dad's uppers, supplied by a local dealer. Made a routine of visiting the dodgy off-licence for cheap wine so he could get to sleep. 'He *reeked* when he came in to say night to you,' she said, before a painful cough contorted her face. He always spoke to her from another room. He grew his beard out, but there were patches missing. He was saying so little, by the time he left, that his lips would be too dry and bleed when he yawned. She never saw him eat.

Boyd nodded along, understanding the feeling if not her exact circumstances. The two of them, stray and stray. He wished he could squeeze her hand, but he was scared to try. Then, as if it might compress the ordeal of his own home life into one line, he admitted to her: 'My mum drank, too.'

'Mine's in the hospice now,' Leigh said. 'She won't see me. Says she feels too guilty. Feels like I'm all her fault, either way, and can't stand to be reminded.'

Then quiet. A silence both loaded and hard to bear. Leigh broke it by coughing, went inside the van to pee. When she returned, her eyes were puffy. 'Why don't you write about what we've done today?' she asked. 'Doesn't matter if it makes no sense. It doesn't need to. Nothing makes sense, if you think hard enough.'

Boyd told her he wasn't sure. The recent past was a hot blur, impossible to capture in language.

Leigh wasn't having that. 'It doesn't have to be *poetry*,' she said, chuckling. 'Say how you felt when you woke up. Our breakfast. "*Observations*." I made porridge with unfiltered rainwater because I'm a lazy bastard; you must've tasted the difference. Or it was too hot in the van last night, because I forgot to turn off the heater.' She paused, annoyed with herself for making what she saw as another confession. 'Any old shite, to be honest. Cos it's for you, remember? I don't give a toss. Put, "This sad prick Leigh made me go and plant *flowers* with her."' She sniggered at her own coarseness, then suggested, 'We ate a crap pastry, she spun me a sad story, and then I had to do homework.'

Well, sometimes you smile and can't help what it gives away. Boyd stood there, gormless, and let an idea unfurl.

That night, past their usual bedtime, he tried to record it. Only a page, painfully slowly, while Leigh – unaware he was listening – wept almost silently on her bunk. He tried to articulate a desire to comfort her, offer himself, as he once had to his mother. Equally, he lamented that her façade would so easily come back, that her tears would go unmentioned tomorrow. Because Leigh liked to hide her sadness the way Maureen used to hide hers. He half wondered if Leigh had wanted to weave her sadness into the soil with her seeds, so that it could grow separately from her.

He considered their conversations, their distance, their sudden closeness. His stomach twinged. The last thing he wrote was, *Leigh probably doesn't want to know me.*

As if that was a bad thing.

When he was sure Leigh was sleeping, he took his notepad outside and threw it in the burn barrel, trying not to look at the feathers piled at the bottom. The mound loomed, a great shapeless mass. Some of the other gulls were still circling, and in the quiet their shortened cries sounded even more like children. He sat on Leigh's camping chair for a while, noticing her sporadic cough, trying to reassure himself that the small dark patches on the van doors weren't evidence of fresh mould blooming.

But the cold night was a fluid thing, leaching in. When he touched the doors, and smelled his fingertips to check, he couldn't be sure.

The next morning, Boyd found Leigh and Gaff in a quiet but terse conversation outside the van. It was Gaff who noticed Boyd skulking at the window.

'Out here,' Gaff said. 'Bloody earwig.'

Boyd moved his attention to Leigh, but her stance was closed off, and she wouldn't make eye contact. Her face was drawn; she looked even more ill.

Boyd came out onto the scrub, pulling Leigh's blanket around him. There was a hard lump in his throat.

And there was a newer white van parked behind the kennel.

'It's a good runner,' Gaff said, by way of introduction. 'Goes on red diesel, and my mate's sorted the MOT.' He opened the new van's side door. The cargo area was ply-lined and there was a filthy mattress in there. 'Hose this down, scrub it good, stand it to dry with the blowers on,' Gaff said to Boyd, 'and you'll have your own kennel.' He gestured over his shoulder to Leigh. 'The best bit is, you can drive it up to town so I don't have to pay her cab fares no more.'

Leigh could barely contain a scowl. Boyd nodded to Gaff, but hated the idea of sleeping on that mattress, without Leigh's company, her presence. He thought of the chewing gum she'd used to cover the holes. He wondered if Gaff would ever do that to him, or whether he and Leigh should just take the white van and go...

'Also,' Gaff said, 'we've been chatting about these dying birds of ours.'

'Leigh told me,' Boyd said.

Gaff squinted at him. 'Oh aye? Funny, that, since I've only just told her myself. You seen anything dodgy up there at all? Cos me, I could swear I saw a big old dog-fox up there yesterday. And I'm telling you, sunshine: whatever's done for the poor bastards, it's turned their insides black.'

Boyd didn't say anything.

'It's not right, any road up,' Gaff said. 'So, I'll need you both to pay attention.'

Boyd nodded.

Leigh didn't.

Gaff made a face at them. 'I'm going away for a few nights,' he said. 'Maybe a full week, if I get lucky – let's just say I've made the acquaintance of a lovely lady in Scarborough. It means I'll be relying on you both to make good on your promises. Hard work and persistence. When I get back, I want to see a nice pile of sellable goods, and this new bus scrubbed up nicely. And Leigh, I want you to have this pile of noodles in line.'

'Sure,' she said.

'Good girl. So get grafting, both of you. And mind them birds. They might be like rats, but they're *my* rats – and they keep this place tidier than you do!'

When Gaff had gone, Leigh turned to Boyd. 'Van. Now,' she hissed. They went inside, where Leigh made a show of slamming the door behind them.

'Way more gulls copped it last night,' she said, biting her thumbs intently. And that wasn't all. She'd forgotten to refuel the dozer at the end of their last shift, so she'd gone up with the jerry cans before Gaff could notice. 'I'm there,' she said, 'pissing diesel all over my hands, and the gulls start fighting over scraps, screaming like mad. The rest of the buggers are up in the air, barking. I hike up, and they're all fighting. And trust me, I had a mate whose dad ran a butcher's floor, so I know bright blood means a fresh kill. I ran at them. They shifted. There were two left in the middle of a crater. Gull chicks. Not much to one of them, and its head was *hissing*. The second was more alive, one wing torn so it's hopping about in a circle, a right state.' She paused and rubbed her eyes. 'I couldn't stand it, so I went to grab something, found a steel tube. I had to close my eyes; kept missing. It took a few goes. Then I pushed them down a hole, and I swear I saw purple twigs pulling their carcasses deeper down. When I stood up again, there was a fox, or I think it was a fox, going over the other side. Like it had been watching.'

'That's nasty,' Boyd said, shifting his weight.

'Look at them now,' Leigh said.

He peered out. The birds were settled, barely moving.

'Like they're *scared*,' she said. 'But it can't have been a fox. Because I know a fox doesn't move like that. Those birds were killing each other.'

'I'll go up,' Boyd said.

Leigh was shocked. 'Will you?'

He nodded. He had to.

Because he was convinced he knew what he'd find.

The wind strengthened as Boyd ascended. It was insistent, unbalancing. The light was flatly grey. Heavier weather was scudding in over Neighton Prangle, and the first spits of rain crackled on his father's waterproof jacket. All else was internal, everything switched on at once. He couldn't shift the feeling he was being tracked, hunted. When he swallowed, he heard himself squawk. His breath was shallow.

As Boyd drew close to the top, some of the gulls took flight. A flutter of lazy wings and disappointed-sounding calls; a slow clattering, like sarcastic applause. But the majority stayed in their divots as he passed, and even those in flight seemed to give up quickly. As these gulls landed, stilted and awkward somehow, Boyd noticed that many of them were missing wing feathers.

From the summit he looked across to Sile, down to Leigh and the vans, and tried to massage away the tightness in his chest. He could hear Leigh coughing, even from here. He knelt and took up a handful of top-fill – loose soil, plastic beads – and saw what he feared he'd see. Strands of bright vegetation, damp and tacky. Balls of fungi, strung together with pale threads. The past tore in, flooded him. He fell back, grazing his hands, crushed by the truth. He'd never been good enough. He'd abandoned what he should've stayed and fought for. He'd been wilful enough to think he was the only one who'd got out. That none of it would catch up with him.

Because now the house was blooming here, too.

Heavier rain swept in. The mound seemed to tremble. Boyd got to his feet, wincing. Leigh was by the door of her van, hands on hips, and coughing, coughing, coughing. Boyd was sure he could remember the exact scene, as if he'd lived it before. Not in dreams, or in pictures, but for real. He was undone by the sensation of recalling the *future*. And now that same force, the same knowing, compelled him to the other side of the mound, towards a sharply familiar smell, and a pile of fresh scat.

There he locked eyes with Red, whose ginger coat was torn and wild, and whose whiskers were thicker and moving independently of her. She was glowing, vibrant against the dark cloud base behind. Her fur had the shivering lambency of the column in their living room. Between her forepaws was a bale of wet moss. It was the colour of fresh liver.

'Don't,' Boyd said to her. 'Please don't.'

But Red of course left, leaving only the moss, and a scent. Sweet cucumber, sweet death.

Leigh was rinsing pots with the hosepipe when Boyd returned.

'Boyd?' she said.

He didn't have time. He dove straight into the van, grabbed the kitchen roll, and tore off several sheets. With these he went about wiping and sniffing at the windows and seals, before studying what had come off.

'Boyd,' Leigh said from the door, unimpressed. 'You're soaking!'

He was aware of her, but his task was too important. He kept going, chest burning.

'Boyd!' Leigh shouted. 'You're acting possessed! What's going on?'

Frantically wiping. Sniffing. Wiping. Checking—

Until Leigh caught his wrist, held his arm against his chest. Vanilla perfume and hot fear in her eyes. He turned his head so he wouldn't breathe on her.

'There's no time,' he said.

'Tell me,' she said. 'Jesus Christ, Boyd, what's wrong? You look *awful*.'

He didn't want to tell her, but he needed to tell her—

'Please, Boyd! For Christ's sake!'

'It's Mum,' he said. 'The gulls. The site. It's all...'

Leigh let go, stricken, and spluttered into her sleeve. It was as if their dynamic had changed so quickly, it had given her whiplash. 'You mean your mam? What the fuck are you telling me?'

'Up there. The birds. We have to go... we need to. Pack up. We can just take the new van. While Gaff's gone. Just go.'

Leigh laughed, incredulous. 'What are you *talking* about? We don't have fuel. Gaff's still got CCTV streaming. Even if I wanted to, you know I can't just—'

'Siphon the dozer. He even said – the new van runs on red diesel. We can sort it.'

And now came Leigh's anger. 'You'd better explain what the hell you're playing at.'

Boyd shook his head. Adrenaline had put a spice in his nose. He was shutting down on her. Numbness spreading from his fingers up. There was a real threat of losing her, but—

Leigh was shaking him. 'Boyd! You have to.'

He looked at her. He looked away.

'Please.'

He said, 'I don't even know. But if it's on us, if it's on you, then we have to clean up, fast. We need to sleep in the other van. I keep hearing things, weird things, and I don't know whether it's safe.'

'With no heater? On that rancid mattress?'

'It doesn't matter. It doesn't.'

She said, 'Are more gulls dying? Is that it?'

And Boyd thought of Red in her new form, landfill queen, and all the gulls lined up in rows. When he spoke again, his voice was even, reduced. He said, 'No.' Then, after a hesitation, he added, 'Not yet.'

Leigh stood up, brushed herself down, and said, with fiery denial, 'Do what you fucking want, then. I'm going out to work.'

She managed less than an hour. Boyd, meanwhile, continued cleaning what he could of the van's cabin and living space, filling the burn barrel with soiled paper as he went. There wasn't much mould inside the kennel, admittedly; the corners of the windscreen carried the worst, and that could've been there anyway, but it still needed to be done, and would again.

He only stopped on hearing a frustrated yell. He saw Leigh throw her gear down, her gloves and respirator mask, and come stomping past the kennel.

'Don't follow me!' she said, coughing thickly.

Boyd filled two mugs from the rainwater bowser and followed her anyway; found her squatting by the crossed aerials, hugging her knees. He passed her the mugs and said, 'Here.'

'You know I can't leave,' she said softly.

'And I don't know what comes next,' he said. He was glad she wasn't looking at him. He knew, in himself, that he wouldn't hide how gutted he was. The lump in his throat was still there, large and sore. He lacked the guts to tell her that nothing decent would ever grow here again.

'Do you think they've been poisoned?' she asked. 'The birds?'

'I think so.'

'And us?'

'We're both coughing, aren't we? I don't know.'

Leigh emptied the mugs and watched the water soak into the soil. She turned to him. 'You're different,' she said. 'In your eyes. Like whatever's inside you has started reflecting back.'

He said to her, with some finality, 'It wasn't a fox, up there.' Then, 'It doesn't matter.'

They drifted into the evening, silent and afraid. Neither had much appetite for supper. There was stasis and there was this: treading water, seeking distraction, attempting to find the right way through, and failing. For Boyd, it was a fear of forces unseen, working on another level – or beneath them, in the ground – drawing their strands through the rotten soil, moving inside the mound. Red, in her new and terrible majesty.

At two in the morning, when they agreed to try and sleep, Leigh was still coughing in fits. Boyd – staring up the mound with keen apprehension – made her promise they'd move across to the white van tomorrow.

Leigh went to bed fully clothed, face turned into her pillow. Boyd kept his vigil as faint, harrowing cries drifted down from the mound. A little later, Leigh woke sweating and panting, and asked what he was looking at. What he could see.

'They're all over the place,' he told her, meaning the gulls.

Leigh hadn't the energy to join in. She spluttered and cleared her throat and said, 'All of them?'

He didn't answer. Didn't need to.

'And you really think it's your mam?'

Because maybe they could be honest, at last.

'It's our house. The smell,' he told her. 'I can't explain it any better than that.'

Leigh shook her head. She was still angry. She said, 'What can we even do, right now?' And she was right, of course: they weren't about to go outside, wouldn't so much as light a fresh candle.

When the gulls finally stopped moving, the muted crying continued. 'I keep thinking I can hear a baby,' Boyd confessed to Leigh. But as soon as he'd said it, he was grateful she'd gone back to sleep.

Boyd was awake and ready to leave before dawn. Leigh stirred and asked where he was going. He said, 'Up there again.'

To where the dead gulls were.

In dim light, he collected as many birds as he could, adamant that Leigh shouldn't see. Flies had set in, but the carcasses were otherwise clean, strangely colourless. He took them by their necks and dropped them in bags. When seven or eight were piled together, he wondered if he should try to burn them, but decided the feathers were too waxy, wouldn't take. He went to himself: *I'm so stupid. I'm so stupid. It's not even Mum – it's me.*

Remembering the bathroom, finding Maureen. What she'd said.

Oh, little light. It's all coming off you…

Something clanged, then: Leigh had come up the mound behind him – either quiet enough to go unnoticed, or simply beyond his focus – and was climbing into the dozer. As he watched, she brought it across the mound. It was like cutting grass. All the gulls he'd missed, gathering against the dozer blade. Maybe some were still alive, but she wouldn't have heard over the engine. Leigh made stripes and she made piles. She kept at it till the birds were back together, a quiet flock.

Then she got out and poured a thin fluid all over them, lit a match. The flames burst. A dense, oily smell thickened the air. Boyd dropped his face into his jacket and stood and smelled it anyway. When the pyre was well ablaze, Leigh looked up to him, vacant, forlorn, and went back down to the kennel.

That cry again. Boyd heard it very clearly, this time, and knew it was close. It had come from behind him, a wail that rolled into gurgling, which made him feel cold. Further up, he found the source. On a bed of purple moss, partially concealed by dead flowers, lay the smashed doll he'd seen days before. Except it was reaching differently, vibrating with strain. Closer, he saw its fingers were moving. Two tiny hands, grasping air.

Standing over it, he saw the face, soil around the eyes and in the creases.

Not the doll, but a baby.

There was a baby.

Boyd waited for Leigh in the back of Gaff's new white van. Sitting on the dirty mattress, wrapped in tarpaulin, holding the baby. When Leigh found him, she immediately rubbed her arms, as though his appearance had given her goose-bumps.

'I didn't know what else to do,' he said.

Leigh came to him. Knelt there and lifted Boyd's chin.

'What is that?'

He showed her. The baby in his arms – an actual baby – under the tarp. He said, as though from far away, 'It's sleeping.' He wanted to throw up. His ears hurt. It couldn't be real, but it was.

Leigh didn't react at first. Then her confusion manifested in an odd, dreamy smile. She asked him, 'What have you done?' And, quickly afterwards, 'Where has that come from?'

'On the mound,' he said.

Silence. The baby keening. Leigh still staring at him.

'We'd better get it out of here,' she said.

Boyd shook his head, but Leigh tore away the tarp and lifted out the baby with both hands. It seemed even smaller against her. A pinched, grubby face and dirt around its mouth. Leigh sucked her finger and cleaned its lips. 'Is it a boy or a girl?' she asked. But Boyd couldn't speak for shaking. 'We better get it warm,' Leigh added. And he could see her processing it. The sheer speed of her thoughts.

'I didn't know what else to do,' he said.

'I don't know, either,' Leigh said. 'Here. Wait. I can't. I think I'm gonna puke.' She passed the baby back to Boyd and marched over to the kennel.

Boyd took the baby into him. The baby stirred and tried to open its eyes. It saw him and stopped blinking. His heart ached and his teeth ground together.

'Don't pretend this isn't happening,' Leigh said, returning. He nodded, because he wanted to pretend it wasn't happening. Leigh had gathered towelling, a saucepan, a fleecy blanket. She took the baby and wrapped it. Sucked one corner of the towel and used it to clean the baby's face. 'Is it a girl or boy?' she asked Boyd. 'We can't call it an *it*.'

'I don't know,' Boyd said. 'I didn't look.'

She tutted at him. Babies had to be changed. That was what you did. 'They piss and shit a *lot*,' she said, as if she hadn't been clear enough.

Boyd unwound the blanket, wet and sticky. The infant's skin was damp and sore, spotted with a purple rash. There was a greenish stain all over her back. 'A girl,' Leigh said. Which she was. Boyd took in the girl's semi-spherical stomach, her minute, miraculous fingertips. Leigh wiped away the fluff sticking to the girl's wet face and dabbed the towel across her body. 'I think we should call her Lamb,' she said. Which the girl instantly became. A girl called Lamb, fluffy from the towelling, lying there in Leigh's arms.

'You're going to have to help me,' Leigh said. The girl – *Lamb* – staring at the light, the corners with the most contrast, blinking almost too slowly, and already more content. Boyd stroking her face and shushing her as Leigh did what she thought she was meant to. Lamb didn't cry once, and refixed her focus on Boyd, and held his gaze for an uncomfortably long time. Her eyes were more intent, more intelligent, than he could account for.

Leigh said, 'Let's get her to the hospital, then. Or they'll think we've done this – that we've stolen her. Or they'll think she's ours, and we've neglected her.'

A feeling stirred in Boyd. He said, bluntly, 'No.'

While Lamb watched on.

'What?' Leigh said, her voice quivering. 'She's a baby, Boyd. A baby.'

'I know,' Boyd said.

The girl's impossible nose, lips, shoulders.

'So, we can't,' Leigh said. 'This – we can't.'

But a sureness in Boyd told him they were going to. Had to. Deep knowing.

Lamb.

PART TWO

MAUREEN

Maureen entered the world unknowing yet already full. Even as a newborn, she had the sense of her mind being part-occupied by a person who'd come before her, that her thoughts were pre-mixed with memories from a previous life, of which she caught glimpses through a gauze. At first, these were dangled hints, things she could never quite grasp. But as she grew – and she grew fast – she often experienced impossible visions, an unresolvable sensation of floating, and sharp impressions of places she'd never visited. Sometimes there were fields and gullies and sheep rotting in empty reservoirs. Sometimes it was a tarpaulin shelter stretched between the legs of an electricity pylon. Sometimes, the distinctive face of the gaunt man she'd come to know as her mother's redeemer, only he was happier, rounder in the jaw. But always – always – Maureen remembered the manner of her birth.

Maureen was born to her mother Joan in a cold lock-up, delivered over oily rags on a cold floor. Her birth was neither heralded nor celebrated; it was savage and bloody and, impossibly, she experienced it all. She opened her eyes inside her mother's body; she saw pink light, a gold corona, blood vessels like filigree. Emerging, she saw two faces: her mother's, peering over her own distended belly, and then the gaunt man's, his features severe in the light of a halogen lamp. The man said, 'There you are.' But while Maureen's head was free, the rest of her body wouldn't pass, and the man had to cut around her, caught her in chamois leather and gore-slicked hands, wiped her of vernix.

'There you are,' he said again. He didn't smile – not the way she *remembered* him smiling, not the way she often saw him in the deepest past. And Maureen writhed in his hands while the afterbirth followed. The man placed her on Joan's hollowed belly, where she rooted instinctively for a breast. The milk was electric in her mouth, her mother's scent familiar and close, a clarity that surged through her. And as it flowed, the stranger inside Maureen swelled, and fresh memories glimmered and took shape. Maureen turned within. She found the gauze and pushed it aside, moved deeper into the labyrinth. Horror lit the walls. She had the cleanest thought: *Another body occupies my own.*

But no, it was worse. Maureen had been out here before.

Maureen and Joan slept a lot, those first few days. Joan wasn't right – the man had stitched her wrong, had to do it again. Boiled needle and bright-red string. Afterwards, the man came and went, bringing sheets and clothing stolen from washing lines, saucepans of rainwater, a wind-up torch. Maureen wriggled and fed. Joan took water through a muslin, a makeshift filter. She was weak, her skin was molten, and she couldn't hold down her fluids. The man fed her tablets. He was worried about sepsis. Sometimes he sat on the other side of the lock-up and cried. Each night he slept under his coat beside them, like a loyal dog. He brought them tinned food and even scavenged wheelchair parts from a dry canal, announced his intention to make something of them, something to help Joan get about. The man changed Maureen's towelling, swaddling and re-swaddling her until it was just right. There was rarely affection in his eyes, only disquiet. He squabbled with Joan about their status, their confine-ment; there were no days and nights for Maureen, but what else could they do? Joan was too weak to move. At her most desperate, Maureen wailed and wailed until Joan jammed a finger between her gums to soothe her, or offered a scabbed nipple from which the sweetness weakly came.

'She's already going too fast,' the man said of Maureen after several days. Joan agreed. It was the reason they kept arguing: his instinct was to get out of there. Meanwhile, Maureen's brain was developing rapidly, receiving more memories that shouldn't be. She had the maddening sense she was used, borrowed, *pre-warned*. Because the freshest memories were even starker, more claustrophobic – she was trapped inside a tank, a curved vessel, under ultraviolet light, and nobody ever came.

All the while, her face was changing, already filling out. Her limbs were lengthening. When she dreamed, she found she could look down on herself, observe her downy hair, the precious soft divot in the top of her head, as if she shared her mother's eyes. And there she caught herself thinking, *Push hard on that hole and end it now*, and tried to convince herself, *I'm just an infant*. But Maureen wasn't an infant – she was simply wearing one.

When Joan grew strong enough, they left the garage. Maureen saw the world from a gap between breast and woven wrap. Dilapidated lock-ups behind a row of terraced houses. The last cold light of another day. The man wrapped them in rags and tarpaulin and guided them along the pavement. 'It's still not dark enough,' he whispered to Joan. 'She shouldn't be out in this.'

Joan demurred. 'Out in what?'

It was a question that stuck – it carried implications. That Maureen even understood the man was disturbing enough; that her mouth and tongue wouldn't form a reply made her stomach hurt. Her tiny body held her captive.

The three of them hurried along back roads until Joan planted her feet and made the man stop.

'The stitches,' she pleaded. 'It's all coming down.'

'We're not far now,' the man said, urging her on. 'I promise. I made sure.'

So on they went, just slower. They reached the edge of the town, where her mother walked with one hand between her legs, the other on Maureen's back, until the buildings dropped away and the wind rose and tore at the tarp. Open space. Dense brown grass and buckled walls running with water, silvered with old lichen, frilled with feather moss. A range of hills stepped away from them, grading right back until they were indistinguishable from distant islands, then the sky itself. Goldfinches flashed between hedgerows. After a hard ascent, they reached the ruins of a hilltop church. As Joan leaned against the wall, Maureen placed her tiny fingers against the stone. There was coolness and movement, as if the stone were weeping. The man tapped her hand away, panicked. 'No,' he said, reproachful. 'Don't do that, little one. Don't touch anything.' Then, scowling at Joan: 'Not till we've enough pills for her. And don't give me that face, either. You know why.'

They walked on to harsher moorland, through peat groughs and sucking mud, and disturbed a grouse that made a horrifying scream. The landscape was empty in all directions. Maureen had the feeling that Joan was weeping as quietly as she could.

*

Maureen was cruising before long. During the adults' breaks from walking, she'd lean on the man's rucksack and Joan's knees and stagger round them, occasionally slipping on the wet ground. The adults never laughed or indulged her. They didn't help her at all, come to that. In truth, they didn't want to believe it was already happening. Maureen was two weeks old, yet she'd already thought of the word *abomination*; it had come to her in one of her visions, a word pushed through some membrane from her ghost-self, the past her. Vignettes of women standing on the far side of a mesh fence, chanting and waving placards that said things like NO EARTHLY ABOMINATION SHALL SUPPLANT THE LORD.

They moved by dusk and before dawn, in the blue hours between worlds. They slept by day, below ridges and in valleys, beneath overturned feeding troughs, huddled against dry-stone walling, and always above the waterline. They cleaned in gentle rivers. Dead heather and bracken crackled underfoot. When the weather shifted, the man shared his waterproofs. Each morning they woke in their stinking clothes, the inside of the tarpaulin dripping with condensation, the exterior sometimes varnished with frost. If they were careless, one of them would knock the tarp so all the collected rain and muck came in on them. The man pH-tested the water they drank, filtered and boiled it, added droplets of iodine. He said life was about weighing risks, and that he was trying to weigh them in their favour. When he went away to forage, Joan would hum to Maureen and say things like, 'You're so grubby,' while stroking her nose in awe. Sometimes the man went without breakfast, so Joan had more to share out for dinner. So Maureen herself, still breastfeeding, could get what her body needed.

And Joan confided in Maureen that she was worried about the man. Didn't he look like a bundle of sticks, in his sleep? Maureen got it, sort of, but still had no facility to reply. The man always deflected Joan's concerns, but admitted he wanted for hot tea, a spoon of honey to cover his tongue. Later he stole powdered milk and chocolate from an unattended tent. He'd have taken the tent too, he explained, were it not a stupid colour. But he did find a luminous orange insulated jacket for Joan. It was so big she could wear it around Maureen's sling. Its padding smelled mineral, musty.

They continued. Maureen taught herself to form deliberate sounds and practised them loudly. Joan and the man did all they could to shush her – Joan's new jacket helped a little. But in her sleep, Maureen couldn't help but scream: she kept dreaming of her tank, a thick liquid coursing in to drown her, the smell of scared animals or rotting plants. It was a constant reminder that her other life would always hang there, beside her, behind her, like the out-of-focus sections of a bad photograph.

They observed their rituals. The man gave Joan injections and pills. He rubbed a sweet-smelling balm into her belly, and draped a muslin dipped in steroid cream over her face. One morning they were doing this routine inside a stone bothy beneath a run of gnarled crags. Sunlight crept up the rock, heather brought out like rust. The man said of Maureen, 'She'll be talking properly soon, won't she?' to which Joan nodded. The two adults held each other's gaze until they both smiled grimly. That night, when Joan cried out in her sleep, the man cradled her stomach and tightened the tarpaulin around all of them. 'You never have to go back there,' he whispered. 'They won't – they can't – find us.'

And Maureen wondered, with a feeling deeply seated behind her ribs, if the gaunt man was in fact her father. If he were talking to Joan, or to both of them.

*

When Maureen was three weeks old – by then walking almost solidly and babbling in strings of consonants, longer in her body, larger in the head, her hair coarsening and darkening – Joan's exhaustion got the better of her. The man, panicked at first, insisted they carry on. But Joan took off her boots to massage her feet, which were bleeding through her socks, and they spent a whole night in the hills above a city, dressing blisters and watching traffic on an overpass below. The man talked of losing time, falling off plan. Joan was too tired to care. The man, visibly frustrated, gave in. He pored over a large map, hunting solutions. Close to dawn, he announced he'd found one.

They came down a scree slope, walking parallel with an intimidating fault in the hill's flank. Howling wind dropped away to reveal rain beating on the tarp. Maureen faced forward in the sling, legs frogged, with her mother's wet hair tickling her forehead. Beneath the overpass, they reached the wall of a used-car lot. The man ordered them to crouch and hide while he surveilled.

Daybreak brought a searing light. Maureen fixated on the damp slabs of the underpass, saw life in the moss that clung to it, and felt an affinity. The adults were tired and hoarse. After so long moving by night, it felt unnatural to be awake for the sun. Joan rested against a large bin to readjust the tarp, breath hot on Maureen's crown. At last, the man returned with a cheap phone to his ear, into which he said, 'We're coming,' before he helped Joan to her feet. 'See there?' he asked her. He meant the dozens of white and silver vehicles parked in rows. 'They're all ex-police,' he added, in case Joan hadn't noticed the ghostly impressions where their decals had been stripped. Joan nodded, but for Maureen the negative spaces brought to mind a memory of an old finger.

A circle of smooth, paler skin, where a wedding ring had once been. She looked down at her hand, then at Joan's, and the image strengthened, reframed itself: it was a recollection of her *own* hand, captured from another past. Despite everything in front of her, she was certain she'd once worn the ring. So what had she forgotten? And what else would she remember?

They stayed by the wall, by the bins, as the sun rolled up. The man kept checking his watch. Maureen's gums hurt, because her first teeth were already coming. When Joan next nursed her, Maureen bit down as if to punish her.

At no particular signal, the man said, 'Time.' And he bent back one of the fence panels, climbed through the gap, and picked his way between the cars to a cabin on the far side. Maureen and Joan watched in nervous wonder. He had a tool in his hand, and there was a popping sound. The cabin door stuttered open, and the man went inside. A minute later he was back and bending the fence panel back into place. They waited to see if anybody would come. Nobody did.

'It's the white one,' he said, dangling a car key. It was the first time Maureen had seen him grin.

Joan took a deep breath. Through the carry-wrap, Maureen could feel her mother's heart thrumming, a tiny bird in the small of her back. The man guided them into the lot, to the right car. Maureen sat on Joan's knees, just tall enough to see through the windscreen. The tarp and jackets in the footwell. The man started the car and immediately stalled it. 'Bit rusty,' he said.

Joan was silent. The air was dense and soundless, as if they'd been caught in snow. The windows fogged. The man drove them across the city, out the far side.

'How long?' Joan asked.

'Rest of today, if we make up lost ground.' He tapped the phone in his pocket. 'But they'll wait for us.'

Joan didn't reply, but Maureen could tell she'd smiled.

The roofs became trees, then cloud. Maureen stuck four fingers in her mouth to soothe herself, and woke again to a starless night. They were on a motorway, and her mother had tightened the seat belt around them. Gantry signs flashed words she vaguely recognised. She looked at the man. He was breathing through his nose. His knuckles oozed from recent wounds. Great slab-sided vehicles merged, loomed over the window, and roared on beside them. Something about one of them terrified her, a wretched pain in a deep part of her she couldn't touch or rub better. Joan, meanwhile, slept behind her, and for some time it was only Maureen and the man, his face lit red by the rear lights of the vehicles in front, sweat glistening in his thinning hair. The three of them, pocketed up, bound together, and constantly moving.

They dumped the ex-patrol car in a layby the next morning. The man set a fire under its seats while Joan explained to Maureen that they'd have to walk again from here, speaking in a way that suggested Maureen might understand why. On they went, down the thin pavement of the carriageway, until they reached a leafy village. A sign read THE HEART OF THE COTSWOLDS.

'Is that her?' Joan said.

They stopped. A grey-haired woman was emerging from a yellow wooden gate partially hidden by thick-flowering wisteria, and greeted them warmly. She cooed at Maureen and stroked her face, as if she knew exactly who Maureen was. She stood back, teary-eyed, and hugged the man again. 'I can't believe it,' she said. Then, with a wink and a turn of her wrist: 'Bit late, mind.'

The woman ushered them through the yellow gate, her wild garden, and into a stone-floored cottage. Downstairs was being warmed by a cast-iron wood burner. A steaming pot of tea and fruit loaf were arranged on a table. As soon as she'd locked and deadbolted the door, and checked through the window, the grey-haired woman said to them: 'Safe at last.'

The man ignored the refreshments and flopped in the armchair closest to the fire. He took off his boots and his socks, and his trousers, and rubbed at his stringy thighs. Joan, trembling, took a kitchen chair, while Maureen bunched and unbunched her mother's top in her fists. The grey-haired woman came to them. 'Let's give Mummy a break, shall we?' she said, and placed Maureen down on the rug, where she sat upright, alert, as the woman shored her up with cushions. The woman poured more tea, handed Maureen a bottle of cow's milk and said to Joan, 'Grown fast, hasn't she?' Maureen stared up at the woman, who now wore a thick multicoloured cardigan. As if on cue, the woman removed the tie from her bun and shook out her hair. It was surprisingly long.

'Have you brought much of anything?' the woman asked. The man said they hadn't. The woman said, 'We've plenty in,' and pointed around the kitchen, out to the pantry. The shelves were well stocked – dry food, tinned stuff, long-life milk. She'd come back in the morning with a spare key, some fresh milk, clothes and sanitary pads, and a word that Maureen took to be 'suppressants'. She stroked Maureen's arm and said, 'I'm only sorry I can't stay with you longer. But here – your mother will control things now.' At which the man frowned and studied his feet like a scolded child.

'Thank you again,' he said.

'Yes,' Joan said. 'Thank you.'

The grey-haired woman didn't take her eyes off Maureen as she unlocked the door again. 'You're welcome,' she said, pulling on a bright yellow anorak. 'Good luck to you, little one.'

*

Upstairs there were two bedrooms and a tired but cosy bathroom suite. Joan carried Maureen face-out, perhaps so she could orient herself. One of the rooms had obviously been made up for Maureen. There was a nest of cushions on the bed, a shelf of old children's books, and some candles on the bedside table. A pair of matching rugs laid over the lacquered floorboards. A dresser, cleared except for a brace of hair pins and an unusual cameo brooch, its pale face in profile, with the finish of fresh soap. Joan lay Maureen down on the bed to change her, arranged the pillows around her.

The bed linen smelled peppery. The woman's home was warm and safe and lived-in, and now it would be theirs. With Maureen cleaned and freshly changed, Joan stretched out next to her. Maureen's hands sought her mother's breasts for comfort. She suckled in biscuity warmth, seeking patterns in the cracked ceiling. Joan stroked her hair, began to hum, then sang softly: '*Oh these memories that should not be; hold them to light; see they're not of me.*'

It was only late morning, but sleep came heavy for both of them.

They slept for sixteen hours straight, waking to a vivid dawn chorus. Joan brought Maureen downstairs. The shopping and keys were on the kitchen top. The man was in the armchair, exactly where they'd left him. His trousers had been folded neatly across the chair's arm, and his socks were still wet in his boots. The blanket had fallen away from his legs. Joan said his name quietly, as if not really trying to rouse him. Maureen only heard the first of two syllables, a hard *toh*: Thomas?

As her mother put a saucepan on the hob to warm and knelt to tend the fire, now mostly ash and embers from a long cold night, Maureen climbed onto a kitchen chair and watched the man. His skin was blue. The hair on his legs looked frozen. She could see her breath, but couldn't see his. Intrigued, she slid from the seat and went towards him. Some dim sense of implausibility; of trusting her feet while believing they couldn't really be hers. When Joan returned from the fire, she found Maureen with a hand on the man's chest. She said nothing of Maureen standing. Not tentative, nor worried, nor even surprised. Maureen kept her hand where it was. Joan nodded to the kitchen chair where Maureen had been sitting. 'You can walk, now, can you?' And Maureen, ashamed, sat back on the cold floor, her belly squashed into her arms. From there she could see the spilled powder on the floor around the man. 'He made us a promise,' Joan said, by way of explanation. 'Because they'll be searching, and he can't keep running – can't give us away. He made a promise to both of us.'

Maureen went to her mother and stood against her. The fire was already hot. She kept her arms outstretched. There were new shapes in her mouth, full and pushing. A familiar sensation: soft palate and spit; she was trying to speak but the words wouldn't come; it was all bunched up behind her lips; it ebbed away on a breath through her nose. Then she was crying. Joan scooped her up and held her tightly and said, 'It wouldn't have hurt. I asked him to be kind to himself, so he wouldn't suffer. I just have to change him...' Joan looked away, past the pause, out to the window. The garden was hued purple. 'Yes,' Joan said, surer of herself. 'I have to change him.' Then she exposed a breast. 'Come on, you. What a big girl already. You'll be on rice come the weekend.'

*

Joan started the changing before lunchtime. She slid out a heavy padlocked briefcase from under the stairs, which contained still-packaged tools and rolls of plastic sheeting. She laid the sheets flat, smoothing the edges and weighting the corners with cushions. She heaved the man from the chair and rolled him over the floor, onto the sheets. It took a lot, and she was slick with sweat when it was done. There was fresh blood in the gusset of her leggings from the strain. Maureen watched as Joan arranged the man, face rumpled with concentration as she made minute adjustments to his arms and legs, until she was satisfied.

'Don't be frightened,' Joan said to Maureen. 'He told me exactly what to do. But, here, I want you to remember him resting. Peaceful, like this. So when you nap, that's when I'll work. And when you next wake, there'll be a bottle close by. Don't try and come downstairs, big as you are. Hold your ears if you must. Imagine the sound of snow under your boots – I know you can remember it. Or think of the sea, like I do. By tonight, he'll be gone, like he never was. And then we'll take good care to remember him, and all he's done for us.'

Maureen looked at him, the man. The way his cheeks had sunk, and his hair was still. She watched her mother cut away his clothes. The way she sponged down his body with warm water from the saucepan, humming to herself. The water turning dark where it pooled on the plastic, as the grime ran away and his skin shone. The way his feet were turned outward, toes torn and blistered. And how, slowly, his matted chest hair untangled and straightened.

By evening, as Joan promised, the man was gone, the plastic sheets too. Joan had swept and mopped. All the downstairs windows were open, and four canvas bags stood by the kitchen door. There were knives and saws in the draining rack. At some point during the afternoon, Maureen had felt Joan's presence over her, smiling down. There'd been a dark smear across her mother's forehead, where she'd wiped something from her forearm. She'd lain on the sheets next to Maureen, offered a breast. Brown flakes had fallen from Joan's hairline onto the pillow.

Maureen had rolled over, refused, frightened. Joan hadn't forced the issue; she'd closed the bedroom door and slipped back downstairs, still humming. The house smelled strongly of metal and, later, cooking. By suppertime, the saucepan Joan had used to clean the man was back on the hob. Joan didn't eat much, distracted. They went back to bed, where neither of them could sleep. Maureen practised making shapes with her mouth. Her bones ached. Somewhere an owl hooted, and the cottage's roof tiles rippled in the wind. A distant *crack*, fox screams, passing headlights.

Maureen thought of being inside the vessel, drowning painlessly. Her mother cried out in her sleep.

They were all safe, now.

BAD COPIES

In only a few months, Maureen's body had grown tall and gawky. Her speech, so malformed at first, had clarified, and now full sentences flowed naturally – the more she said, attached labels to, the sharper her mind became. In turn, she found she could better distinguish between now and before – the part-remembered life she'd once lived – and better accept what was going on. Joan smiled encouragingly through it all. There were no shocks for her, it seemed – only a vague acknowledgment of Maureen's rapid development as each stage arrived. And just as the man had for her, Joan gave Maureen pills, unwrapped from plain packages delivered in the dead of night.

Maureen mastered the potty, then the toilet. She lost her baby teeth and developed mild acne. Her hips, she complained, hurt constantly. The two of them spoke cautiously, and only ever of their day, of their food – never of the man. Maureen learned her times tables. She loved to count, to make Joan proud. She liked to watch insects, like the fruit flies dallying over their apples. She asked Joan about materials, about the formation of clouds, about the forces that had shaped their views of a valley, or about what grew in the heat-browned fields in the middle distance, where tractors were constantly working. She learned to identify birds and kept a chart.

She understood that lots of these things fitted together and made up her world, and that Joan's explanations for them deepened her relationship with her surroundings, unlocking new territory and richer meaning, while pulling dark sheets from memories she couldn't claim but still carried inside her.

They never saw other people. They lived a tiny life, though it ran deep. Then one day Maureen entered puberty, and the growing pains became unbearable. Sanitary towels were left on her bed. One evening a razor, the next a bra. In the mirror, Maureen saw a shorter, softer impression of her mother, confined on all sides. If she looked for too long, though, the mirror became the tank, and she could picture herself inside it, screaming; and it was clearest to her then that her inherited memories were her mother's, that it was *Joan* who'd once been the one trapped.

She wanted to ask but wasn't ready. At the same time, she accepted that she'd never need to. One Joan lived beside her, another inside her.

Routine was the lathe of time. Maureen and Joan ate sparingly and worked long hours in the yard behind the house. Its high walls only allowed for sunshine in the late afternoon, for which they both wore strong sun cream. They shared the old woman's bed and made marmalade and processed hogweed when its shoots came up under the fence. They each took their little pills, and ate apple crumble, spotted dick, and what passed for a roast dinner if the week's ingredients weren't too beaten up when they arrived. (Food deliveries, like medical deliveries, came overnight, unseen.)

Maureen, knowing little else, rarely questioned what modelled their existence in the cottage. But then some combination of her rapid maturing and curiosity began to unpick things. One time she came down and caught Joan making notes in front of the television, and realised with a start that there was a performance involved, that the way they were living was a form of mimicry. It hurt her to admit it, but she made herself: Joan's concept of domesticity, her stoic motherhood, was actually being informed by the soap operas and cookery programmes she watched alone in the evenings. And through this, Maureen remembered she'd seen programmes like them before, from inside the tank. An aperture in the tank's wall, through which videos were streamed. Yes: Joan had come in here believing you had to do things a certain way. That beyond England's dead collieries and heaving motorways, its boarded-up town centres and rusting railways, this was how to exist here; this was the only way to protect yourself from the sin and corruption of other people, or the government, or from the country's very soil.

The rupture came when Maureen was a year old by sunsets but pushing eighteen by development. By now her stretch marks were fading and her hair had grown long and thick, and so many chores had strengthened her bones. Joan, on the other hand, had grown frailer. Each was becoming the other's inverse, and their quiet resentments were setting hard. Sometimes Joan called Maureen *Reens*, and soon Reens was ready to question her.

They were in the kitchen when it started. Maureen was rolling pastry as Joan washed dishes beside her. Maureen abruptly stopped, touched her mother's arm and said, 'Mum?'

Joan turned from the sink, face flushed, soap suds in her hair. 'Yes?'

'Am I real?'

Joan frowned and wiped her brow with the crook of her elbow. 'Of course you're real, silly.'

'Then what else am I?'

A quizzical look. 'Well, you're my girl.'

'And how old am I?'

Joan turned back to the sink, hesitated, then let the water out. 'I'm not… A woman shouldn't have to think about her age. You understand, don't you? You're special in your way. That's your blessing.'

'So, I'm a woman, too?' Maureen asked.

Joan cleared her throat. 'Oh, yes, of course. Of course you are, for heaven's sakes. But listen, I'm told it'll slow now – that you can't grow quite so fast from here. But yes. Yes, I promise, you're a woman too.'

Maureen took that in. Then she said, 'And how old are you?'

No response.

'Or, who's *your* mother?'

The last of the sink's water squealed in the plughole. Joan stood silently as though stuck for a moment. 'I was an orphan,' she said. 'I lost my parents when I was very young. I told you this. You do know.'

Maureen shook her head.

'Then maybe you haven't remembered yet,' Joan said. 'Which is fine. I do think it's fine to accept it's just there, inside you. You don't have to pretend to me, either. I know what's happening, and that you'll get to remembering it. You'll always feel as if you *partly* know. We are connected, you and me. You remember little slivers of what I remember. Because when you were titchy-tiny, not so long ago, you'd babble to me in your sleep, and I'd hear myself talking. I'd hear my own memories.'

Maureen swallowed. Her throat was full. 'It scares me,' she admitted.

Joan nodded sadly. 'It must do, yes. It's a lot to bear.'

'Then why's it happening?' Maureen asked.

'Because…' Joan shook her head. 'Because that's what they did to me. That's what they've done to us.'

'Who, though?'

'That I wish I knew,' Joan said. 'My only desire is to remember it all properly.'

'But what about your mother?'

'I don't know,' Joan said. 'I don't think so—'

'Or the man?'

'Who?'

'The thin man. Father.'

Joan flashed a kind smile, as if this had taken her by surprise. 'Oh – oh no,' she said. 'He wasn't your father. He was Tomasz. But Tomasz has gone, and you're my life. You.'

'Am I?'

Joan nodded sagely. 'You are. You're all there is, Reens. You and me. That's what matters. And one day I hope you'll know how that feels for yourself.'

So now it was in the open that Maureen was unlike other children, and unlike other women, and curiouser by the day: the changes to her body, the pills she had to take, her ability to synthesise and order information; and to see her mother's weaknesses, the blurred outlines and boundaries of Joan's constructed identity.

Secretly watching television only reinforced what Maureen could piece together. While Joan guarded the TV remote, carried it everywhere, autumn's shorter days meant she often went to bed earlier, during which time Maureen took the opportunity to learn. She got into the habit of sneaking back downstairs, kneeling in front of the television, and dialling its sound down to one. She liked to hop between channels and take on the lies of the outside world. A world in which, Joan insisted, people would never be able to understand Maureen, or what she was, or what she could do. Where she could never be safe.

Until Maureen was caught in the act, anyway. In need of water, Joan found her with her nose pressed to the screen, and instantly cuffed her round the head. Maureen was plunged into hot shame, more shocked than pained. 'It'll rot you!' Joan shouted, meaning the TV. 'It'll get in you and rot you from the inside out!'

Maureen stood up, scolded, and instinctively hid the remote behind her back.

'Is that it?' Joan said. 'Is that all I'm getting? How long's this been going on?'

'What do you expect!' Maureen said, her eyes filling up. 'You keep me like this! It's a prison!'

Without hesitation, Joan threw her glass at the wall. They both watched it burst over the sideboard, then stared at each other. 'You selfish little cow,' Joan hissed. 'Prison!'

'Like *you* were,' Maureen said. 'In that tank.'

Her mother slapped the chair beside her. 'How could you know what that means?'

'Because I do,' Maureen insisted. 'I can smell it. Taste it.'

'Taste it!' Joan yelled. 'And you still think you know!'

Now it was Maureen's turn to be angry. 'You have me live as you lived. It's all you know how to do.'

Joan veered forward with a hand raised. At the last moment she stayed her worst urge, the one Maureen could see clearly, and shook her head. Still, she was fearsome, and the lesson for Maureen was that frailty can hide a life-won hardness. 'Go on,' Joan said, breathing hard. 'Say it again.'

Maureen scowled. Held herself. Straightened. She pointed the TV remote at her mother and said, 'You. Have. Me. Live. Like—'

Joan barged past Maureen. She grabbed the television in both hands and rolled it off the top. The plug socket sparked, the house electrics tripped, and darkness fell in on them. Joan became a drab grey mannequin, a coat on the door, an abstract shape against the wall.

'Don't *test* me,' Joan said softly, leaving to go back upstairs. 'And clean up this mess before you come to bed.'

Maureen paced, then swept up, then lay on the rug for what felt like hours. She didn't know where to start, whether to apologise, or how to reconcile her anger with the sense she was *right*. Moonlight edged the hardwood furniture. She was so still she wondered if the room's dust might settle on her. When she closed her eyes, she was in the tank, howling into her sleeves. The front room, by comparison, was much larger, but it was no less desolate.

As the air cooled, the rug released a smell of mildew.

Maureen slept in the second bedroom and dreamed of being back in the stolen car with her mother and the man, Tomasz. His eyes were closed as he drove; her mother had one hand steadying the wheel for him. Maureen was feeding, and her mother's milk tasted of metal. As they overtook another vehicle, she heard Tomasz whisper, 'Time!' before he turned to wax, the same as the morning she'd found him in the chair, and their car lurched across the road, towards the central reservation—

She woke to her stomach griping badly. There was a dark patch of moisture on the ceiling directly above her, as if something had leaked through. Her back felt hot, wet, and she drew back the duvet. Between her legs was a slick of dark blood, like fresh paint. She went to touch it but found she couldn't move. Fear coursed through her; her whole abdomen was on fire. When she called out for her mother, it came out strangled, a yelp. She didn't want her mother to see her in this mess, to admonish her for not using her pads properly. But she also knew this was different. She called again, managing the *M* of Mum; then endured fresh agony as her leg muscles cramped. The stairs creaked, old slippers on hardwood, and Joan tried the door, which Maureen had locked.

'I can't get up,' Maureen croaked between breaths. 'Mum,' Maureen said. 'I can't—'

'Open this door right now,' Joan said, her tone the same as the night before. The pain seared on; Maureen wanted to be sick. She tried again to move, shifted one foot fractionally. She looked again at the moisture on the ceiling above her, and then at the blood. The two patches reflected each other.

'I can't get up,' she sobbed, as her mother rapped on the door. 'I can't.'

'I'll show you *can't*,' Joan shouted. Her footsteps thundered away; the landing fell quiet. The moisture was creeping right up behind Maureen's shoulders. Soon it would touch her hair, soak in. Perhaps it would come up over her face, enamel her. Get inside her and suffocate her. Which was when the blade of the garden shovel came directly through the door, sending great splinters of wood and paint across the floor. Again and again, until the door split and a livid Joan came twisting through the hole she'd made. She was wearing the old woman's dressing gown, and her hair was tied up in a bun. Her expression was sour until she saw the sheets.

'Oh, Reens! Oh, God, no.' Her mother immediately put her hands on Maureen's stomach, as if she knew. The pain was horrendous. 'There?'

Maureen, wincing, nodded.

'Oh, oh no. Can you sit?' She peeled Maureen away. The blood stretched like mastic. 'Let's get you— Oh love.' Joan perched Maureen on the end of the bed and baled up the sheets around her. 'How long was that there?' Joan asked, meaning the patch on the ceiling. 'No,' she added, 'don't *look* at it,' as if Maureen had anywhere else to look. 'We'll get you cleaned up.' And they staggered over the debris and through the broken door, and Joan had Maureen sit on the toilet, flecks of blood on her thighs, her mother's hands under her elbows for support. 'I'm getting hot water,' Joan said. Maureen nodded weakly as another wave of pain broke over her, and her mother descended the stairs. The toilet filled while she stared at the tiles, at the mould. She listened to the quiet rhythm of water droplets forming and falling from the cold tap, and the sound of the kettle whistling on the hob.

Then her mother was coming back up the stairs, each moment drawn slowly from the last, until Joan was there and pressing a hot water bottle into Maureen's gut. The heat spread through her, instant relief, and she clutched at it desperately. Joan took Maureen's hand and massaged her palm, the pads of her fingers. She fed her two pills and said, 'It'll pass soon. Hold this close – you can cope. Oh, dear girl. I'm sorry, Reens. This is my fault. It was fear that brought this on. But it's only a bad copy.'

'A bad copy,' Maureen repeated, dazed.

Joan wiped her eyes on her sleeves and flushed the toilet over Maureen's shoulder. 'They never take,' she said, quietly. Maureen concentrated on the fresh blood spots on the mat, a knot working its way out of her, uncoiling and untangling itself. Joan touched the hand still holding the water bottle. 'Breathe with me,' Joan said. 'You push and you breathe. Oh, Reens, I'm sorry. I shouldn't have shouted. It's my fault – last night. I'm so sorry. I made you afraid.'

'Last night...' Maureen said. And she remembered the fantasy she'd entertained as she came up the stairs from the cold lounge: wrapping her hands around her mother's throat and pushing down till the thrashing stopped—

'We can change it,' her mother said. 'And I'll clean. It can't go down there. We'll bury it with the seeds, so it can grow in another way, away from us.'

Maureen stared at her mother. What *was* 'it'? But there was a lucidity, and of course she knew; she only had to look inside, consult her occupier. Because this had all happened before, in another place, to another body. It had happened to her mother – to Joan. The shame, the guilt, were exactly the same. Two bodies, two minds, entwined and recursive within her. She caught the echo and isolated it. A rush of relief as the last of her bad copy fell free, and her body felt emptied. She shook from release and exhaustion, waning adrenaline. She felt obliterated. Joan ushered her to her feet and fished something from the toilet before flushing it again. She pushed the wet, stray hairs back behind Maureen's ears. The feral smell remained until the water in the sink ran clear. With a warm flannel, Joan cleaned Maureen's legs. There were fresh pyjamas on her mother's bed.

'There you are,' Joan said, tucking Maureen back in, before she sat in the old rocking chair opposite. Maureen had no idea what time it was. It wasn't dark, but it wasn't light.

'Mum,' Maureen said. 'I was scared.'

Her mother shushed her and smiled quickly. 'I'm here,' she said. 'They just don't take – not those ones.'

True dawn was another kind of relief; they'd made it. They were up early, aware of their renewed bond and the unexpected intimacy that follows a crisis. After breakfast, Maureen sat on the settee wrapped in towels while her mother worked in the garden. She was feeling better, if remote – Joan had given her two extra suppressants. The lounge was stuffy, and her stomach still griped intermittently. At its worst, she closed her eyes and tried to picture being in a white box, swaddled in fresh linen. Then her mother was coming inside with two handfuls of wildflowers. These she washed and stemmed, placed in a vase for the coffee table. 'A posy for your loss,' Joan said. 'Now, would you like to come out here with me? It'll help you, I think. It will help you grasp things.'

Maureen gathered herself and shambled through the kitchen. She paused before the door and tapped her mother on the back. 'How old were you, the first time?'

Her mother turned. 'I don't remember.'

'How many more were there?'

Joan sighed. 'I don't know. But they took it as a protest. My body was their property, and it was letting them down. They couldn't see that my fear equalled failure.'

'Please, tell me who they were?'

'They didn't like you to know their names, Reens. They were mostly men.'

'And what about me?'

Her mother took her arm and tugged her towards the door. 'You saved me,' she said. 'I learned to close my eyes, and my ears, to not let them in. That's how I knew I'd keep you. How to hold on, so that when I found my way out, you'd be safe.'

Maureen let her mother lead her outside. Early light danced on the plastic covering their tomatoes. She saw that Joan had been trowelling soil from the raised bed beside the runner beans. The hole was narrow but deep. 'To help you grieve,' Joan said, producing an envelope from her pocket. It was made from thin, brown paper, and was studded with flower seeds. The bottom edge was dark and wet. 'Hold it at the top,' Joan said. Maureen took it to the hole and pushed it in, rolling it. A numbness. She left herself again; saw herself from elsewhere, taking up the trowel and scraping the mounded soil back over the hole. Patting it all flat. Her mother nodding approval with a hand in the small of her back.

'It's only cells,' she heard Joan say. 'Only cells.'

Maureen swayed. She felt a strange sense of forward-projection, as if she were somehow in the hole with the thing that had come out of her, with soil under her nails. It spoke to her: the rain would water it; its cells would multiply. It brought her to the idea that three of them were now living in the cottage.

'Let's get back inside,' Joan said. 'I don't want you out in the sun today. I'll make us French toast. I could read to you. There's ice cream in the freezer. And I'll see what our host can do about replacing the television. We'll take on the day all over again.'

Maureen liked the sound of that. But when she went upstairs, the bedroom door was still broken, and there were faint streaks of blood in the toilet bowl, and she could smell mud. She curled into a ball on the landing carpet, and stroked the rough carpet with her fingers, questioning whether her mother was afraid to confront what her daughter had done. Or what else her mother was holding back.

Later, Maureen stood at the bedroom window, watching the raised beds where the bad copy was buried.

Maureen's second miscarriage happened in the daytime. By then, she and Joan had fallen into a routine that saw Maureen preparing their food and mixing Joan's dose of suppressants into a glass of water. Their constant use had started making Joan bilious, and lately she preferred to take them alongside food. They also made her incredibly drowsy, so as Maureen cleared the table, Joan would sit in her chair and watch the windows until she drifted into sleep.

Unlike watching TV by night, there was much less risk in Maureen stealing this nap time as her own, and it wasn't long until her whole day revolved around what she could do with it. A gift became an indulgence, became an obsession: Maureen had been given another chance to explore, and she wasn't going to waste it. So, she'd put on her mother's coat and shoes. She'd apply sun cream to her face, tuck a small umbrella under her arm. She'd come to sit on the stairs opposite the front door, with all its locks and reinforced hinges, and will herself to leave, reach the yellow front gate, and pass it, onto the street, and into the world she was forbidden from discovering.

Over successive days, Maureen took steps towards her escape, until at last she held the door's brass handle in her hand. It was a transgression impossible to rationalise, and of course guilt worked against her. Ten times she tried, and ten times she forced herself back, with a jolt, to stare confusedly at the floor tiles as though she was stuck to them, held there.

Until Maureen, like the inner-woman before her, overcame herself. It was a cold, bright day when the door finally opened. Metallic sky, a hot seam on the horizon. She checked one last time that her mother was snoring, and, before she could rethink, took her first step beyond, her breath shallow and skin buzzing.

Which was when it happened. Her stomach twinged and gave, a deep rending sensation. As if a spell had been broken. Blood came down through her tights and thickly through her fingers, and the soreness of it split her in two. She fell back into the house, noticing the horrible fidelity of fresh blood on clean tile, and slipped. Her vision hazed. The contractions intensified. She lay there, foetal. She knitted her hands and made a compress for her abdomen. A gust swung the door shut, taking the light. Her blood dulled, ruby to brown, and in her grief her tears tasted saltier than should have been possible. She couldn't get up. She could barely move. She would wait to be found, like a broken bird waits for a fox.

'It's inside every parent to want to carry their child's terror,' Joan told her afterwards. 'It's the thing they never tell you about. Watching your child grow up, watching your child learn to suffer – it's a slow death.'

What she seemed to mean was that Maureen's pain was unabsorbable, and Joan was powerless in the face of it – she'd watch meekly as Maureen endured the horrors she'd lived through herself. And so the tragedy of Maureen's accelerated development was exposed. There would always be some degree of resentment held by one towards the other.

Neither of them ate that evening. Before they went to sleep, Joan suggested they bury the second bad copy with the first.

'And what is it I'm supposed to grieve?' Maureen said.

'Heredity,' Joan said.

Maureen hadn't been back in the garden since the first burial. Joan guided her to the raised bed and wrapped her hands around the trowel handle, and asked her to share in the ceremony. 'Angle it down,' she said. Maureen, in clean pyjamas, comforted by fresh cotton and barrier cream, allowed her mother to guide her. The trowel blade slipped into the soil. Halfway, Joan released Maureen's hands. Maureen pushed again, but the trowel stopped abruptly, as if something had gripped it.

'It won't go,' Maureen told Joan. 'See?' She wiggled the handle.

'It's only rubble,' Joan said. 'Crushed stone. Turn the soil.'

Maureen glanced along the raised bed, realising her mother had stepped further away. Her arms itched, and when she looked, there were crimson blotches up to her elbows, as though she was having an allergic reaction. 'Why are you over there?' she said.

'Turn it!' Joan urged.

So Maureen did, and immediately leapt away in terror. The trowel rang on the patio flags. Her mother said nothing and went to the corner of the beds, where the tubers were growing. She groped around in the soil and pulled out a wrinkled black sac, oozing with cream. A potato. 'Small wonder,' she said. 'They won't take like this, either.' She continued, rooting through mulch to pull the others. Each new potato was more hideous than the last. 'It's all spoiled,' she said, flatly. 'So tell me what else is in there, little one?'

Maureen was shaking. She returned to the raised bed, and what she'd turned out. Just below the surface ran a seam of what looked like sinew, shot through with gleaming purple threads and something more fibrous, bronchial. Fat marbled the soil. She could smell sweetened charcoal. Was it that the bad copy's cells had divided, just as she'd pictured from her bedroom window? Joan came forward, snatched the trowel, and dug a trench that ran the whole length of the bed. The soil was riven with bodily structures, ligaments and capillaries. When Joan turned out what could've been a claw, or the draft of a hand, neither of them knew where to start.

'What do you think it is?' Joan asked.

Maureen was speechless. She was disgusted to have had any part in it.

'Roots?' Joan tried. 'Like when you pull out a weed? Because it was a weed, in its way. Don't you think?'

Maureen shrugged despondently.

'There's a bag of quicklime in the pantry,' Joan said. 'Fetch that – we'll set a fire for the other one.'

Maureen went inside. The cottage smelled earthy again, as if the roots had taken in the house, too. She thought she saw rhizomes in the tile grout, mistook cracks for mould. When she opened the pantry door, she imagined joints and ribs moving, gristle flexing in the hinges. On the shelf, she pictured the fletched orbits of a skull, propped between jars of foraged leaves. Was the whole house rotting? She found the sack of quicklime and dragged it to the back door, which had closed itself. The sack was heavy and chafed her calluses. The door's seal was fraying and there was a white mould growing on the inside of the glazing. She touched it; there was a resistance, as though it *responded*. She rubbed, but it wouldn't wipe away. She opened the door and watched her mother working the beds, the sound of potatoes splashing on the flags as she dug them out.

'Don't dawdle,' Joan said. 'It's getting faster.'

Only the fresh air was stopping Maureen from being sick. Faintness came and went. Joan began trowelling the quicklime into the trench she'd made. Then she covered it over and patted it down. Lastly, she went to their woodpile, pulled away the dirty blue tarpaulin she'd once carried Maureen inside, and nailed it over the beds.

They stood there looking at her work.

'Will it work?' Maureen asked Joan.

'I don't know.'

'Will there be another? Will this happen to me again?'

No answer.

Maureen couldn't sleep. The air was oppressively warm, and she was convinced the raised beds were keening and chattering, even if it was far more likely to be the house shifting, a draught playing the roof tiles and the old floors. Recently they'd been putting pillows down the middle of their bed, and Joan was adrift on the other side. Their candles had all burned out.

Maureen got up and brushed her hair. Her scalp itched. The starchy pyjamas tickled her ribs. She brushed her hair at the window, watching the raised beds. The tarpaulin rippled as though fingers were stroking it from beneath. Downstairs, she made toast. The plants on the windowsill were wilting, and dozens of fruit flies were dead in the sink. The front door key was on the table. She sat in silence, caught between three places: her mother's womb, the tank that haunted her, and the cottage.

Her chest tightened. She was drowning, but not afraid. Languid, not lost. There was security in confinement, and she didn't want it. She pulled her knees up under her chin and rubbed her ankles. There were spots of blood in the gusset of her pyjamas. She was meant to wear dark pants and pads, for dignity, her mother said. But really it was about saving on needless shame, should anyone see. Another way to be invisible.

She didn't want to be invisible.

Maureen went back upstairs and dressed in still-damp clothes from the maiden. She returned to the bedroom to check on her mother, who was snoring softly, eye mask perfectly set. She wouldn't stir, Maureen decided – and it was always a bigger dose of suppressants before bed. She did, however, want to take a piece of the cottage with her, as a tether. So at least she could say, if she were caught, that she'd taken home with her. She settled for one of the old woman's multicoloured cardigans from the airing cupboard. Beneath it was a grey wig, heavy and realistic. Maureen took both items into the bathroom. The wig was the same colour as the old woman's hair. Was it intended as a disguise, for her mother? Or was it the old woman's, a spare? She tucked it under her towel, telling herself she'd hide it again later. Because if she didn't go now, she never would, and returning to the bedroom was a risk too far.

In the hallway she pulled her mother's raincoat over the cardigan and opened the door. She held her breath until she was at the gate. The garden flowers had shed their petals, and the path was soft and fragrant, all shades of blue under the moon. The gate creaked, but not quite loudly enough to worry her.

Those first steps were the hardest, but only because she knew she'd never experience them again.

DEPOT

Maureen wound east from the cottage, edging a large woodland. A biting wind came and went, but she felt good and warm, remembering what it was like against her mother's chest, over the moors, through the fields, with Tomasz. With each turn away from the cottage, a greater sense of freedom charged her. Only there, walking the empty road, did she notice how much the voice inside her had quietened. She picked up her pace until she was running, and her lungs were burning in her chest.

She left the woods, and the village, behind her. The countryside rolled on and away, seemingly infinite. The road narrowed to a single track, which shone with a milky glaze. Sweating and panting, she wasn't sure how long she could keep going, but she already knew she'd do it again. And she was smiling.

Maureen stopped at the sound of rushing water, which drew her into a copse of twisted oaks, through which could be seen a series of bright white lights. She stepped through long grasses and found a fast-flowing river, separated from her by barbed wire. Further along was a bridge with a signed footpath, where she saw that the bright lights were mounted on a warehouse unit. There were voices, dogs barking, and she thought about turning back. Were people working down there? Through the night? She crossed the bridge to an access road which ended with a red-and-white-striped barrier, warning signs. Beyond this lay the warehouse, where six men were huddled by a vehicle. They wore blue overalls and yellow helmets, and were gesturing to each other above the sound of an alarm.

As Maureen watched, a series of roller doors opened in the warehouse wall. Four articulated lorries drew across the apron, their lights sweeping out through the woodland. She clacked her tongue, dry-mouthed: seeing the lorries made her afraid, as they had once on the motorway, and she still didn't know why. Each lorry took its turn reversing towards the roller doors, where the six men guided them in. The drivers climbed down from their cabs. Rough laughter and greetings, obtuse shouting. She thought of Tomasz, in his chair, where he'd died. The black bags in the kitchen, after her mother had changed him. Were these men like him?

A rustling nearby made her lose her balance. She fell sideways into muck and leaves. She dared to look.

A man was standing there.

'Oh,' he said. 'What you up to?'

Maureen seized up. He was right next to her. She rolled and pulled her knees into her chest, forcing the air from her lungs. She made herself as still as possible.

'I can actually see you,' the man said, chuckling. He was smoking a thin cigarette. He wore a grubby woollen hat, but his face was smooth as a candle in the light. 'Are you pretending to be something? A rock?'

Maureen stayed where she was, hoping he'd go away. She drew half a breath through her nose and tried to ignore the bramble thorns scratching her cheek. When she checked again, the man was gone. She stretched out and turned over and exhaled.

'Hiya,' the man said, now in the thicket behind her.

'I wanted to see,' Maureen replied. 'I saw the lights.'

The man cocked his head, then frowned. Was she scaring him? She had no idea what time it was. Much less how to actually explain herself. The man looked even younger up close. There were two scars on his cheek, thick dashes. But his eyes – he had kind eyes.

'See what?' he asked. 'A bunch of lorries unloading pallets?'

'I'm Maureen,' she said, shaking her head.

The man shifted his weight. 'All right,' he said. 'You look a bit cold, Maureen, if you don't mind me saying.'

She nodded. 'I got lost.'

He offered her a hand. 'I can believe it. You'll catch your death, though. Where's home? You know what time it is?'

She didn't take his hand, but stepped out of the thicket and brushed the thorns from her face. One side of her mother's coat was damp and covered with a stringy weed which stuck to her fingers.

'I'm Dougie,' the man said, undeterred. He went to relight his cigarette, but it seemed to Maureen that his hands were too cold, because they were trembling. She tried a smile in return. He was clearly thinking about what to do with her. The way he kept glancing off to the side as if the crew might be watching. The lighter came on, and he inhaled deeply. The cigarette smelled fruity, a little like her mother did whenever she came in from scrubbing the yard. 'You want a lift back to somewhere?' he asked.

'I can walk, thank you,' Maureen said. And then, to really make the point, 'I'll be completely fine.'

'Right,' Dougie said. 'That's all right, then.' And he straightened his back and swivelled to the warehouse. His jacket carried a sheen, well-worn. Its elbows were patched with denim offcuts. His trousers – heavy canvas, multiple pockets – were spattered with white paint. 'See you later,' he said.

Maureen wiped her nose on her sleeve and started back up the path towards the bridge. She had no way to tell the time, she realised; it was rare she needed to attach any importance to it. Still, the dogs had stopped barking, and the birds were silent in the trees, and it was dark.

'It really is late,' Dougie called after her, as if he understood, or had read her thoughts. 'You look after yourself.'

When Maureen turned again, Dougie was watching her, still smoking. Blue clouds suspended in floodlight. He took off his hat, scratched his head in puzzlement. The men by the loading bays were remonstrating with him for skiving. He waved at Maureen once more, squinting, and went back to his own world. And she went back to hers.

Inside the house, Maureen found Joan sitting on the stairs with the old woman's grey wig in her lap. She'd been waiting, Maureen saw, and her expression was far more cutting than any reproach.

'Mum,' Maureen said, feigning a yawn, innocence. 'What are you doing up?'

'Where were you, Reens?'

'Hey? I was just in the kitchen, making hot milk.' She flapped the old woman's cardigan. 'I was cold, so I borrowed this – whose is it?'

'How long were you out?' her mother said, ignoring the question.

'Out where? I meant, why are you holding a wig?'

Joan shook her head. 'Are you joking? I've just *watched* you come in.'

Maureen stopped talking. The mood shifted.

'Who have you seen?'

'Nobody—'

Joan shook her head. 'It's too important,' she said. 'Don't.'

'I'm not lying, though.'

Joan stood up. 'Come here,' she said.

Maureen went to her. Her mother squeezed her cold cheeks, blinking tears. 'We can't let this happen,' she said carefully. 'It's not safe.'

Maureen rubbed her eyes. 'But why?' she said. 'There are never any proper answers.'

'Because there are people who want to harm us. Because of who we are. Please. I don't want to upset you again.'

And Maureen allowed herself to be held in silence, until Joan turned her mouth to Maureen's ear and whispered, 'Tell me who you met?'

Maureen shook her head.

'What did you tell them?'

'I didn't *see* anyone—'

'Don't you think I can *smell* it? It's coming off you.'

Dougie's funny cigarette, Maureen thought. 'I don't know,' she tried.

'I want to trust you,' Joan said. 'I have to.'

'I walked. I just walked.'

'And have you been walking before?'

'Not outside. Never.'

'Promise me.'

'I promise.'

'But you've wanted to?'

Maureen nodded. Of course she had.

'I understand,' Joan said. 'But you're too precious. Think about Tomasz. You think you're invincible, when you're not.'

Maureen pulled away from Joan's embrace. She was shocked at how casually Joan had used Tomasz's sacrifice to make the point.

'Nobody knows who I am,' Maureen said.

'And we should keep it that way, Reens,' Joan said sharply. 'But I don't want to cause upset. It's the middle of the night.

Let's talk again in the morning.'

Maureen, seeing no other way, capitulated. She lay beside Joan with the pillows between them, aware of what more had been broken, not least the last of her respect, and questioned whether it'd been worth it. She decided it had. They'd have to live in opposition, from here. Too much had frayed. Too much of the world had opened up to her. If her mother refused to give her what she needed, she'd go after it herself.

For all Maureen's frustration, the incident had clearly altered Joan's view of Maureen, too. She now talked to her daughter as if she were a sensitive toddler, much less of a friend, and was content to let her suspicions dictate her actions, almost to the point of harming herself. Her lunchtime nap was out – she took her suppressants earlier, to avoid a slump – and in the evenings she stayed up much later, as a means to make sure Maureen was asleep first. New locks were fitted to the front and back doors. Certain topics – feelings, vulnerabilities, anything demanding maturity – were no longer discussed, and hung heavy around the cottage. Tighter boundaries were inferred rather than drawn. And tellingly, Joan was ever-present, ever-calm, and much, much colder. She was reinventing herself as a watchful eye, a guiding hand, and taking what she considered the moral high ground. She would treat Maureen politely, yes. But she would be diffident.

Maureen was Maureen, however, and had other ideas about what came next. She was self-aware enough to know that her private hour after lunch – her space to plan, learn and dream – had become vital to her health. She also knew that she possessed the patience and doggedness to get it back. Seeing her mother's reliance on controls, she began by steadily adjusting all the clocks in the house to show slightly different times, effectively training her mother to ignore them. She knew it could take weeks to have any effect, for Joan's annoyance to give way to apathy, just as she knew it wasn't even guaranteed to cause or lengthen Joan's naps – merely confuse them. But it was a start. Then, whenever there was chance, she forwent her own suppressants, and pocketed one or two of her mother's, adding the unused pills to a jam jar she kept hidden in the pantry.

The strategy was simple: work up enough goodwill to be trusted with certain tasks again, offer to make her mother's special solution, and double its dose. Joan wouldn't notice, and soon she'd go back to napping. And so Maureen went at it: a week of impeccable behaviour rolled into a fortnight, which became a month, then another. Cottage life calmed down again, with Joan believing that Maureen had paid attention to her warnings and was making good on her promises. She was oblivious to Maureen's deceit, of a new arrangement being negotiated, of having no stake in the terms.

Then Maureen's day came.

'Reens?' she heard her mother call.

Maureen bounded downstairs, half-expecting trouble. She found Joan reading a book in her armchair with her feet in a new foot spa, which she'd ordered from a shopping catalogue she was increasingly addicted to.

'Be a love,' her mother said distractedly, 'and mix up a dose for me?'

Maureen couldn't believe her luck. Without hesitation she went straight for her jar in the pantry, taking great care to mix in the extra powder until it was dissolved and the solution had clarified.

Within a week, Maureen had her solo lunchtimes back, and from there saw an opportunity to reclaim the night. And all the while she went on daydreaming of the warehouse building, and the crisp air, and the quiet kindness of Dougie, the man she'd met there.

LAMB

*

Maureen found her way back to the warehouse, in the peace, and kept on returning. Sometimes she saw Dougie working, and sometimes he was off. Whatever the situation, she took mental notes, created a kind of filing system for him, into which she placed important observations. Dougie drove a small brown car with a red stripe down each side; he always wore his hat (and always took it off to rub his head in the same place); his hair never looked to grow. He was committed to his job, and he smiled easily. When he concentrated, he furrowed his brow, which changed his face a lot. There was a pattern to his shifts, and the breaks were long enough for him to smoke two funny cigarettes over a steaming flask. One night, he sat up in the cab of a parked lorry and smoked three out of the window. He reminded her of somebody, and nobody. He was young, and placid, and ignorant of her; or so she convinced herself. On other nights, he'd stand with his cigarette and scan the road, the thicket where she liked to hide and watch. It made her stomach feel strange to imagine he might be thinking of her.

Unlike Dougie, Maureen was changing her hair and clothes daily, inspired by advertisements on the television, and by a growing desire to experiment. She wore her mother's coat religiously, but the outfit beneath was carefully prepared, and often put together by subterfuge.

Never once would Dougie see her. Never once would she slip up and let him. Until, inevitably, it happened.

Maureen was walking back up the hill towards the main road when Dougie caught up.

'Hey,' he called. 'Wait!'

Maureen's heart could have cracked. Hadn't she just watched him go inside, and left satisfied there was no more to see? Now look – she'd ruined it. Ruined everything. She trudged on and wouldn't let herself turn around.

'You're not lost again, are you?' he asked.

He was right there behind her. She shook her head, annoyed.

'Maureen, wasn't it? Please don't walk off! I'm just saying you can't hang about down here. It's no good for anyone. Hang about, will you? I can't keep up.'

She stopped.

'Hiya,' he said, drawing alongside her. He'd had to jog, and he was out of breath. 'What's going on? You shouldn't be out here—'

'Because I'm a woman?'

Dougie stared at her.

'I shouldn't be out here, because I'm a woman? Is that what you're saying?'

Dougie grimaced, embarrassed. 'Not that, no. I didn't mean to—'

'It just reminds me of something,' she said, pointing behind him.

'The depot?'

'The lorries. I don't know why.' She tapped her head. 'I can't talk to you, anyway.'

Dougie grinned. 'Nothing else going on out here, is there? You don't have to be so panicky, either way. I'm soft as shite, me.'

'I'd still better go.'

'Where to, though?'

'Home.'

Dougie chuckled. 'Wouldn't mind that myself.' Then an awkwardness as he searched for something more to say, a way to stall her. 'Can't go getting the boot, mind,' he started. 'I'm hanging on till I can drive one of these bad boys. One day... Before the robots take over, that is. Out there on the M6, foot planted – I swear down.'

Maureen tightened her mother's jacket around her. Dougie lit another cigarette and turned his boot in the gravel.

He pointed the glowing tip at her. His hand, with its long fingers, was more emphatic than the rest of him put together.

'Still look cold,' he said. 'So how about I walk you over the bridge? And not because you're a woman. Just because I hate my manager tonight, and the cameras can't see this far up the track.'

Maureen and Dougie started walking together when he finished his shifts, and sometimes during them. It pushed Maureen's time out, increased the chances of her mother waking and finding her out, but she wasn't about to stop. She learned that Dougie was eighteen and had grown up north of Manchester before moving south to help care for his ailing grandmother. He had his small brown car with its go-faster red stripes, and lived between a bedsit and his grandmother's bungalow in Cheltenham. Driving, she learned, was his point of reference for almost everything, his way to explain or deflect attention from himself. For instance, he invested a lot of time in telling Maureen that his drive to the depot, to this remote part of the Cotswolds, was fine in the summer, but a lot sketchier in the winter. The car's washer fluid froze, and road salt coated the windscreen on the M5; you had to drive too close to the lorries in front so their spray could clear the glass. He was very proud of the car, despite its age. He'd learned how to repair the essentials, perform a light service. The oil change was the most satisfying job. He had a friend whose brother had a ramp, so they'd make a day of it. He paid his friend's brother in beer and cigarettes and something he called 'ganj', and they'd use all the big lights in the garage, the full jig, so Dougie could see how his small brown car was put together.

'And how's your nan been doing these last few days?' she'd ask him, to bring him back.

And he'd always say, 'Oh, she's trooping on.'

Maureen, unguarded, felt as though she could bring all of herself to him. She told him how she'd been put together, too. Despite herself, or Joan's warnings, she told him about her mother, and the man Tomasz, and the suppressants, and the cottage. She told him because he liberated her, because she felt so accepted in his company.

And when he didn't so much as wince, she told him more. About the exact colours of her birth, and the cold garage, and the empty moors. The old woman and the wig she'd found in the airing cupboard. Her visions of being inside a darkly lit tank, this awareness she had of being *reincarnated*, a word she'd learned from a TV programme about a medium. Her isolation, and learning about the world through abstractions of it. And when they'd been walking and talking for many nights, and it was comfortable to thread her arm through his, just as they did on the television, she told Dougie about her two bad copies, and the raised beds in their cottage garden, and what they'd found in the soil.

This time, Dougie stopped her. He'd been listening to her story graciously, but his face told her it was painful for him. He said he was grateful she was here, now, and looked oddly contrite. 'Nobody could do anything about all that,' he said. 'Didn't your mam say it wasn't your fault? It's on her to put that part of you right. That's what my mam always did, Nan says. When I got it wrong, she blamed herself. When I first got to Nan's, she told me I was just like Mam. It made us fast friends.'

Maureen didn't fully understand. She said what it felt safe to say, which was to repeat her mother. 'They were bad copies.'

Dougie bit his lip and stretched his mouth open. She wondered if he was trying to stop his eyes from watering.

'What is it?' she said.

'You're just a bit of a weirdo, aren't you?' he replied, and tenderly drove a fist into her shoulder. 'Aye, well, so am I.

Everyone's weird when you really see them. And you don't scare me, Maur. You think you will, but you won't. You can't scare me.'

She pursed her lips.

'Do you have a phone?' he asked.

She didn't, of course. She wasn't allowed one; they were trackable, and unfilterable, and would lead to things her mother called impure. 'Why?' she asked.

'We've no way to stay in touch, is all. And I fret about it. Because what if something happens?'

'Like what?' she asked.

'An accident. Or—'

'I don't have those,' she said, confidently.

'And I guess it would be all right to chat. To say hi, once in a while. See how things are.'

'I know,' she said. And she did know. The yearning was there for her, especially the morning after seeing him. Sometimes it sat so heavily in her gut that it was hard to tell apart from an illness. 'But I really can't.'

Dougie sighed and left it there.

Maureen prodded him in the sternum.

'See?' he said. 'Weirdo.'

Then came a night when Maureen left the house without doping her mother first. Their food and medical deliveries were two days late, their pills were all but used up, and Joan, despite fraught phone calls to persons unknown, hadn't been able to find out why. Maureen, even despite her stash, suspected her mother had been drinking too much, then forgetting how many suppressants she'd taken. But she didn't mention anything. Their companionship was transactional: they saw each other but didn't speak; they smiled but rarely meant it. Maureen sat there in the lounge until the cottage's only accurate clock chimed for midnight, and then she blew out the candles. Dougie was finishing at one a.m., and she didn't have long to make it up there.

Dougie met her at the top of the access road. As usual she was sweaty in her jacket and flustered by the possibility of being late. He shushed her. He looked mischievous. 'I wanted to show you this before we go off,' he said, pulling her towards the depot building. She tried to stop him, full of nameless dread. The cameras, the other men – it was too far. 'It's all right,' he said, reading her. 'Hey. Maur, I promise. Please. Trust me.' The warehouse shutters were all closed, but the floodlights were powerful, and her shadow was thrown long across the apron.

'They'll see me! They'll catch us!'

Dougie laughed. 'You daft bloody bat,' he said. 'It's the middle of the night, on Boxing Day – they're all at home, cosied up. Me, I left Nan asleep with her brandy and the cat. It's only us here. No bugger else.'

He directed her to an empty lorry cab. There were blue fairy lights strung across the dashboard inside. Its driver, Dougie explained, had struck up a relationship with a local woman whose kids insisted he join them for the whole Christmas break. He wasn't sleeping in the cab for now, didn't need it, so Dougie had asked to borrow his keys for evening, and here they were. He helped Maureen up. The cab smelled of latex and old food. It was warm, too, though Maureen still took the blanket Dougie offered, because he'd offered it.

Dougie made sure she was comfortable and drew his knees up under his chin. He put his hand on the gearstick and said, 'Sometimes he lets me sit up in here, on a shift, I mean, so I can work it out. Your gearing's all different in a lorry, for a kick-off.'

Maureen watched his hand jerking about; the gearstick certainly looked awkward to manipulate. She thought about the times she'd watched him sitting in a cab, smoking out of the window. Despite their frankness, their growing closeness, she didn't know when – or if – she could ever admit she'd been watching him.

'I told you,' he said. 'One day I'll have a crack at this. Then we'll see what's what. Hauling stuff up and down, east to west. It'll be right, that. It's my calling…'

She smiled at him. 'So, what are you trying not to say this time?'

'You what?'

'When you're nervous,' she went on, 'you yammer on about your cars and lorries and driving as if they're the only things that matter.'

And maybe Dougie seemed a bit hurt by that, but he laughed anyway. He said, 'Aren't they?' Then, 'It's a bit late for Christmas presents now, but I did grab you something.'

Maureen shook her head in mock disbelief, yet she felt awed. She wanted, in some way, to be able to get inside him. She stared at the warehouse roller shutters, the weak green emergency lighting high up on the walls. What was she doing?

'You have to actually look at me, though,' Dougie said, smiling.

She turned to him. He turned as though to retrieve something. 'Close your eyes and put your hands together, palms up,' he said. She did, and, when he was sure, a weight came into her hands.

A phone.

Maureen exhaled through her nose. Her guts felt twisted. It wasn't the thought of it, or the gesture, but the sudden fear of what he expected from her, and so of disappointing him.

'I can't,' she said.

'Course you can! It's tiny. They use these in prisons. One of the lads here – he told me about them. Wasn't mega expensive, if that's all it is…'

'I mean I'm forbidden,' she said. 'I told you. My mother—'

'Isn't even here.'

Maureen shook her head. 'You don't see. Out here, I can do as I please. She only wants to keep an eye out for me.'

Dougie took back the box. 'Sorry. I should've… I thought it'd help. That's all it was.'

'I'm grateful.'

'Plus, there was one other little thing.'

She smiled at that. 'And I need to do the hands thing again?'

'Maybe only one of them.'

Maureen obliged. This time a warmth entered her palm, and Dougie coughed softly. It was an old copper coin. 'Mam's penny, that,' he told her. 'Right back from when I was a nipper. She used to put it inside the knot of my school tie, so the older lads couldn't peanut me – you know, over-tighten the knot? I only had to have it on me, and then I'd be all right. And, it's nowt, not really. Pretty daft, in actual fact. But I've kept it on me ever since. It's for luck, and I wanted to give you some. You deserve some.'

Maureen turned the coin over. For some reason she sniffed it. It smelled like blood, which was to say it smelled like what had happened to her. But the coin was Dougie's, and something different, which made it good. She placed it on her knee. The Queen's head in profile, like the face on the cameo brooch left on the old woman's bedroom top. She sniffed her fingers, where the smell had stuck. She held the tips right under her nose.

'Happy Christmas,' Dougie said.

'Happy Christmas?' Maureen replied.

He blinked at her. 'I—'

She kissed him on the cheek. It happened quickly. Then, more urgently, she said, 'I want to sleep in here with you.'

Dougie didn't know what to do with himself. He'd gone red, and his hat was wonky from where her face had pushed it up. He said, 'There's a bit of room behind here?'

'And you'll sleep next to me?'

'I don't – I can't,' he said, clearly worried about upsetting her. 'I'm still on nights when I go back properly. Kipping now'll mess up my pattern, and I can't afford another strike against my name. Are you sure?'

She shrugged. She knew what she wanted. She said, 'If I sleep, will you watch out for me?'

'I don't follow.'

'In the mirror. To save your neck. I'll sleep here, and you can wake me in two hours and tell me if I look any happier.'

'*Happier?*'

'Or at least as if I enjoyed it. So I'll know, so that if I'm ever worried, I'll know that having a sleep can bring me back. Because I don't want to be afraid of my dreams anymore.'

'Maur,' Dougie said, almost desperately, 'I don't know what you're on about, when you talk like this. I just don't get you.'

'Then try harder,' she said. And she took his coin from her knee and held it tight against her chest.

PACT

They arranged another rendezvous at the depot for New Year's Eve. Dougie was there minding the unit, having accidentally-on-purpose pulled the short straw to cover the firm's party shift, and his colleague's truck cab stood empty again.

So far, Maureen had napped in the back for an hour, released from herself, from her leash of guilt. It meant a lot to her, being watched over. Dougie being who he was, grounded and gentle, if not inscrutable at times, meant there was never any threat, nor sense of a concealed motive. He did what she asked him to, and never – she hoped – from any sense of duty, or because it might mean she owed him in return, but because he *wanted* to. He snacked and drank his coffee and smoked his sweaty-smelling cigarettes through the slot in the window. And Maureen revelled in the fact her mother couldn't see, wouldn't begin to understand. That her mother was irrelevant, out here – the same as the tank, as her secondary memories, which barely troubled Maureen when she spent time with Dougie, because he was a dam against it all.

The cab with the fairy lights and his funny way of breathing. The cold air on her nose when she had a blanket wrapped around her. The way Dougie silently handed her a soft tissue when she woke up, and helped her tie back her hair, and kissed her forehead solidly, as if to welcome her, or from pure relief she'd returned. Together, they had a simplicity – something more natural, or even more inevitable, than either of them would be able to explain. Their time together was lived, and alive, a tangible *thing* they shared, and which stood in opposition to the bad copies under tarp in the raised garden beds, to Dougie's dying grandmother, and to pain elsewhere in their lives. Dougie, for Maureen, stood for vitality and decency and escape, and apparently this was mutual. Patience radiated from him. She saw points of fairylight in the knots of his arms and across the bridge of his nose, where the dark hair of his eyebrows ran fair, and in the grey-hued, mottled skin he carried from his nightwork. And soon, she promised herself, she'd have to tell him all of this, if he didn't already know. And even then, he might as well; it would be fun to embarrass him.

The watching he did gladly. These picnics and the flasks he prepared for them, all unselfconsciously, without routine or emphasis, with no purpose except to try and make Maureen feel safe and contented. And how she savoured the crackle of his cigarette lighter's wheel, the way he exhaled away from her, every tight *O* of smoke he sent through the window. And later would come the thrill of taking Dougie's penny back to the house with her, hiding it as though it were dissident materiel, or keeping it in a pocket as a ward, a superstition, the one thing that made the cottage's silence less alienating, Joan less overbearing. Phone or no phone, she knew they'd go on like this, for as long as they could, and with no need for any discussion about what they were together, or what they were becoming, because the process was so effortless. The penny was her portal to him. Any time she was alone, or felt it, she could turn the penny over in her hands until her palms glistened, and its metal was warm again. Because when she carried its bloody scent on her fingers, and inhaled it, she knew she belonged somewhere.

'You missed the bells for New Year,' Dougie told her, after her sleep. 'Oh, and a few piddly fireworks, over the other side of the valley. Meant to sing "Auld Lang Syne", not that I know the bloody words. Nan, though, she'd still love that, except the home, miserable sods they are, have her in bed by ten. So, happy new year to you, Maur.'

'I don't trust years so much,' she said. 'Not actually sure how many I've seen.'

'Seen enough of this one, though.'

She laughed.

'I made a resolution this time,' he went on. 'Not packing in the wacky-baccy, or owt mad like that, but...'

He pulled a soft nylon sports bag from the footwell and held it across his knee, which she saw he couldn't help bouncing.

'Please don't freak out,' he said, undoing the bag's zip, 'or judge me too much.' He showed her – inside it were three wigs. 'They're decent quality,' Dougie assured her, 'but I'm skint till payday, so I had to rob them.' He waited for a response, a disapproving look.

'Why?' she asked.

Dougie pulled a sheepish smile. 'Remember you saying about that grey wig at the cottage? It gave me this idea.'

'Right...'

His smile widened. 'The basics of it is, they'll help us escape together,' he said.

Her stomach started fizzing. It wasn't the first time – Dougie had an effect – but his sincerity, his intent, was new, and it was unsettling. He said, 'I'm like any old potato round here. Nowt special, that is – seen the state of me? But these'll help you disguise yourself. And there are places we can go. There's this firm down south I found. Labouring work, at first, but they offer HGV driver training when you've stuck it out a few years. You come with me... we get our own flat... we make do. Start over. And I know it's mad, I do. But I have to get the car MOT'd next week, and then I'm good for it – it's only a week's notice at this place, if they'll even see me out. And I've got a few quid stashed in the piggybank, enough for a couple of months' rent. And Nan won't care, either. I chatted to her. I told her about you. All she says is we're to mind one other.'

Maureen looked over the keenness of Dougie's posture and the way the wigs were perfectly spaced, placed, in the bag. A red one. A yellow one. A brown one. Before she spoke, she tried on the red one. She regarded herself in the cab mirror and saw a new person, no longer her mother, perhaps a cousin instead. Then she kissed Dougie on the mouth. He took it, surprised, before he tugged playfully on her sleeve to stop her.

He said, 'You're enough without it,' and pulled off the wig.

Maureen reared back from him, stared unblinking. She said, 'The only thing is, next week's too late. Let's go tomorrow. It has to be then.'

Maureen didn't sleep much when she got home, naturally; then Joan stormed in at nine to throw open the curtains and assail her with a list of chores. Maureen tackled each of them gladly – perfectly, in fact – seeing each one completed as part of her goodbyes. Scrubbing, polishing, sweeping, chopping... all jobs she'd never have to do for Joan again, and that she and Dougie would go on to share. She even pitied Joan, for not seeing what was coming. There was dirty rain on the windows, and the yard was bleak, but inside her it was late spring, and she was filled with the promise of summer.

Maureen didn't bother doping Joan over lunch, having

decided that with a lifetime of exploring ahead of her, she had no need for another selfish hour. They sat and watched the weather, eating soup, taking their pills, and occasionally turning to check the other was still engaged. Joan only raised her eyebrows when Maureen came and sat beside her, tucked herself under her arm, and placed the side of her head against her breast. When Joan whispered to her that she was sorry, Maureen had already fallen asleep.

The rest of the day ran away with itself, and Joan went to bed as she normally did – again with no extra dose. Maureen took out her bag before she got into bed, aiming to pack it so that later she could slip from the house in silence. But all she could think to take was Dougie's penny, some sanitary pads, as many tablets as her coat pockets would take, and one of her mother's scarves. Dougie had the wigs and his brown car, and both of them had the will to try. She reminded herself that nobody else apart from her mother and the old woman even knew she *existed*. In this case, having no presence in the world was its own blessing, and Dougie had already reassured her that there were people who could create fresh identities for them, if that's what they needed. He'd told her about people sitting in the quiet corners of pubs, who had friends of friends, and lists of favours owed. Through need came ingenuity, and while Dougie's hands often shook, and his eyes were endlessly alert, he still faced forwards, and believed their future together could be shaped if not assured. Plus, when she thought of her mother, their life in the cottage, she saw it would never be a permanent goodbye. On the old television, in scenes of sunshine or rain, scenes set against sad music or uplifting chords, she'd watched children leave their parents in droves. It was a rite, and now it was Maureen's turn. She'd write to her mother, or in time, after forgiveness, she might visit. This was what it meant, what it would take, to quieten the other voice inside her.

LAMB

Joan was sleeping soundly when Maureen decided she was ready. She stood over her mother for a last time, wanting to map her, to make sure she'd remember. Sleep softened Joan's face so much; Maureen had a sense of there being a fresh beauty in her skin, sudden and obvious – as if something had sharpened the musculature beneath. She traced the shape of her mother's face with one hand, careful not to make contact, and matched the movements on her own face with the other. The mole on Joan's left cheek was in the same place. The curve of Joan's septum matched her own. Maureen pushed her tongue in front of her top teeth, where a piece of thick tissue connected the lip to her gum. Carefully, she peeled back her mother's top lip. Even their lip-tie was identical.

'Thank you,' she said, and touched Joan's nose with her own.

Maureen marched through the woodland and across the bridge, giddy with desire and nerves. At the fence behind the depot – Dougie had taken to leaving by the rear of the building, through a flap in the mesh, to avoid the gatehouse cameras – she sat on her favourite trunk, a felled oak, and waited for his signal. Two pips on the horn. Footsteps. Their now-standard embrace…

Fifteen minutes passed. Then half an hour. Maureen began to fret. Suddenly having no phone was not only idiotic but cruel. Her thoughts accelerated to such an extent that the surrounding woodland appeared to blur, and she convinced herself she was sitting in the wrong place, at the wrong time, having missed him, or having misunderstood their plan. But it couldn't be. That was only last night, and this was today, and they'd agreed. They'd done everything right, to make it happen. They'd made their pact. She checked her watch and checked the fence and paced to the corners for a look, to try and see him. She could only see the others. No broken twigs or swift movement. No Dougie at the fence or in her arms.

An hour. The longest of her life. An hour in which Dougie had died a hundred ways and betrayed her in a thousand more. An unravelling, uncompromising, deathly-cold hour. Her loneliest since the first bad copy, in her bed, trapped in her own blood.

Sitting there was no use. She got up and brushed away moss and bark and promised herself that, even if Dougie should appear right now, she'd never forgive him for taking this night from her. And without a care in the world, she went through the flap in the fence and marched round the side of the depot and across the loading bays, to hammer on the nearest roller door and shout for him.

'Dougie! Doug! *Doug!*'

There was a commotion inside – tools on concrete and someone swearing in surprise. There was a knocking and a deep mechanical groan, and the roller door swept upwards. Behind it were five men of various heights and ages, staring at Maureen as though she'd just climbed out of a pond.

'You all right, there?' asked the youngest of them.

'What is it, lover?' asked another, glancing at the mud on her feet.

'Dougie,' she said. 'Where's Dougie?'

The men looked between themselves.

'You tell us,' the youngest said.

'Never turned in for his shift,' said the other. 'Can't get him on the blower. Left his charger up in the office, as well. Boss said he asked for his pay packet a day early. You ask me, I'd say he's vanished.'

Maureen couldn't believe it. The pain was white-hot, paralysing. She went to speak again but only squeaked. She wanted to explode, or dissolve, or tear them all to pieces—

'Here, you're not his bird, are you?' one asked.

Maureen's face burned. 'Bird?'

'The lad said he was seeing someone,' the same one said. 'But we thought he was pulling our legs. I wouldn't have said he had it in him.'

'Dark horse,' went another, scanning Maureen up and down. 'Always the quiet ones, though.'

Maureen shook her head.

A third man said, 'So who are you, then? Have you brought us tea?'

'I'm not anybody,' she told them. 'I'm nobody.' And she turned and left, surer than anything she'd never return, and shattered to admit it, and so angry her jaw ached, and doing all she could to ignore the men's mild jeers and mocking calls, and the one who shouted, louder than the rest: 'Give him a kiss from us!'

Across the bridge, heavy rain swept in. Maureen opened her jacket and hoped she'd drown.

When Maureen returned to the cottage, breathless but steely, soaked to the bone but still holding back her tears, there was an unfamiliar car parked beside the yellow gate. It was early morning now, the sky deepest red, and slats of sunlight were breaking through the cloud as though somebody above were searching the village.

The front door was off its latch, and all the lights were on. A bright yellow anorak was hanging from the coat hooks. Maureen padded across the hall tiles and left her socks and shoes and sodden coat in a heap by the stairs. Faintly, there came voices. She cracked the lounge door to see. The grey-haired woman – the cottage owner – and her mother were sitting by a dead fire, a candle burning between them. Burnt clove spiked the air; the old woman had made tea, and its smell took Maureen immediately back to the night they'd arrived with Tomasz. The women stopped talking. She watched them for a moment, floating almost, as though watching herself squirm, before she turned to try and go upstairs.

'You will not,' her mother said.

Maureen was sweating. The residual heat of walking. The shame of being caught. It was all humiliating enough; their interrogation, a trial, would be overkill. She put one foot on the first step of the staircase, then glanced over her shoulder, at the door, and considered running back to the depot. It was all a mistake, she thought. A big misunderstanding, and Dougie hadn't stood her up.

'Come in here,' her mother said.

Maureen went.

'For the record,' the grey-haired woman said sincerely, 'it wasn't so obvious. You've been a clever fox. Just not *quite* clever enough.'

And that was when Maureen saw the brown paper bag on the table, the torn cardboard boxes, and the stash jar of suppressants she'd been keeping in the pantry.

'Data doesn't lie, Reens,' her mother confirmed, tapping the jar. 'The maths trapped you. So now you'll sit with us, please. I think you owe us that. Though, let me say this now: I'm already over the worst of it. I promise.'

Maureen entered the lounge, scolded and sheepish. As an invite, her mother tapped the arm of her chair, which sent up a plume of dust. But Maureen couldn't bring herself to sit that close to her. She sank to the rug, crossed her legs.

'I'll only ask once, this time,' Joan said. 'How long?'

'I don't know,' Maureen said. 'A while.'

'And have you been taking yours properly?'

'Sometimes.'

The old woman frowned. 'You have to,' she said. 'You can't lose control.'

'It doesn't matter,' Maureen said. 'It's done with.'

Joan and the woman shifted awkwardly.

'What have you shared of your life?' the woman asked.

'Absolutely everything,' Maureen said.

'And what do you do with him?'

Maureen's mouth was too dry. Suction against her palate when she opened her mouth.

'Go on,' Joan said.

'We walk, and talk,' Maureen said. 'How have you—'

'Eyes in the back of my head,' Joan said, smiling in pity, before she gestured to the grey-haired woman. The candle flickered, caught itself. 'I know it's not enough to meekly want someone,' Joan went on. 'I know you must sacrifice a part of yourself. And so I – *we* – we don't blame you for chasing after boys. I can't blame you at all. And, of course, I don't want you to feel trapped with me. But our nature, our blessing – we do have to take care. We have a responsibility. You know what happens when we don't.'

The grey-haired woman nodded cautiously.

Maureen scoffed. Her bad copies? So her mother *was* blaming her, after all? The room was spinning. She felt woozy in the candlelight. And the grey-haired woman, so assured, was now hunched and staring at her shoes.

'I made a friend,' Maureen said. 'That's all it is. I like being near him, because it's enough.'

Her mother's eyes were brimming. 'And does he know?'

'About me?'

'About your gift.'

'I should hope so.'

'Then I have to remind you that you can find something like it again,' Joan said. 'Douglas is a nobody. He has nothing. You think I don't know? You think I haven't seen it all before? You think you're in love, but you can't be. You're too young for the depth, and you're too old for that much optimism.

It's all happening at once. They say the heart wants what the hearts wants, but it's so often wrong.'

Maureen didn't think she was wrong at all. She looked at her mother levelly and said, 'And how would you know? I've seen your wedding ring.' She tapped her temple. 'I've *felt* it. I know what came before me, what you've felt yourself.' Then, as though struck by lightning, she leapt to her feet and dug her nails into the back of her hand. 'Wait,' she hissed. 'How do you know his name?'

Her mother blanched. A visible surge of panic. She searched the other woman's face for support, then stared across the room, at nothing.

'I wasn't—'

Maureen shook her head in disbelief. She could believe the whole world was coming apart. She wanted to be sick; she wanted to scream. There was a pain behind her pelvis, a memory-bruise. Her insides were roiling. 'You followed me? You watched us?'

Her mother shook her head. 'Not me, not us. You led yourself away. We had to let him know about the potential consequences of that.'

'What?'

'Only a polite word.'

'You've *threatened* him?'

'No,' the older woman said. 'No, Reens.'

'Then where was he, tonight? At the depot?'

'Dougie understands better, now. All we gave him were the facts.'

'The *facts*?'

Her mother let out a desperate moan. 'It's dangerous,' she said. 'And he gets it.'

'So, you've taken this from us? You've taken him from me?'

The grey-haired woman got up.

'Stay over there,' Maureen told her. 'Don't you dare. No! What have you told him? Where is he?'

'He's with his grandmother,' the older woman said.

'You *bitches*.'

'Maureen!' Joan cried.

But Maureen had heard enough. She only cared about getting back to Dougie, who was another life away, and who was going to take her with him.

'Reens,' her mother pleaded.

Maureen didn't answer. She was back in the hall, pulling on her wet boots, her wet coat, trying not to slip on the tiles.

'You'll always be running,' Joan said, coming to the door with the grey-haired woman. 'If anyone ever found out who you are, it'd all be for nothing. All of it. And these people who watch out for us—'

'Joan,' the grey-haired woman said, cutting her off. 'It doesn't matter.'

'There's no guarantee you'll be safe,' Joan added. 'Our life here is so *deliberate*.'

'I don't want it,' Maureen said. 'I don't care.'

The grey-haired woman sighed. She was holding the paper bag that had been on the table. She held it out and said, 'You do have to manage yourself, Reens. Here. To keep yourself from—'

Maureen shook her head. No more suppressants, either. No more of this. *Dougie* was the one who made her normal. When she was with him, the tank and the memories and the pain were pushed right back, like everything else was. The living pasts inside her had no force. With Dougie, she fitted, so if she couldn't be with him, then she'd let herself go, let herself feel every moment of it.

Now it was Joan interrupting, waving a hand in protest. 'I won't beg for her loyalty,' she told the older woman. Then, addressing Maureen directly: 'I love you. Wherever you go, wherever this takes you, there'll be help.'

The old woman nodded in agreement. 'We'll be here.'

'I was never choosing him over you,' Maureen said. 'I was choosing for myself – for once.'

There was a loud knock at the door. All of them stilled. The house creaked and Maureen's wild heart could have filled every corner. More knocking, insistent. A neighbour, maybe? Somebody had heard them fighting, and it being so early in the morning, was coming to see…

But they had no neighbours close enough, and there was another sound outside. An engine idling.

Maureen sprang to the door and opened it. Dougie fell into the house, hat and jacket dripping and face drawn. He brought with him the sweet scent of burnt castor oil. His little brown car was half mounted on the kerb, driver's door open.

'The lads at work said you'd been over,' he blurted, ignoring the two older women glowering at him.

Maureen took him by the collar. Heat radiated through the cotton, from his neck. Were it any colder outside, his back would be steaming.

'I thought you'd bailed on me,' he said.

'What?'

Dougie glanced behind Maureen. Maureen turned so that she and Dougie stood shoulder to shoulder, their backs to the open door.

'What did you tell him?' Maureen asked.

'Maureen,' Joan said.

'You lied to us both?'

'No lies,' the grey-haired woman said.

Dougie touched Maureen's waist so delicately it made her shiver. She smiled at her mother and then at the grey-haired woman and then at Dougie, his head in profile, like the old Queen's on her penny, his eyes full of purpose. She squeezed the coin in her pocket. The smell of blood and the promise of summer. A night of endings. Holding the penny diffused the pain and anxiety. She moved her hand to her abdomen and imagined what a good copy might be. Warmth spread from her hand across her belly. A bubble of sunshine, expanding. She closed her eyes and saw the rawness of another birth, but this time it wasn't her own, nor Joan's before her. She wanted to take a final look at the raised beds in the back, the burial ground, so that she might better grieve, while seeing there was no need; the house and her bad copies were entwined and under the care of Joan, her mother, and she was her own person, and able to go on. And from there she entered another space, from which it was possible to forgive, and to see *forward*. And there she was, glimpsed through the veil: another Maureen, an *older* Maureen, sitting with her own child, a boy, in her lap, and both of them laughing.

She found Dougie's arm. She was ready; they could leave. One day, she swore, she and Dougie would have a son together.

PART THREE

SURROGATES

Even through hard rain, Boyd could hear Lamb's wailing from the top of the mound. She'd been asleep with Leigh when he set out, but now – as he used the shovel and yard brush to work the charred remains of the gull pyre into the landfill's crevices – her distress was more like an alarm call, pulsing and ebbing over the wind, and he was starting to worry about who might hear.

The sweeping was futile, either way. Rather than washing the pyre away, the rain was turning its ashes into a black paste, and each stroke of the broom was only extending the problem. When Boyd stood back, stinking of it, he wiped his nose, shook the rain from his hood, and winced. Trying to hide it wasn't going to work. Gaff's return was still a few days away, yes, but there'd be no escaping how bad it looked. And all this before Gaff found out about Lamb—

Lamb. Even acknowledging the girl's existence was shocking to him. They'd spent a single broken night with her, and yet this tiny girl, with her brutal newness, and their responsibility for her – the weight of it all had come down on them. And while Lamb wasn't a burden in herself, not exactly, her being there was still generating an ugly feeling in him, an aversion that ran all the way out to selfishness. Most of all, he had the impression they'd entered alien territory. Wanting to run, having to stay.

LAMB

Coming back towards the van, Boyd could hear Leigh coughing while trying to soothe the girl. She was repeating Lamb's name as if she were willing it to stick. An incantation, almost sung. Her tone was melancholy and gave a new dimension to Leigh entirely. Boyd wondered how it might feel to be on the other end of it, knowing equally that any chance of that happening had passed. When he opened the van door, and Lamb's crying intensified, he stood there dumbfounded. Leigh was struggling to hold the girl, and was staring bleakly at the pictures of her own family on the walls.

'I was going to move your bedding across to the new van,' he said gently. 'Away from the mould, I mean. To make it cosy.' He picked up a blanket, as if to illustrate his point. He was desperate to be useful; felt he owed it to Leigh, and more besides, for her hospitality. And in some way, he *was* being useful: Lamb, on hearing his voice, had settled.

'Leigh?' he said.

Leigh didn't say anything – didn't even look over. He felt guilty. She was having to shoulder so much without even knowing why.

'I think "Lamb" really works,' he tried, removing the trunk, the baled-up fairy lights, then the compost toilet. The girl had wriggled into the crook of Leigh's elbow. She was so small and pathetic, uncomfortable in her own skin. Her name *was* right, he was trying to say. For one, she was still attracting fluff from Leigh's fleece blanket – but the meaning also ran deeper, spoke to her cuteness as much as her uselessness.

Lamb, Lamb. Sing it or plead it. This scrap of a thing they'd found on the mound, made cherubic against Leigh's chest.

Leigh, finally noticing Boyd, turned and smiled absently. But she couldn't find a way to shed her startled expression, and her eyes were bloodshot. There were too many possibilities, too many worries, and Boyd could see she felt them as acutely as he did. In turn, he saw his parents' own responsibility for him in a new light; recognised some sliver of what it meant to have to care completely. The anxiousness of it. The desire to get everything right. The dread for things that might never happen. Had he been like a bomb going off in the middle of their life, too?

Like Dougie's death, Lamb had applied a pressure they hadn't asked for, much less prepared for. The girl was a force. An imposition. A test. And so far, it seemed as if they'd both lost something in the transaction.

'We'll work it out,' Boyd added, barely believing himself. If nothing else, there was at least a contract: they weren't Lamb's parents or guardians, nor her *grown-ups*. They would make do, which in the moment meant writing a big shopping list of necessities, holding to a kind of patience or mercy for the other, and pretending they each held innate childcare knowledge, something more than the books or television programmes or films they were actually drawing their ideas from.

When they finished the shopping list, Leigh was restless. 'We need this stuff *now*,' she said, jabbing the paper. She hated being out of control, Boyd saw – it wasn't enough to feed the girl with boiled water, treated or not.

To try and calm herself, Leigh started stroking Lamb's face, the fuzzy down of her cheeks. The girl smacked her lips in hunger. Soon enough she'd wake again, and then they'd have to change her, feed her, resettle her.

'How old even is she?' Leigh whispered.

'Few weeks?' Boyd tried.

They double-checked their shopping list. Milk powder and nappies, wipes and cotton wool, towelling and bedding, rash cream and clothes. There was a minimarket on the edge of Neighton Prangle.

They were trying.

'What about cash?' Boyd asked.

'Gaff's got a float in his caravan,' Leigh said. 'Some jewellery I could pawn, if needs be.'

'And then we'll leave?' he said.

Leigh's hard stare. 'You're not winning *that* argument.' Then, after coughing away from Lamb: 'Ah, shit, not again…'

Lamb had woken and was watching them, blinking slowly.

'I could swear she listens,' Leigh said. 'Aren't they meant to just… cry all the time?'

Boyd shook his head. He didn't know.

'Oh my God,' Leigh said. 'Work it out, Boyd. I really don't think I can do this.'

Boyd would stay in the van with Lamb, and Leigh wouldn't be long. There was a shortcut through the estate, and she had a skeleton key for Gaff's static. Boyd reminded her to scrub the CCTV or turn off the cameras. If Gaff spotted what was happening, had any clue at all, he'd likely cut short his Scarborough trip, and they'd have another problem to deal with. It was unspoken, but they both knew he wasn't going to put up with a baby on site.

Leigh settled Lamb on Boyd's knee, facing him. Fully open, the girl's eyes glittered with adultlike perception, and the way she held herself convinced him she was almost *too* solid. It was something like pride, a certainty.

Leigh left the side door open and set off for the shop. Her shoulders relaxed the moment she started walking away, and she didn't turn back once. Boyd found himself envying her until Lamb poked his nose, wanting attention. He took her across the scrub to sit under the old van's awning. She mewled in the breeze, so he closed Dougie's jacket around her and brought her head against his ear. Her skin had an addictive warmth, a doughy texture. He shushed her, as if that was the answer to everything – and it amazed him, because it actually worked.

Lamb relaxed again, her ribs against his collarbone, and he scanned the mound, lingered too long on the smudged gull pyre. Lamb exhaled for a long time, became subtly heavier. There was moisture on his neck. Dribble, her breath, or both – he didn't mind. Even the churning in his stomach was slowing, as if Lamb herself were an anaesthetic. As if she alone could protect him.

He closed his eyes and bowed his head. The ground and the wind. Their breath and the rain. A little girl, a lost boy.

Leigh returned with a more determined outlook. She'd scored hand towels, safety pins, a box of powdered milk, a wash-ing-up bowl, two baby bottles, and terrycloth for reusable nappies. 'Easier to strip-clean, apparently,' she said, voice mettled. 'Whatever *that* fucking means.'

She touched the back of her hand to Lamb's cheek. Boyd wondered whether it was involuntary, another baby-thing you were just compelled to do. Lamb's skin was hot and her cheeks were rosy. Reacting to Leigh's coldness, she turned her face into Boyd's chest and stayed like that until Leigh handed over her milk. 'It's fine,' Leigh said, of Lamb's ungratefulness. 'I'll remember.' Yet when Lamb finished the bottle greedily, Leigh duly prepared another.

'Powder won't see us through a week, at this rate,' Leigh said. 'She's a beast.'

'Yeah,' Boyd said. 'So we're going to have to make some decisions before Gaff's back.'

Leigh didn't need to reply. She wasn't going to entertain it. She nodded at Lamb, who had begun to writhe, emitting little whimpers. 'Needs winding,' she said. 'Watch.' And she mimed how Boyd should put Lamb over his shoulder.

Mystified, he gave it a go, patting and rubbing, until Lamb belched and vomited green cream down his back. Leigh sniggered, then fell into laughter, which caught them all off guard. Boyd, hopeless, joined in. When he held Lamb away so Leigh could remove his top, she was grinning too. It was a moment, binding. Leigh threw his top in the wash bucket and prodded him in the chest.

'You're too thin,' she said, as if to close herself off again. 'Eat.'

They went to bed in the new van, all three on the mattress. Boyd had done all he could to clean it, lain newspaper under the blankets to separate them from the cover. He pictured them from above, from beyond himself. They made an unlikely family.

'Stoppit,' Leigh kept whispering to Lamb, faux-annoyed. 'Stop!' Then, to Boyd: 'You seen this? She won't stop pawing at my tits.'

He turned over to find Lamb giggling.

'If it helps her sleep,' he said.

'Ohh-ho,' Leigh said. 'Is that how this is going to go?' Lamb's hand on Leigh's chest and her mouth against Leigh's shoulder. 'We'll have to cope for tonight, then, won't we?' Leigh said to Lamb. 'Yes, we will – ignore dickhead over here. Ah, look at you. Cute, cute, cute.'

They slept in fits and starts, Lamb especially. At some point, milk bottle in hand, Leigh nudged Boyd and said, wide-eyed with distress, 'What should we do? When should we take her to hospital?'

Boyd pretended to stay asleep. Leigh's priority was Lamb's welfare – he got that. But in the dark, in their closeness, the idea of them separating choked him up. 'I don't want her to be scared,' he mumbled. He had to believe that as long as one of them was here, with Lamb, she'd be safe.

'Never saw myself having kids,' Leigh said quietly. 'I doubt you've even had that chat with yourself. But I see you, pal – how you look at her, even when you try to hide it. What do you think they're going to do at the hospital? Honestly? They'll understand. They'll know she isn't ours. They'll be able to tell. They'll be able to *test*. And we can't get in trouble for wanting the best for her, can we? For doing what anyone would. We found her; we don't know where she came from... I know that hurts. But she can't stay here, can she? This can't be enough. *This* – seen this place? We're living in a fucking *bin*.'

Between them, Lamb rolled over and parted her lips to make the tiniest click.

And Boyd said, 'Why can't we?'

Neither of them could face the inbox. The mess and the mud made it hard to tell where you'd even start, and in any case it was pointless now, not much more than a game, a distraction. As Boyd dressed, Leigh said, 'I'll tell Gaff we've had the shits, or something.'

But Boyd, distracted, didn't hear her properly. There was already mould growing in the new van. It was in the roof carpeting, in the window seals. Mildew on the cold surfaces. He'd been trying to rub it away before Leigh woke up, but he'd only managed to stand on her leg.

'Can't you smell it?' he asked.

Leigh shrugged him off. 'I've stopped coughing, haven't I? And this is with three of us in here – there's zero ventilation. It's cold, it's what happens.' Lamb, meanwhile, was whingy, pleading for more food. Leigh pointed at her and said, 'She's being a right greedy bastard today.'

Boyd made a sling for Lamb using one of Leigh's hoodies, tying and retying its arms until he found the right knot. It wasn't a ploy, but maybe there was a thread of possessiveness about it. Seeking control, even if he'd never take it. Wanting to be close to Lamb because it felt right.

After their breakfast, and another two bottles of formula, Boyd wandered around the site until Lamb nodded off in the sling.

'Fair play,' Leigh conceded. 'You're good at it.' Except she said it with sarcasm – half envious, half offended. Boyd was clearly acting beyond her expectations; this wasn't like searching through the inbox.

Boyd offered to do the afternoon shift with Lamb, too. He came back with his boots and legs caked in mud, none the wiser about where he'd taken her, other than to say the woodland behind the site, away from the squalor and the rot. 'Never too far,' he said, as if that might offer any assurance.

'What if someone's after her?' Leigh asked. 'Or what if they changed their mind? Someone better than me, than you, than us. Than this. What if her parents...' She let that hang, and so did he. They both knew Lamb was working as a wedge, a reminder they didn't truly know each other.

Rougher weather swept in after dark. Lamb wailed and burrowed into Boyd's front while rain lashed the van. He laid her down and smoothed her chest. 'We can't trust anyone else,' he told her. 'It's only us.'

Leigh shot him a look. 'So tell me why, will you? Tell me about your mam. Tell me what this is. Because I can't lie here all night, again. I can't be next to her, in my head. I can't keep wondering.' She dropped her voice to a whisper: 'When you're asleep, all she does is stare at you. So, please, Boyd. Please, tell me.'

And suddenly Leigh seemed so young. Just as Boyd must have appeared to her, that first time they met. In the super-market, with that boy. His eyes filled with tears. There were things in him, drawn from the depths of another place, a well of strange consciousness. And he was sure it wasn't Leigh doing it, but Lamb.

Boyd said, when he could: 'Do you know what it's like when you love someone, and they're in the worst pain you can think of, and you can't help them? No matter what you do?'

Leigh didn't answer.

'That was my mum.'

They slept better, but Lamb had a temperature and threw up all morning. She couldn't hold anything down – not even water – and screamed whenever Leigh came near. In the end Boyd suggested Leigh do another supplies run, so he could stay and soothe Lamb.

'What?' Leigh said.

'To try and calm her down,' Boyd explained. 'Maybe try another walk.'

Leigh rolled her eyes and snorted.

'Wouldn't it be best?'

She glared at him.

'Leigh?'

'Sure, Boyd,' she snapped. 'Except it's *your* fucking turn.'

He recoiled, shocked. 'But I thought I'd keep her—'

'So take her in your precious bloody sling. Go down there with her and play the big daddy, why not? But clean up first, else they'll think you're on for smack, the state of you.' She scratched out a quick map of Neighton's high street and slapped it on the mattress. Then she went outside, where she also slapped the van.

Lamb looked up at Boyd, expectant.

'I don't know,' he said. 'It's a lot.' Then, 'I don't know what we're going to do with you, either.'

Lamb wriggled until drool swung across her chin. He wondered if he was meant to be able to feel her ribs, if that was another indicator of growing. He laid her on the bed, where she rolled onto her belly, and ignored her whimpers while he rubbed new mould away. Outside, Leigh was pacing up and down beside the inbox, head low. She *was* denying this. Their realities were in conflict.

'I don't know how to get her back,' he said to Lamb. What felt like a sudden break in his alliance with Leigh was making him queasy. He'd only wanted to do right by the girl and didn't fully understand how he'd caused upset. It was as if an old, sad pattern was re-emerging, and he couldn't do anything to stop it.

When Leigh noticed he was looking out at her, she went inside the other van and slammed the door shut. Lamb went silent, as if she was reading Boyd's mind. Or as if Boyd's rift with Leigh was somehow reassuring to her…

He shook his head. No – this had always been bound to happen with Leigh. He'd been holding in too much, and he'd opened himself enough to inundate her.

'Stay there,' he told Lamb. And he went over to Leigh's van.

'I'm still sulking,' she said through the window. 'When I've got over it, I'll go into town – obviously you can't take her. And I'm sorry, all right? It's so… I just feel like I'm losing myself.'

Boyd and Leigh were calmer, more present for each other, in the afternoon. As if they were agreeing, tacitly, to hold on. He'd asked Leigh to grab sun cream on her Neighton run, and now he was rubbing it into Lamb's cheeks and neck and ears, and trying to explain himself. 'Habit?' he suggested. 'Mum used to put it on me.'

'Like a security blanket,' Leigh said.

'I guess.'

Leigh smiled wistfully. 'Mam used to knit new gloves for me, once a year, till I was eight or nine. Told me I'd lose my fingers if I didn't wear them when I was cold. I'd even wear them to bed, after that. The stuff you learn young sticks hard, doesn't it?'

Lamb was brighter, too. Since Leigh had come back, she was smiling consistently – too easily pleased, if anything. Leigh bopping her nose or pulling a face, peek-a-boo – trying to build something, make her own play. Every grin a joy. They also managed to feed her, and she kept it down. 'She's definitely growing,' Leigh said, with a note of vanity.

Lamb's consistent growth was irrelevant to Boyd, however – just another facet of her oddness. He wanted to relax but couldn't; the prospect of Gaff finding Lamb was what mattered, and the longer they played here as a trio, a near-family, the worse his dread became. Because Red had been out here, and the mould wasn't going anywhere, and there was clearly a power in Lamb, something intoxi-cating, something that made him reminisce about his own childhood, and something that scared him. All of which took him back to his mother and Watford and the day the police officers had arrived to announce his father's death. All of which trapped him in the past, with all its feelings, when he wished most of all to remember sitting beside his father, in their caravan.

Lamb was due a nap soon. Maybe they should nap when she napped? Each day forever divided into micro-shifts. You make up the bottle, you feed her, you rest her…

'Like a pair of knackered parents?' Leigh said, winking to mask her distaste. Some investments clearly troubled her, and now she was explicit about it: 'Given how much she's taken a shine to you, maybe it's better that only I play with her for the rest of the day,' she said. 'You do the chores, serve the milk, sure. But at least give me a chance. Let me see if I can carry her in your clever-dick sling.'

Boyd agreed; it wasn't the worst suggestion. So far, Lamb was sleeping easier, deeper on him. Far better they both master it.

Then Leigh said, 'Seriously, though. You know she stares at you the second you come into view? And it's *different*?'

Boyd nodded unsurely.

'I'm not even sure she blinks when you're about,' Leigh went on. 'Got your measure, pal. Got you wrapped around those diddy fingers of hers, hasn't she—'

From nowhere, Leigh screamed and pushed Lamb across the mattress. 'No!' she shouted. 'Shit!'

Boyd locked up. Instant adrenaline.

'She bit me!' Leigh cried.

'What?'

'Right here,' Leigh said. A red welt on her hand. 'We *don't* do that,' she told Lamb. '*No.*'

Lamb lay there, looking pleased with herself.

'Are you sure?' Boyd asked.

Leigh leaned forward so he could see it in the light. Then she carefully ran a finger across Lamb's gums, before retracting her finger in shock. 'There's bloody *teeth* in there,' she said. 'Is that right? Is that normal?'

Boyd floundered for something trite, something supportive. Instead, he grimaced. They both knew it wasn't normal.

In the night, Leigh found Boyd in the driver's seat with a bottle of milk prepared for Lamb. Leigh looked annoyed – this time the jet stove had woken her up – but when she checked the time, her anger dissolved into concern.

'It's four a.m.,' she said.

'So get back to bed,' Boyd said. Because he didn't know how to tell her what else he'd been thinking about, the new thing, the latest facet of his knowing. She asked again, but he ignored her. She said, in a drawl, 'I'm not pissing about, Boyd.' And he was too young again, scolded, staring back at his mother.

'Hang on,' Leigh said. 'Where's Lamb?'

Reluctantly, he pointed. The girl was behind Leigh, playing with the van's double doors.

'She started crawling,' he said.

Leigh swung back to him. 'You're joking?'

He wasn't. 'Last hour, maybe longer. Woke me up. I don't know what else to tell you.'

Leigh clutched her jaw. 'What's going on? What the fuck's going on?'

Boyd swallowed. The window had already narrowed, and he knew he was going to say it, tell her the other thing, even as he knew that saying it might break things beyond repair. He rubbed his throat and spoke quickly: 'I have to go back, Leigh.'

'What?'

'I have to go back to Sile, with Lamb. I've left something at home.'

'What do you mean, with Lamb? It's four in the pissing morning, Boyd. You can't tell—'

'I'm taking her with me. I have to.'

Leigh narrowed her eyes. It was all there. The fracture between them becoming a crack, and still widening.

'Why?' she asked. 'You can't do this to us. She's crawling. You can't just—'

'We'll be back here before breakfast,' he said. 'Please, please, don't fret.'

And behind them, at the doors, Lamb was laughing at something, and in the scant light they both saw her single tooth shining.

Lamb, crawling now. With teeth.

But that was only half the story, even if Boyd himself could barely glimpse what might come next. There were concepts in orbit, orderable only through complex equations he couldn't solve. His knowing came and went – as if all the answers were being placed inside his mind and snatched away when he noticed. But if he was right – if he saw a plain truth at all – it was that returning home was the only way to close the loop Maureen had opened.

Strongest of all was his mother's voice, which kept coming to him: *You missed something.* After all, had there not been a calling-back, a hint, in Maureen's apology on the morning she vanished? The way she'd said she *did* love him? Because Dougie had done nothing like that, only shut the door and allowed them to suffer in his wake. Whatever Maureen had done, she'd at least tried to acknowledge how it would mark her son, change him, scar him. That last morning – her last sentence – had been meant as a confession.

I do love you, you know.

So, the fuller story went like this: a recurrent dream had been haunting Boyd ever since they'd found Lamb. In this dream, Boyd was up on the mound, clawing at it with bare hands, coldness to his elbows, trying to find his mother's hand, her shoulder, a shoe. He'd uncover her face, her mouth and nostrils stuffed with filth and worms. And she'd speak to him – reach into him – and say, 'Silly boy, silly boy. It's all back there!'

He'd tried to discount it, but it kept coming back. A longing too big and searing. And so his interpretation of it changed: the dream wasn't a dream at all; his *knowing* was pulling him back to Sile, and Lamb should be with him, guide and ward, strapped to his front in his makeshift sling. Because having her there would make the difference. Because Lamb was part of the equation. And there'd be bile in his throat and purpose in his stride; and swiftly, as though he'd slipped and fallen through time – it was already *happening*, total dislocation – he'd arrived there with Lamb in the sling, and they were outside their changed house before dawn, going back along its side alley.

At the back gate Boyd paused, stranded for a moment by the fact he wasn't scared, that this was true and real and needed. He felt shielded by Lamb, and righteous; he was certain this was the thing he was meant to do. And when he looked down at Lamb, she was sleeping. And when he pushed through the back door, into the kitchen's crumbling mass of branches and dead vegetation, Lamb smiled softly, as though breathing the stale air had put her at ease. And all this despite a sense the house was still being contested.

It came to him that being here, back here, was part of the dream. In the darkness, in the quiet. And in that odd space between, he realised why at last: *Lamb* had directed him all the way, simply by leaning. Lamb might even have put the idea inside him. A magic to it, and a naturalness. Which was how he went on, following her as she fell away from him, tugging him through the half-taken house. Over the fibrous mat of the downstairs flooring, circling Red's dead column, grey and wilting, and up the rotting staircase, on past the column on the landing, now a kind of desiccated nest filled with bone-coloured powder. To the bathroom, door open again, every surface caked with black residue. And to Maureen's room, where Lamb's breathing shallowed, and her weight changed. The room dry and teeming with dust.

'What now?' he asked.

But he wasn't to question anything. Lamb had him circle the room, head lolling left to right, until she zeroed in on the spot where Maureen's suitcase had lain open. Boyd exhaled. There was a warmness, delicate, in his feet. Leigh and the landfill felt a long, long way away.

'Okay,' he said.

Lamb roused and fought against him until he had no choice but to unstrap her. At his knees, she picked and pulled at the dead moss with a dexterity beyond her age. He knelt to help, and when she saw he was making progress, she moved off again, sat against the bed frame, posture unnaturally straight.

The moss came apart like old rope in his hands, releasing an aerosol of violet dust. Deeper, he found the cool metal of a clasp, the fabric of the outer cover, and some cardboard that felt like wet leaves. His eyes were watering; Lamb silently urged him on. He made a hole big enough to drag out the suitcase and emptied its contents onto the floor.

'You stupid, stupid prick,' he told himself.

How had he not seen? How had he not noticed?

He knew these socks. These T-shirts. The warm layers...

And Lamb closed her eyes, as if she was paying her respects.

Maureen hadn't packed the suitcase for herself. She'd packed it for Boyd. And in his wilfulness – after all their disconnection – he'd missed it. It'd been here this whole time. Her wigs, the bank statements, the money... Maureen had left it all for him, as close as she could go to an explanation, pulled together in her final moments of lucidity.

Lamb came to Boyd's side. He felt a pang of recognition, then futility. Lamb touched his neck, gestured loosely.

Because there was more. A line of crude red stitching in the dark lining of the suitcase, where Maureen must have opened the back panel and sewn it closed again. He pushed a finger through, got his hand in. The perished material tore easily. Lamb wasn't blinking. Inside was an old e-reader. It was long dead, but tucked inside its case was a sun-faded photograph: a young Boyd on Dougie's knee, in the driving seat of his cab. Boyd gasped and fell back into the dry moss. He'd never seen the picture before. In it, Dougie's boots were planted on the cab floor while young Boyd was swinging his feet so much they were blurred. He must have been seven or eight, grinning easily. Dougie was vacant, shoulders forward and head turned, focused on something out of shot. The slight smile spoke to his quiet discomfort at being the subject; it didn't come across as sadness. That his mother had kept this photo so privately… it must have captured the essence of her boys, her grumpy husband and eager son, a sliver of their sometimes-fraught relationship, their bond. And Boyd saw the old Boyd, the before-Boyd, and not himself now. And he wanted to reach back, hold that younger Boyd, and say it would be all right.

On the reverse of the photograph was an address: *Bright House 3, Peterborough.* Taped underneath this was an old penny. Boyd recognised it as the coin Maureen had played with during the inquest.

Boyd took the photo with its coin, the e-reader, and wrapped Lamb against him. At the point of leaving, back at the kitchen door, he stopped and turned. Only relief. Only space. And nothing left to forget – there'd be no need to return. For this, he could thank Lamb. Through this – their visit – he could better accept his strange link to her.

Above all else, though, it had to be final.

Boyd returned to the kitchen, turned on all the gas hobs, the oven, and left. Outside, in the street, he hammered on the doors of neighbours either side of their house, and yelled in falsetto, 'Gas leak, gas leak!' through their letterboxes. The rest he'd leave to luck. He tightened Lamb against him. She was silent.

Up ahead, a ginger tabby crossed the street and vanished.

WHITE VAN

The door to Gaff's static caravan broke easily. Boyd rifled the collection baskets for a cable to fit the e-reader, and, finding one, rigged it to the generator. First light broke – a mauve sky, choppy cloud. After ten minutes the e-reader still wouldn't come on, and he accepted that Maureen had had every right to hold her secrets. What he was meant to find, he'd found. He pushed the e-reader aside. The photograph of Boyd and Dougie was just as much a summary of their life; the address on its reverse had been Maureen's parting gift. He pulled off the penny, pushed it down into his sock. Lamb slept on, one hand occasionally pawing his chest as if to check he was still there.

Leigh appeared with a mug of tea. 'Back, are you? I mean, I've only been scrubbing puke stains for the last half hour – thanks for letting me know.'

Boyd blinked at her.

'You could've asked for the key.' She pointed to a camera in the corner of the room. 'Gaff'll be charmed – that's the only feed you can't loop, or wipe. Have you got a locksmith's number? Cos I haven't.'

Boyd drew a sharp breath. The caravan felt too small. Dirty and grim and sad. 'Where's Peterborough from here?' he asked her.

Leigh was puzzled. 'What?'

'Can you look on your phone?'

'No credit. No data. Only Gaff or Mam ever call me—'

'Then what about an A to Z? Has Gaff got any?'

'You think he's a big traveller?'

'He went to Scarborough.'

'And he was a courier in his old life. He'll know those roads. The proper question is why, surely? I mean, I think Peterborough's near Cambridge. The deep middle, some-where. But why—'

'I need to get there,' Boyd said.

'Need, or want?'

At this, Lamb turned to Leigh with curiosity, as if to spectate. Her palms were still grainy with dirt and fibres of moss. Boyd carried her towards the door, stepped outside.

'Need,' he replied.

'Oh piss off,' Leigh said. But there wasn't much conviction in it, and he saw her fear. He readjusted his jacket around Lamb and took Leigh's hand.

'I'm not being a dick,' he said. 'I'm not even asking you to trust me.'

Leigh resisted, then relented. Boyd squeezed gently. He didn't want to let go. He led her all the way back to the white van, where she pulled away.

'We don't have long,' he said.

'You're like someone else,' Leigh said, her face contorted. 'I don't know what to—'

She was interrupted by the rainwater bowser rattling. There were vibrations under their feet, like a washing machine running in another room. A dissonant chorus rose from the mound, as chunks of metal scrap danced together. Leigh shook her head.

'I told you,' Boyd said.

He knew what it was – he'd been expecting it. Heavy

vehicles were coming off the carriageway and looping around the site, on towards the haze of blue smoke rising on the other side of the boundary wall. At last, a set of blue lights strobed the road, and three fire engines tore past the gates and down the main road into Sile.

Boyd wasn't proud. But it wasn't a bad feeling, either. Lamb became fidgety, burrowing into his chest.

Leigh, visibly cold, was trying to read him. Perhaps she wanted to work out what she'd sacrificed to take him in, take this on. He wondered if she was close to giving up; the past told him it was all he deserved. While Leigh's emotional intelligence far outstripped his, she'd underestimated his capacity for self-interest.

'Grab a blanket,' he told her.

'No,' she said.

'Then take Lamb for a minute.'

Leigh and Lamb stared at each other. Leigh pinched the bridge of her nose as if she was deliberating. 'Fine,' she said.

Boyd passed Lamb to Leigh, who held the girl in one arm at her waist, Lamb's legs clamped either side of her hip.

'Too big,' Leigh whispered to her. And Lamb touched her face in response.

Boyd had climbed on top of the van. The smoke over Sile was thickening. They could smell it – wood, brick dust, plastic. The cloud base glowed faintly orange.

Leigh said, 'I'm too tired for this.'

Boyd went to answer, but she was already trudging up the mound for her own vantage point. He jumped down and followed them with a blanket. Partway up, a sound more like thunder. Lamb began to howl – a piercing, mournful noise – which turned to subdued babbling as Leigh jiggled her against her hip. Leigh tugged Boyd's arm – hard – and said, 'Hey – did you hear that? Did she just say "*Mum*"? Did she? She did – she said "Mum"!'

LAMB

Boyd swayed on his feet. A second *crack* scattered the birds in the hedgerows, and moments later a warm breeze came over them. A black pall was rising over Sile, and Lamb continued to whinny as it grew. Leigh hugged herself with her spare arm. Boyd screwed his face up. He hoped the neighbours had got out. He hoped there'd been time.

The cloud base was solid red now. The smell of burning was choking. A huge fire was raging in Sile, and Leigh watched Boyd watching it. If she didn't already, she understood now. Whatever he'd been trying to find in his mother's house, whatever was left of that life, it was all up there, in that smoke.

'I won't say sorry this time,' Boyd said, as a curtain of ash began to fall away from the plume.

This time Leigh looked too defeated to argue.

Boyd drove. The van, being an old-fashioned diesel, was simple enough to operate once you got it running, and torque-y all the way up to fourth gear. Leigh held Lamb in her lap, no belt. Neither of them checked the mirrors. There was nothing said, nothing offered. Boyd had moved on quickly before; he understood that you totalled your costs later.

'Are you hungry?' he tried. 'Is she?'

Leigh didn't answer.

They were only as far as the trunk road when a police officer on a patrol bike swept around them, one arm out. No helmet, but heavy-duty body armour. He was young and agitated. Without a word – recognising that without a car seat for Lamb they'd be in trouble – Leigh took the girl into the back and started swaddling her, shushing her softly before Boyd opened the driver's window.

'Where you off to in a hurry?' the officer said.

'Heading home,' Leigh shouted through.

The officer appeared put out by this, and asked Boyd where home was. Before Boyd could answer, he said, 'Not Sile, no?' and laughed awkwardly.

'Why's that?' Boyd said.

The officer grew sterner. His eyes were scanning the cab. Boyd pictured himself, gangly, an implausible white van driver. Then the officer said, 'There's a fire. Some kind of gas leak. You won't be able to get in.'

Boyd glanced in the rear-view mirror. Leigh was still stooped over with Lamb, rocking her desperately, another whispered song. At the same time, the officer didn't seem to notice, didn't give Boyd the impression he was owed anything. In the end, the officer said, 'Don't hang about.'

'Anyone hurt?' Boyd said.

The officer shook his head. 'We're told someone warned them. We're checking CCTV from the high street.'

Boyd swallowed his guilt and gave his best sympathetic smile. Leigh came through to the front seats. He couldn't see Lamb now, realised she must have been under their duvet. He'd have to drive slowly until they were clear.

'What's happened?' Leigh asked. 'I couldn't hear.'

'Serious incident,' the officer said, nodding. 'Fire.' She and Boyd shared a glance. He was still kneading his thighs.

The officer gave Boyd a last scowl. 'You two haven't got a little one in there, have you?'

Leigh shook her head theatrically.

Boyd told him it was a cat.

They kept to the back roads. Leigh kept Lamb in her lap, clearly hating Boyd for all of it, for making her complicit, almost as much as she might have hated the quiet. She didn't want to be alone with this, with him. Yet he knew she wouldn't have wanted to be alone on the site, either.

A few miles later, Boyd stopped the van beside a shallow river – he was desperate to wash his face. And it was a chance to clean Lamb as well.

'Just in case,' he offered.

'You gonna help me understand what's going on?' Leigh said.

Boyd nodded as if she'd asked a different question.

'It doesn't happen, this stuff,' she said. 'Whatever that was, back there. The gulls and the fire and whatever this is. With her. It doesn't.'

Boyd leaned over and tapped the side of Lamb's nose. She gurgled inanely. Straightening, though, he noticed the fuel gauge and swore. Leigh turned in surprise. 'Diesel,' he said. 'We'll have to fill up soon, or we'll never get clear.'

'Can't we nip back that way?' Leigh asked.

He shook his head. Cooed at Lamb and stroked her temple, where sweat was matting her fine hair.

'She's too hot,' he said. 'We'll have to sort the van later.'

Leigh didn't join them on the bank, and Lamb wouldn't put a toe in the water, squealing in anguish, then in anger. They drove on. Further away from Sile, and from Neighton Prangle, where the weather improved but the roads narrowed. Boyd kept scratching the van's sides on brambles. There was a brief exchange: Boyd tried to convince Leigh that even though the main roads were quicker, they'd be under drone watch, and ditto for the motorway camera network. Going the slow way, they could be assured that nobody would find Lamb, or him, the missing occupant of a burned-out house the authorities were likely now searching. So, they'd drive east, between the fields, which they did, until they stopped again to rest beside dense woodland, where Leigh plucked half-rotting apples and chanterelle mushrooms from the leaf litter, and Boyd took stock. He'd not planned at all. There was hardly any baby formula left, and more terminal was their lack of cash. They'd have to sort that, and soon.

When Boyd went to pee in the woods, he watched the van from afar. The girl had propped herself by the side door, avoiding Leigh, who was hovering close enough to catch her in case she fell.

'What pact have you two signed this time?' Leigh shouted over.

'No pacts,' he said, coming back.

From her perch, Lamb smiled at him. She huffed and rattled when she was contented, like an old man clearing his throat. It must have seemed to Leigh like facetiousness, though, because her patience was waning.

'Are you gonna tell me properly, then, or what?' she said. 'What we're doing out here? Why you want to go to Peterborough?'

Boyd frowned.

'You don't think I deserve to know? Is that it? I didn't even leave a note for Gaff. I don't know what he's going to think – God knows what he'll do. I don't think you realise what you've done, come to that.'

Boyd reached out to stroke Lamb's cheek, an act of evasion, or self-distraction. 'I'm sorry,' he said.

'Course,' Leigh said. 'You always are.'

They went a fair way despite the van's slow going. Close to dusk, the fuel light came on, which restarted the conversation about filling up. They pulled up in the shade of young horse chestnut trees, which stood on one side of a steep valley. The van idled roughly when it was standing, and Boyd wondered if he could've done more to prepare. He hadn't checked coolant or oil or tyre pressures, and they only had Gaff's word that it had passed its MOT. Leigh was napping in the passenger seat, coughing gently. He opened her window a crack, rousing her.

'The sun cream isn't working,' he told her.

'Huh?'

'Lamb. I think we've got to keep her out of the light, out of the sun. It's making her grow faster.'

Leigh frowned. She was desperate, he saw. To unlock him. To reassert herself.

Boyd realised he had to give her something.

He said, 'I had to stop her spreading.'

'Lamb?'

He nodded. 'And Mum. The house.'

Leigh swallowed audibly. 'So you set a fire?'

Boyd nodded, then hesitated. 'I told you I'd forgotten something, at the house. There were things Mum had left me.'

'And?'

'She'd definitely gone,' he said. He couldn't begin to describe the house. 'She's with Nan, I hope. I… that's where I want us to go. But Peterborough – that's why I was asking you, in the static. I know you deserve to know, but I don't get why myself, not fully, not yet. It's a question in me, nagging. I feel as though I remember things that I shouldn't be able to remember. And Mum left an address, and I thought, let's do it. We can see. And you'll be safer, away from Gaff. Away from the stuff he does.'

'Stop there,' Leigh said.

But Boyd wasn't done. 'I knew if I told you this at the site,' he continued, shaking his head, 'you wouldn't come. And I didn't want… we can't—'

Leigh roared, somewhere between incredulous laughter and pain. 'We! Who's fucking *we*? This is all about *you*!'

Boyd looked down. 'I need to finish what she started,' he said. 'Here.' He went into his pockets and passed her the photo of his mother.

Leigh held it a while.

'She's lovely,' she said, a little calmer. 'But you can't – you can't just decide for me.'

'I know,' he said. 'I know.'

Leigh nodded, then nodded again. It was how she took measurements. It was how she evaluated things.

'It's getting late,' she said, nodding into the darkness of the valley. 'Let's get some rest. This feels like a decent spot. You could try and wedge us further into the trees.'

Boyd smiled gratefully. 'I'll go for fuel first thing.'

'With what cash?' Leigh said.

He didn't answer.

'You little twat,' she said. 'I've literally just explained this. *Tell me* stuff. And don't dare say you're sorry again. You're not.'

'Okay,' he said. And he could see Lamb, clinging to Leigh's front, was suppressing a smile.

Too wired for sleep, Boyd was restless through the night. He felt shame for wrenching Leigh away from the site, for not telling her enough, and annoyance that he had an address and no way of knowing what was actually there – not yet. He also wished they'd travelled further – they'd only managed eighty miles, going by the fuel gauge, and it didn't feel enough.

Towards dawn, he noticed Leigh carefully reaching out for his jacket, his bag. He wasn't bothered, and let her: the bag was only full of nappies and wipes, used sachets of sun cream, empty bottles of pre-mixed baby formula, while his jacket only contained the photo of Maureen. The photo of Dougie and him was in his jeans, which he was wearing, and his mother's penny was still down his sock. He wondered if Leigh was searching almost unconsciously, desperate for clearer answers, or making her own plans. Either way, he understood.

When he was sure she'd returned to sleep, he checked Lamb's backside under the blankets. She was dry. Maybe this was what it felt like to drink too much, to start an affair, to turn your rage inwards? To deceive yourself, as Dougie and Maureen each had? He'd let Leigh down, and didn't know how to come back from that. He wondered what else would surface, and how else she might act out.

Sleep, though. He closed his eyes and thought of moss, emerald-green and impossibly soft. It didn't work.

The morning brought inverted cloud. The bulk of it was suspended in the valley, a heavy phantom of the water that had once carved the landscape, and the rising sun bleached in over the top. Leigh ushered Boyd outside, leaving Lamb asleep. The strength of the light surprised him.

'I love how small it makes you feel,' Leigh said, without sarcasm. She tipped her face back, basking. It wasn't forgiveness for last night, nor for anything else – merely a few moments to be, to pretend. To be as they'd been, briefly, before Lamb arrived.

They sat with their backs against the van and fried up Leigh's chanterelles in a dry pan. The sky glowed red and orange. Their feet were wet, their fingers cold, and neither of them remotely cared. Soon the inversion had dispersed, revealing the valley's far side in soft pinkish light, a stepped bluff. A gaggle of bewildered-looking sheep stood in the crags. 'Idiots,' Leigh said, picking soil from her next mouthful. When they were done, she pushed herself to her feet. 'I'm glad we did this,' she told Boyd. 'Because today you're gonna know what my temper really goes like.'

Her red line was clear: she'd absorbed Boyd's crisis without being permissive, but she wasn't going to indulge it any longer.

'I'm going for diesel,' he said.

*

He was back for ten. Leigh's eyes were red. Lamb was settled on her front, frog-legged and dozing, a good clump of Leigh's hair bunched in one fist. Leigh asked where he'd got to, concentrating on picking grime from Lamb's skin. He swivelled to show her the jerry can of diesel strapped to his back. He was all too present, aware of the state of himself. There was drying blood in his hairline, from a gash above his forehead.

'Had to go a fair way,' he said. Which was honest, at least.

Lamb stirred and scrabbled at Leigh's top as if she were about to be dropped. Leigh, looking at him now, gasped. 'What have you done to yourself?' With her other hand, she swept the van keys from the floor beside her and put them down her top.

'Okay,' Boyd said. He went to the fuel inlet, opened it, poured in the diesel. Then he came back and asked if she'd let him hold Lamb.

'Absolutely not,' Leigh said firmly. 'No.'

Boyd shook his head.

'What the fuck, Boyd? You're *bleeding*.'

He loaded the jerry can. 'Can't hang around,' he said. 'There were cameras all over the forecourt.'

Because it hurt him to remember. Because he was trying to pack it down so tightly that his stomach hurt. Because an unseeable thread still drew him on.

'What have you *done*?' she asked again.

'It's not all mine,' he said, meaning the blood. He got into the driver's seat, wound down his window, and asked Leigh for the key back. 'I don't want to talk about it,' he added.

She threw the key at him. 'Did you nick it? Did you rob that fuel?'

He didn't answer.

'Boyd? Are you seriously doing this?'

'I didn't nick it,' he said, and turned the key in the ignition.

About ten miles up the road, Lamb squealed until they were both paying attention. She was staring at Boyd again.

'Mum,' Lamb said, perfectly.

Then silence.

'Stop the van,' Leigh said. 'Stop it here!'

Boyd did as he was told. He turned off the engine, could smell the brakes.

Leigh climbed out, stood in the middle of the road, and screamed.

Then it was shaded council parking beside a reservoir with a cobbled bank. There was a broken tent behind the wall, so Boyd untangled the poles and tried to make an awning for the side of the van, like the one Leigh used to have on the kennel. 'I did pay attention,' he told her, as she set up her stove and kettle. 'Last night. I did listen, about not telling you stuff. And I get it.'

Lamb, meanwhile, was practising her own words. 'Mum!' she kept saying, unbidden. 'Where!' and 'Me!' She was away with herself, deep in some child-only dream space, and didn't care for their concern, nor their interest. She moved freely, with growing competence, in and around the van. Her growth *was* accelerating. She was noticeably bigger and broader. And as he watched her, Boyd felt more and more like his own mother – withdrawing, protecting himself from what was happening, while powerless to stop it.

And Leigh kept saying, 'I told you! I told you it wasn't normal.' As if noticing was enough, could ever be a balm.

Boyd said, 'And you still think we should take her to hospital?'

Leigh nodded tentatively. She obviously felt Lamb deserved someone better qualified to look after her. As they should've done to start with. 'But you keep testing me,' she added, spitting it. 'You think, ah well, Lamb's fine. We're all fine. When none of this is. Nothing about this is fine.'

He sat there. Leigh came forward and traced his forehead, the bruise. She turned his hand over, touched around his swollen knuckle. Her fingers were warm.

'You're a mess,' she said. 'A shiny mess.'

'I was by the pumps,' Boyd explained. 'I'd put a tenner in the jerry can. It was only a small place, a family place. The guy – he must've thought I was going to rob him.'

'And were you?'

'No, or not him at least. I'd already lifted fifty quid from Gaff's static,' he admitted, tapping his pocket. 'But the guy got pushy. I don't – I can't really remember. I think he shoved me, and I fell over.' He flexed his bad hand. 'He got me up and came right into my face.' Which was all true, and had made him think of the boy with the hammer in their kitchen in Sile, and his smallness, and his wanting to prove something to the world. 'So I headbutted him,' Boyd said. 'I don't know where it came from. It wasn't even me. I butted him hard and dropped the money by his feet and... and I ran.'

He stopped there. Was Leigh trying not to laugh?

'Serious?' she said. 'You did that and paid him anyway?'

Lamb turned to her as though Leigh had insulted him. Boyd didn't answer.

Still, Leigh pressed him. 'And here I thought you were a prime bullshitter.'

Boyd sniffed and stepped down from the van. His heart was blaring in his chest. He half slipped, half scrambled down the side of the reservoir and knelt by the side. He put his face, then his head, in the icy water. The cold knocked the wind from him. His dried blood, damp again, ran pink through his fingers. He wished his memories could go with it.

'I was right all along,' she called down to him. 'I don't know you at all.'

That evening she made a kind of broth with young nettles picked not far from the van. It was thin, too thin, but they both finished it. Boyd said nothing, trying not to make anything worse. Come Lamb's bedtime, Leigh lay with her and sang in hushed tones no less beautiful for their gaspiness. Lamb fell asleep, and Leigh came back outside.

'What was it?' Boyd asked.

'What?'

'The song you were singing.'

'Some old song. Mam loved nineties stuff. I don't have any decent fairy tales to hand.'

'Sing louder, next time,' he said.

The following morning, there were dozens of dead trout bobbing at the reservoir's edge.

Rootless, lost, they talked about following signs. Detouring to the Lakes, maybe – into open space, into nothingness, sticking to country roads for as long as they could. They were back to being kind to each other, or at least pretending to be; mutual denial in place of safety, or resignation. Boyd, for his part, was trying to behave more like the boy Leigh had first met, when she'd first invited him to work with her, which in turn had helped a softness to return to her face. There was a time before Lamb, and Boyd being evasive, and all this. Leigh wasn't happy – not under her mask – but it didn't matter. Better this way than open hostility.

'We're better off,' Boyd said without thinking, with the

faint awareness, even as he opened his mouth, that he was lying. It was in the rot setting in behind his ribs, and the van turning mouldy around them. It was Boyd who'd brought this to her, and it was in Leigh's occasional coughing fits.

Lamb chirped at a fly bumbling around the cabin. Leigh said, 'Shall I tell you a story, little one?'

Lamb didn't move, or register Leigh's voice. When the fly had gone, she went back to staring.

'Do you not think she stinks?' Leigh said.

Boyd shook his head.

'Like vinegar?'

'I don't—'

'And you know I found her with my journal, before? She was turning the pages too quickly to be reading it, but if you told me she'd understood it all, I'd believe you. I asked if she was all right. Sat here, asking a fucking baby, like we could ever be on a level. And do you know what she did? She said, "No."'

'Leigh, I'm not—'

'Lamb killed those gulls, didn't she?' Leigh said. 'On the site. And all those fish at the reservoir last night. And you know what? I thought I was dealing with it. But when I see you and her so tight with each other, it's an insult. I keep forgiving her. I keep forgiving you. But it takes the piss that she only wants you, when I'm here, and I'm trying too.'

'It's not that,' he said.

Leigh rolled her eyes.

'It's either Lamb or it's me,' he said. 'We're killing things, yes. It's not my mum.'

'And where does it end?'

He couldn't say what he really thought. He was thinking of Dougie and he was thinking of Maureen. Their house in Watford and their house in Sile. Damp, and mould, and heat. Red, on her column. The men in the house. Leigh coughing into her hands—

'*Vague*,' she said. 'Next thing you'll be apologising again.'

'I'm trying not to.'

'Don't you think she looks like you, anyway? Lamb?'

Leigh turned the girl in her lap. Boyd shook his head.

'You're so far away, aren't you? Sometimes I think you don't even know what you need. I see you, remember – it's like I know when you're about to shut it all off.'

'We need you,' he said. 'Lamb does. You can't—'

'Well, I can't live like I lived with my dad. Or like I lived with Gaff.'

Boyd stopped the van where they were.

Leigh smirked. She was resolute. The gap was now uncrossable.

'I can't stand half-reasons, Boyd. I can't stand it. Mam, see – she never even told me she was having tests. It was in the background, a hum, a *mood*. An aura, or whatever – and I don't believe in any of that shit. I knew Mam was sick, and she still wouldn't tell me. Her little girl. And Dad, with his debt, and the way he ran himself into trouble – all the same. He didn't tell Mam, not till it was too late. And now this. You. And her. With all your secrets.'

'We don't have secrets—'

Leigh shushed him, grinning. 'I've already made up my mind. We'll be driving, like this, and we'll stop. There'll be a few people close by. I'll smile at you, and it won't mean much in the moment, and I'll walk towards someone else, so fast you don't even have time to panic. If I'm lucky, you'll take the hint. You'll see them worry, but me – my face will be blank. I'll tell them it's all fine, I'm fine, my girl's with her dad, she didn't want to come with me. And that's okay.'

'Leigh—'

'Can it, will you? Keep driving.'

'But Leigh.'

'Shut up!'

They set off. The silence lengthened. Leigh waved her journal at him. 'You remember, don't you, how I told you I'd never remember stuff if I didn't write it all down?'

Boyd nodded.

'Cool, well. Now I want to forget.'

And Leigh threw her journal out of the window.

RUPTURE

Leigh fled Boyd and Lamb in another bleak layby – this one in view of a ply-clad shipping container selling hot chai and sweet buns. The ruse was simple enough: Leigh needed to pee, so Boyd pulled over and left the van idling, too preoccupied to worry, to heed Leigh's warning. Lamb was sleeping across the bench seat with her head at his hip, one hand gripping the turned-out label of his T-shirt for comfort. Opposite the van, a family of four were picnicking around a people carrier, two immaculate children perched on the boot sill eating sandwiches, parents idly browsing phones, occasionally adjusting their alpine-fit jackets. They hadn't noticed the white van squeak to a stop, much less spotted the rag-tag bunch inside.

Leigh, having stretched, tapped on the window and told Boyd to keep the engine running. He nodded blearily. They'd been driving for hours, and her eyes were small and red, and so were his. She tapped the window again and mouthed something he couldn't make out; she shook her head and smiled mock-despairingly, before she moved off towards the portable toilet. Boyd was still trying to decode her smile when she tucked her chin and veered away from the toilet towards the family. 'No!' Lamb said, lurching awake and jumping up to the dashboard – the speed of which instantly sharpened the atmosphere. Leigh appeared to notice, and flinch. As she turned, it was all written in her expression, the set of her jaw. Boyd gripped the wheel, cleaving to some slim hope he was wrong, that despite their discord, she'd stick with them. A sick lurch as it all turned over. Leigh was unsticking herself, making good. Her final glance towards the van – defiant, sad, with chai steam billowing around her – was her admission. And she was intentional about it: she took great care to only look at Boyd, not Lamb.

'Don't,' Boyd whispered.

The father glanced up as Leigh approached. He was the earnest sort – Boyd could tell from there. Who was this? Was she going to rob us? A beggar to deal with? But the mother, she'd already read the subtext. She swept in and took Leigh's arm and guided her to the side door of their people carrier, where Leigh sat on the kickstep. Boyd moved to get out, but Lamb put a hand on his arm to stay him, a gesture so mature it left him reeling. Then Leigh had one of the kids' blankets around her shoulders, and was staring into the verge beside the kiosk. For a moment, Boyd saw himself arriving at the landfill site that first time. They were each other's inverse.

Lamb squeezed Boyd's hand. What was he meant to do? Something more, definitely. Lamb, though, had other ideas. She began slapping the seat. 'Don't!' Boyd screamed to Leigh, more urgent. The father, still confused by the scene playing out between his wife and the young woman, heard Boyd this time, turned to squint through the van windscreen. 'Don't,' Boyd said, quieter, touching the bruise on his forehead. The father started towards the van. Boyd met his stare and said, 'What are you doing?' but knew he didn't have another confrontation in him, not like the one at the garage.

The father kept coming, surer with every step that he was only dealing with a youngster. Boyd hesitated, let it go on for as long as he could, then acted. He pulled Lamb down into the seat and slotted the van into gear. A final hesitation as he willed Leigh to go back on herself, return to them. The father raised a hand. Boyd nudged the accelerator. 'Wait!' the father shouted, his intonation making it more of a question. Boyd released the handbrake. The van leapt towards the people carrier. The father swore and dived clear. The children both dropped their sandwiches. The mother covered her mouth. And Leigh stayed perfectly still. Boyd hauled on the wheel to correct himself; the van swerved the family but struck the dividing kerb and drifted into the road with a slew of dust and gravel. A third car peeled around the outside of them, horn blaring.

The white van's cabin stank of burning clutch – Boyd couldn't manage the pedals properly. In a panic, he put it back into first gear instead of third, and the van sheared hard, seemed to slam into itself. They had two wheels off the road, bearing hard left. A low branch struck the van on the passenger side and sent a crack across the windscreen. Unbelted, Boyd glanced his nose on the steering wheel, a blinding pain. Lamb rolled off the bench seat into the footwell, then came back into view. She was beaming at him, gums bloodied. Cracks spider-webbed through the glass. He threw a hand down to Lamb and hoisted her back up to the seat. From behind came the shouts of the parents, who'd gathered themselves to give chase, bolder now the immediate danger had passed. Further back, like a statue, stood Leigh. Boyd found second, third, fourth. Leigh and the family shrank in the mirror. They were still there through the first corner, gone by the second. It was the end of it, the end of them, a cold grief. He squeezed the wheel and took the next right, eyes streaming. A tight farm track towards rows of maize. The track curved round, went long. All he wanted was a place wide enough to stop.

'Shit,' he said, realising the van had drawn up a large cloud of dust. 'Shit,' he said, checking behind. But he had to stop. He'd be sick, or they'd crash again, if he didn't. Lamb stared at him. Her tooth had punctured her bottom lip. A vehicle hurtled past on the road – the family's people carrier, he thought – and was gone.

'Five minutes,' he told Lamb. To make sure the family didn't double back. To make sure there were no sirens. To try and rid himself of Leigh's shaming glare. The idea of her approaching people she didn't know, and it still being a better option than this.

Eyes forward, and clear: it was all on Boyd, now. He opened his door and gulped fresh air. A rain front was rolling in over distant hills. Sunlight broke through the drapery in wide panels, casting the hills with watery gold. He was tired and shaking. Lamb sat there, waiting. 'Not now,' he said, irritated by her attentiveness. They'd have to take their chances while he managed himself. While he let this pass. He couldn't face driving another metre; Lamb was momentarily irrelevant. She wasn't fussed, of course. She nursed her bleeding lip, ambivalent. When his breathing steadied, and his nose stopped throbbing, he turned the van towards the maize and moved forward until a good volume of stalks sprang up behind the van. It would have to do.

Lamb, pulling a face almost like concern, shuffled across the bench and drew into his arm. He put his hand on her back. Against the cold, against the world, he clung to the possibility of being the only person who could comfort her, the only person she trusted. She found his T-shirt label again, exhaled, and settled, eyes on the sky. He stroked her cheek, pushed back against the headrest, and closed his eyes. It wasn't enough. It was better, though, that he wasn't alone. Instead of joining Lamb in sleep, Boyd mourned.

*

Boyd accepted, of course, that his own behaviour had created the rift between Leigh and himself. Were he older, less naïve, he might have recognised how things mirrored the way he and Maureen had drifted in their final months together at home. It was as if he'd learned from that fragile intimacy, the way it had broken down, and couldn't help but play it out again.

Inevitably, though, the rupture had started with Lamb, and the way Leigh had cared for her despite the pain of doing so. He couldn't be angry about Leigh's assessment of him, hurtful as it felt. Strip away her aloofness, her posturing – which in some ways his behaviour actually had – and you were left with a sensitive, incisive woman. Remove all certainty – put her beyond the comfort of familiarity – and you found the little girl she'd masked. Before she'd given in, given up, she'd been losing herself – she'd even said so. There was no malice in any of it – she'd felt isolated and excluded; she'd lost control; she'd been alienated by Boyd's unique bond with Lamb. But it was a bond that, despite his care for Leigh, he couldn't loosen. If there was any comfort to be taken from the situation, it was that Leigh couldn't have resented him – not really. It was hard to believe she was never genuine, never generous, despite her initial deception – the fact she'd identified him as vulnerable, to some extent, taken advantage. Likewise, it was hard to believe she'd made her decision easily.

The two of them were similar, no question. They'd both been lost and found. Between Leigh's father and Boyd's mother, they'd had more in common than she'd have liked to admit. What's more, accusing her of deception would have made Boyd a hypocrite. He'd arrived on the landfill site, gathered hell around her, and ultimately broken her down. Everybody, he considered, has a limit.

*

LAMB

In the van, in the field of maize, Lamb stirred. She was calmer with Leigh gone. Her eyes flickered briefly, then settled on Boyd. She smiled benignly and stood up on the bench seat, head steady. Boyd watched her. She was a marvel. Maybe the crawling had all been a feint; maybe there was even more to it. Alone with her, Boyd made himself accountable. It wasn't parenthood, no, but he was in charge now; and in his clarity, he wanted to be everything to Lamb that his mother wasn't to him, not after Dougie. So, there was terror and there was incompetence. But there was also determination. Lamb deserved to feel safe. He was a stray and she was a stray, and that united them.

'That's new,' he said, meaning the way she was standing. He stiffened in his seat, as if to express solidarity. Her ankles were showing; she'd grown again.

'Mum?' she said.

'I don't think so,' Boyd said.

Lamb leaned over and poked Boyd in the chest. Her hands were clumsy, the movement stilted, but there was a purpose in it – he just didn't understand it. He put his head back. Sleep would come easily, and it was tempting. Lamb came across the bench seat and squashed herself into his flank. She smelled familiar – the smell of the cupboards in their Watford house. He hugged her and remembered his father doing nothing extraordinary, overalls peeled mostly off, a dirty white T-shirt stretched across his chest, stealing a bowl of Boyd's cereal for his supper, eating it dry. On such a quiet night, Boyd would have read while his father watched sports on catch-up, chewing as obnoxiously as possible.

Lamb put a hand over his heart. Boyd closed his eyes, let himself go.

*

He came to hours later, refreshed yet annoyed with himself. Lamb was propped against the passenger door, feet extended across the bench. The sun was going down, and the fluffy tips of the maize surrounding the van glowed orange. The effect stretched out over the field, leaving nothing in focus. It was like a fluid, a burning lake. Lamb chuckled softly. Boyd was both relieved she was awake and disturbed by the possibility she'd been sitting like this the whole time. 'Did you sleep again?' he asked her, rubbing sleep from his eyes. She smiled unsurely, which he took as a no.

He climbed into the rear of the van to pee in a bottle. Coming back through to the cabin, he noticed that a stalk of maize had collapsed over the bonnet and entered the cabin through the cracked windscreen, its head flat on the dashboard. It seemed illusory until he prodded it. 'How's that happened?' he said. Lamb didn't reply. He lifted the head and found the underside blackened and swollen, the leaves curled back. Shiny the way a banana goes on the turn. He touched the dash – sticky – and quickly wiped his hands on his thighs, down the seat fabric. A whine started in his ears. He opened his door. 'Don't touch that,' he told Lamb.

It was the same story all around the van. They were parked in a circle of rotting crops, the infection a metre deep in every direction. His head throbbed. He came back to the open driver's door, where Lamb could see him. He stared at her. He couldn't deny her any longer.

This time Lamb gave what might have been a shrug. Boyd was frightened of her, but recommitted himself to protecting her. It was a powerful decision, less thought through than deeply felt. He wanted to cry, but the release wouldn't come. All of that was pointless, anyway. He'd have to do enough, be enough.

He forgave her.

'We've got to get somewhere, haven't we?' he said. 'This place Mum told me about.'

Lamb nodded, unequivocal. Eyes level. Then, as if to really prove herself, she said, 'We do.'

They drove on. There was no end to the narrow roads, nor the fields beside them. In the absence of directions, he put faith in features: a mothballed wind farm whose turbines stood rotting, towers and blades bronzed in the light, the last of the sun split into red points on every nacelle; a reservoir with an enormous solar farm floating on its waters, panels shimmering like oil; woods and marshland stalked by stooped hikers; broken-up fracking gear; cold steel and rotting canvas behind barbed-wire fences.

Come dark proper, they stopped on the shale shore of a lake, where Boyd squatted to shit by a birch tree studded with plates of pale fungus. From nowhere came the rushing sound of a train – louder and louder – and *high*. Suddenly the sharp silhouette of a fighter jet passed no more than fifty feet above his head, flashing over the lake and out of the valley. He watched it go, mesmerised, then climbed back into the van. It had reminded him of his father – Dougie watching recoloured footage of World War Two in their Watford lounge, eyes wide in fascination. It was as if, facing an uncertain future, Boyd was seeking new ways back to the past, and making new connections. Like footage of a bombing run over occupied France. Like a mountain of smoke over Sile, from their house, which he'd burned down.

These were new old memories, was the point. These were things he'd never remembered – or thought to remember – before.

He found Lamb cowering in the footwell.

'Oh,' he said, surprised. 'Here, it's fine. Was it the plane? It was just practising.' And maybe the girl understood, but she didn't budge, and her vulnerability made his stomach hurt.

'Okay,' he said, 'let me… it's fine. It's fine. They're noisy, aren't they?' He leaned over and took her hand, which gave him a static shock; he jumped and immediately wondered if she'd done it on purpose. Then a bolder idea, a persuasion, that Lamb had somehow shared his response to the plane; that the two of them were linked in a way that ran deeper than language, than carer and charge; that she'd somehow *seen* Dougie's wide eyes through his own…

Particles in chaos, briefly aligned.

Lamb only smiled when he was safely back inside and belted in.

'We're never going back there,' he told her, tapping his chest. 'I promise.'

It was as true as it was necessary, not that he knew how to get to where they were going. Without Leigh he'd have to do it all himself, and his options were dwindling. Given what had happened at the garage, it wasn't a good idea to enter a city. They'd be better off in deep country, where nothing really changed, or where people resisted change, and where facial recognition systems wouldn't pry so keenly.

'Not that I know how to get where we're going,' he admitted.

'Mum?' Lamb said, speculatively.

'What about her?'

'Mum.'

He shook his head. 'Can you say anything else?'

'Nan?'

Boyd scoffed, then laughed at himself, at the absurdity of it. Lamb was plainly more aware than he was willing to accept.

'I want to get to Nan's,' he said. 'But I don't remember how that goes, either.'

Lamb pointed back at herself. That now familiar fluidity to the gesture. Coyly, she climbed back onto the bench and drew herself into him again. Then she pointed up and down, and emphasised the down.

'Down?' Boyd said.

Lamb shook her head, annoyed. She pointed up, then right, then left, then up. Then down again. Slow, measured.

'*South?*'

At which point Lamb lit up.

Boyd rubbed his jaw. How? How was it possible?

'I think so,' he said. 'She would've been south-west of us in Neighton. But we have to find this other place, first.'

Bright House 3, Peterborough.

Lamb nodded, as if she already knew.

On through the night. Lamb knelt on the passenger seat, possibly to avoid sleeping, with both hands on the dash and chin raised, as if she were a gun-dog sniffing for a query. Boyd, hollow with hunger and weariness, was developing a habit of checking for blue lights in his mirrors and couldn't reason her into wearing her seat belt. At junctions, Lamb pointed at the reflective signs, sometimes angrily. Later he began to follow her vague directions, in part because there didn't seem an alternative, but mostly because he didn't care how long it would take. Travel in one direction for long enough, and the signs would eventually show for Peterborough. As long as there was fuel in the tank. As long as they were even in the right part of the country...

Darkness, the concentration required, brought demotivation. He was getting lost in his own head, and for long stretches Leigh's departure preoccupied him, a brick in his guts. He hoped she was at least satisfied with her decision. He replayed their recent conversations, to try and re-sensitise himself to her experience. He wondered if he deserved punishment. If everyone close to him had so far rejected him, was it not for good reason? It wasn't much of leap back to the redundancy notice he'd brought in for his father. Or his mother's insistence that Boyd had distorted their marriage for the worse. Mainly, though, he missed Leigh's smell, her semi-reluctant companionship, and being calmed by the faint sounds she made as she slept. Even her affectionate insults.

He was also missing road signs, now. Alarmed, he became convinced they were circling the same five or six lanes. Headlights running into ditches, left turn after left turn. Sweaty hands and cold neck. The challenge of night driving, which was both boring and difficult. The fear of meeting an oncoming vehicle down a lane no wider than the van. Even the van was flagging – the old rig was losing power through inclines, juddering under braking. He entered a mode where scarce light and engine drone proved hypnotic, lulled him back towards sleep. The night air, whistling through the cracks in the windscreen, made him shiver.

It was hard to say how long they'd been going, as the clock (and all the other instruments) were no longer working. The diesel would be running down again. The fields opened out, uniform terrain. He wished for hills, mountains, interesting landscape. More features they could navigate by. When it started to rain, Lamb began to cry. Boyd saw she was losing her way, too. He reached for her hand and tried to imagine a future beyond all this. Reading. Exploring. Images from childhood stories, misty mornings or nights under moonlight, or blankets around a fire he'd built for them to toast marshmallows. *What would Leigh do?* Lamb whimpered until he pulled up on rough ground under a large hawthorn. They sat there with the engine running, headlamps illuminating a squall of rain so dense that Boyd could actually see the air currents, the wind shifting.

'Another quick nap,' he said. Because if all else had failed, that was what Leigh would do.

Lamb turned to him, face rumpled. 'Leigh?' Saying it

looked painful; her mouth wouldn't shape it properly, and her tongue was swollen.

Boyd swallowed. His eyes stung. 'She isn't here,' he told her. 'You know that.'

Lamb shook her head in frustration. 'Lor-*ry*,' she said.

'Sorry?'

'*Lor*-ry. *Doug*-ie!'

Boyd's skin prickled. '*What?*'

Lamb tilted her face. Drool shone on her chin. She was exerting herself.

'Are you talking about my dad?'

Lamb pointed through the windscreen at nothing in particular.

'You've got to pack it in,' he said, angrier than he thought he was.

Chided, Lamb pushed out her bottom lip.

'No, no,' he said. He was getting this all wrong. Lamb sat there expectantly, then crossed her arms.

Boyd undid his seat belt and lifted her into the back of the van. There he changed her nappy, which was full and smelled like paint. Lamb didn't resist. She was content. He tried to make her a nest, using all the throws, fleeces and soft clothes he could gather. All the while he hummed her a tune, as Leigh would have, except it wasn't a lullaby nor an old song but a melody from an eight-bit computer game he used to play when he was away with his parents in their caravan. It'd been the only thing to come to mind.

Lamb's eyes widened. Did she recognise the tune? Did it stir something in her?

He shushed her, and stroked her face, and she almost instantly fell asleep. He pushed the sweaty hair away from her forehead, and listened to her deepened breathing. He could learn her breath, the way he'd learned Leigh's. Her skin was luminous. She didn't even look real.

He hopped back into the driving seat. He turned off the engine, popped on the cabin light, and tapped at the instruments, hoping they'd start to work again. The bulb's harsh blue light was especially crude. It was then he noticed that the bench seat, especially where Lamb had been sitting, was heavily stained. He touched the covering, and the material sank down. When he rubbed at it, sticky threads rolled up on his fingertips. He smelled them. Cucumber. The fabric wasn't stained – it was burnt. Something primal made him glance in the mirror, and he startled. Lamb was standing at his shoulder.

'Leigh!' she said, tugging Boyd's sleeve towards her nest in the back.

'Can't you stop this happening?' he asked, meaning the chair, meaning the process.

She grabbed his nose.

'Lamb? Can you make it stop?'

The girl chuckled. Boyd stared ahead. The rain had eased to a fine white spray, and the glass was misting with their breath. It was too dark to see the hawthorn's colours, but he saw they couldn't stay here now; they'd already parked for long enough. Soon its leaves would brown, then detach. Its thorns would wilt and moulder. Its trunk would shed its fungi, parasites, bark. Sap would run to brown, slow to toffee, harden to onyx. Slow death would descend into the soil network, into the water table, and whisper out through the woodland.

'Not now,' he told her, and restarted the engine. They wouldn't stop like this again. They couldn't. Now he'd accepted what Lamb's presence was doing, he had an obligation.

Lamb gave Boyd a satisfied look. What did it mean, that a child could patronise him? She stepped back onto the bench and started pointing, Leigh's fleece thrown around her shoulders. He pulled away, following her new instructions.

LAMB

When he opened the window, the last of the rain felt like
needles in his face.

BRIGHT HOUSE

Boyd saw the sign for Peterborough before Lamb did, though by then it was obvious she'd been expecting it. It was almost light out, a drier morning, and even on the busier roads there wasn't much in the way of traffic. A headache split Boyd's face dead centre. Everything was washed out, a muted blue.

'How?' he asked her.

'Yes,' Lamb said.

There'd been nothing aimless about it. Lamb had been directing him the whole time – a realisation that filled him with both wonder and terror. And what was he meant to do with it? Challenging her – *it* – would only give the madness, the deep weirdness of their bubble, more power. Yet Lamb clearly sensed his intrigue. She clutched the dash plastic – it was beginning to deform – and left a set of wet prints there, as if she herself was thrilled and guilty and drunk on what she'd done. They approached the city in apprehensive silence. He eyed her warily; there'd been a single hour during the night when Lamb had finally fallen asleep where she sat. In her dreams she'd murmured softly, hands palm up, as though divining their route. Only when Boyd coughed had she snapped awake, bolt upright, and pointed tersely in such a way as to suggest she felt embarrassed, caught out.

Boyd almost asked how Lamb was feeling, then. She looked intent and dangerous, and he smiled nervously. Her breath smelled loamy, and her skin was mottling.

'What's up?' he said.

With her pudgy fingers, Lamb opened the glovebox and swept out the photograph of Dougie and Boyd sitting in the lorry cab. She'd taken it from his pocket; he didn't know when. She turned the written side towards him. *Bright House 3, Peterborough.* Maureen's stilted handwriting. She tapped the picture, right where Maureen's penny had been taped.

'Home,' Lamb said, surer of her mouth, her voice. As if the photograph was all – or even exactly – the map they'd needed.

As he fixated on a cathedral in the distance, Boyd wondered if he too might have intuited some of the way here. The thought was triggered by a bank of firs crowding a junction. They appeared taller, fuller, more vibrant to him than they once had – except he was sure he'd never seen them before. As he waited on a red light, he found himself trying to reconcile this sureness with a faint memory – more slippery, even, than the stranger's face you recognise but can't place – of passing through.

It was as if he'd found inside himself a fragment of someone else's past. Or as if another person's memory, garbled by time, or maybe the transfer itself, had been injected into his mind. By holding such thoughts at a distance, consciously making them subconscious by continuing to look around – the road markings, the ad hoardings – it was obvious to him that there was far more to them. In full glare, however, the links degraded into mist. Was that a shopping centre he'd seen further along? A run of old office blocks? The problem was consistency. As soon as he connected one road to the next, the vision fell apart. Trying to see his way caused a more primal response, and not quite pain, more a frustrating reset, itchy and maddening. And all of it like déjà vu, with no means to anchor or reassure himself. Look too hard, and he failed. The construction seized up and collapsed. Another new, old memory. And his *knowing*...

Commuters behind the van sounded their horns at Boyd's hesitation on the green light. He came back to the road, and to a sorrow at the loss of something vital. His mother's voice came to him; he fished the picture of her from his pocket and propped it on the speedometer. He looked across at Lamb and allowed himself to let go. She furrowed her brow in concern, an empathy he was sure no other child on Earth could communicate, and began to hum the video game melody he'd used as a lullaby the evening before.

Boyd shook his head at her. He was learning what it all meant, to care for another person in the right way. That fear and self-doubt, and being complicated, were each part of the method. Whatever this was – whatever Lamb was doing – he had to trust in it. And with this, he accepted his own vulnerability in their relationship. He needed to believe her. He needed faith. Because if his own mind had been unlocked briefly to the truth of another life, a portal, or even some underlying structure to the world, then it was shut again now.

He was left with a final, deep impression, lingering as the van accelerated, of ageing too quickly.

Lamb had Boyd turn in at the entrance of an out-of-town shopping centre, which came as a relief. He stopped the van in the middle of the car park and kept his seat belt on. The development stood almost exactly as it had in his mind's eye, yet in reality it was lifeless, its outlets closed and boarded, and bounded to one side by – as he'd foreseen – three grey-brick office blocks. All of them were signed COMMERCIAL SPACE TO LET, COMPETITIVE RATES; several of these boards hung sun-bleached or dangled precariously from strips of rotten timber. Only rushed graffiti and vandals' stones disturbed the blank uniformity of the buildings' windows. From this aspect – full cloud, fragile light – the offices were completely, almost deliberately, anonymous.

'This is the place,' he said to Lamb. Out of the van he wrapped the makeshift sling around his waist and pulled Lamb against his chest. She clung to him as he secured her, the side of her head tight against his collarbone. He kissed her on the crown in thanks.

Bright House One was the closest building to the car park. Its plaza was a series of ramps, neglected laurel hedges and polished concrete walkways, which ran in concentric circles around a dead fountain whose past reach was now described in lichen. Between the façade and the road was a screen of pitiful conifers, every tree slanted or fully stooped over in litter-strewn soil. The one remaining bench was broken.

Up at the main entrance – brown laminated glazing, a seized revolving door – somebody had been fly-postering with soft porn, and local kids had marked their tags and insults on every available space. There was a reception desk inside, but the security gates had collapsed and the floor tiles were carpeted with dust and animal droppings. The lights were off.

'No one home,' Boyd said. Lamb, one ear pressed against him, seemed unfazed. Or at least as if she was concentrating on something else. When Boyd touched her back and said, 'I'm a bit cold – aren't you?' she didn't so much as stir.

He went on. Bright House Two and Bright House Three stood either side of a bollarded walkway that curved away from Bright House One. The ground- and first-floor windows of each building were secured with metal sheet and heavy mesh; their height shaded the whole alley, and the temperature drop was noticeable. A toothy wind buffeted them as they walked. Lamb tried to burrow deeper into Boyd's chest for warmth. He wrapped her with both arms and adjusted the sling so it better covered her neck. She turned her face against him and whimpered.

Boyd, considering it all, was oddly sanguine, perhaps a touch removed from himself. If his awareness was expanding, then so too was his detachment. He kept one hand on the small of Lamb's back as his footsteps caught and reverberated between the buildings, crassly loud. Together, they cut a peculiar silhouette, ungainly against so many perfectly unnatural lines. When Boyd pictured people walking this passage to work each morning, he wondered how Leigh might respond if she were with them. In her discomfort, he decided, she'd over-compensate, walk cocksure, chest out, in loping strides. So that's what he did. Next, he tried a bright 'Hello!' which scattered a line of pigeons up on the gutters. The security cameras, movement sensors and benches were all spiked; with nowhere to go, the pigeons doubled back and resettled.

Guiltily, he thought of the gulls back at Gaff's site and wondered if Lamb would do for these birds too. There was nothing else at ground level except old wet paper, chewing-gum marks and rubbish blowing down the alley from the car park, which was collecting in drifts at the corners of stairways and empty planters.

It started to rain, then hailed. The metal cladding rang around them. Lamb tautened; Boyd did his best to cover her ears and neck and ran straight into a smoking shelter. 'It's fine,' he told her, nauseated by a sour, tarry smell. He noticed how tightly she'd closed her eyes and decided to keep going. There was a canopy spanning the entrances to Bright House Two and Three, so he broke for it. The shelter's rank scent followed him, grew more septic. In horror, to check, he sniffed Lamb. The smell was coming from her hair.

'You're okay,' he said, trying not to gag. 'You're okay.'

The revolving door to Bright House Three was boarded up and well secured, with no obvious keyholes or access controls, and no way to see the lobby beyond. He hadn't expected this, but it emphasised how his mother's note was only a name, a link to a place. In her mind, these offices might have still been open, teeming, far from shelled out. Which was when Boyd noticed that Lamb was gazing up into the canopy above the entrance, her face contorted. In one corner, a small gimbal-mounted camera – much smaller and more advanced than the boxy beige systems surrounding it – swivelled to gaze back.

Lamb twisted and arched her back, trying to escape the sling, then gave a strained howl of frustration. Boyd shushed her, bounced her, but there was a power to her body, a strength he didn't know how to handle. Despite his father's jacket, they were both soaked through. The septic smell was getting stronger, more noxious. 'I know you want to get out,' he told her, 'but you can't yet, not here.' She carried on struggling anyway, until he relented and untied her, stood her on the ground, and took her by the shoulders. She grabbed the hem of his top and wouldn't let go. He shuffled behind her, like a penguin guarding its young. 'It's all right,' he told her, while convinced it wasn't.

And was that movement? Behind the accessible entrance, to the left of the revolving door? He remembered to breathe. A sound like a whisper, above the relentless rain, over the buildings; somebody saying, 'Her!' or, 'Here!' And everything moving with the slowness of a dream. Again, 'Here!' – further away, as if it was coming from back on the street, or a person crossing the plaza, with the rain distorting it. But it was definitely 'Here'; and beneath it was a shambling, the sound of movement in a bare room. And then the next thing, a new thing, right up against the shutters. A glint, or a wetness. It was an *eye*. Someone was standing on the other side of the entrance, behind the metal sheet and brown glass. 'Lamb,' Boyd said, yet in place of fear came confidence. Boyd knew exactly where he was. Lamb's toxic smell was filling him, and with it the world's true colours seemed to be streaming in. He *remembered* this door. He hadn't just approached this boundary before – he'd crossed it. He'd been standing right here.

Boyd stared at the eye. It stared back.

'It's all in here,' Boyd said.

'Home,' Lamb whispered.

The eye withdrew. Weak light described half a face, pallid to the point of ghostly. A woman in dark clothing. She tilted her head, lank hair tumbling with it, then returned to the slat, her eye that bit wider. Boyd felt as though he recognised her. Did she recognise him, too?

The eye closed, and the woman disappeared. Lamb whinged for Boyd to pick her up. As he did, she pushed her wet face into his top, once more clamped her feet around his waist. The smell of her hair washed over him. She was drenched. He had to breathe through his mouth.

'Don't let go,' Boyd said, tightening the sling under her backside. 'You're getting too heavy.' The sheet metal shifted. Mechanisms turned and decoupled. The accessibility door opened to reveal the woman waiting in the gloom.

'My God,' she said. 'You look just like her.'

Inside, Boyd took down his hood and smelled the tang of mildew. What got to him was the fact that the woman herself looked so much like Maureen. She was shorter, perhaps, and older, but there was no escaping it: their bones were structured the same, they shared the neat scowl, down-sloping brows, severe cheekbones. He and the woman sized each other up, breathing heavily, while Boyd and Lamb dripped rain onto the floor. It took all Boyd's will not to cry out and run to her. At the same time, it was hard not to see himself as the butt of a horrible joke. Not to feel this woman was wearing his mother's mask.

Boyd said, 'Who are you?'

The woman cleared her throat. 'I'm Agnes. Who are you?'

'Boyd.' Then, with more nerve: 'What is this?'

The woman called Agnes glanced around and shrugged. 'Home?'

Boyd checked on Lamb. She was listening, unblinking. He took her nasal whistle to be a sign of stress. He pushed the wet hair from her eyes.

'Mum gave me this address,' he told Agnes.

'We don't know anything about her.'

'You haven't seen her? She isn't here?'

Agnes shook her head. 'Never. Why? Are you searching for her?'

He had to look away, momentarily. Agnes's likeness revolted him almost as much as it pulled at him.

'See, though,' Agnes said, 'you're here now, and we're glad of it.' She nodded to Lamb. 'The girl's skin is tight. Is she tired? Did you come a fair way? We ought to find you a towel.'

Boyd blinked at her, suspicious. Agnes's constant use of 'we' bothered him. Wasn't she alone?

'Obviously you've no need to explain yourself,' Agnes went on, this time with a warmth that evoked his mother's tone on one of her good days. Boyd's confusion cycled; he wanted to step forward and hold her; he wanted to go back outside. Worst of all was an instinct to try and hurt her. Agnes wasn't his mother, even if he wanted to believe otherwise. So why did she sound like her? And why could he see himself in her face, as if he stood before his own mother at one remove, gently blurred, just off? He shook his head, but it kept pressing on him. It couldn't be her, surely. Yet if you were to place her in a crowd, at a distance, or in a group photograph…

'We can be patient as well,' Agnes said. 'It takes all sorts, doesn't it? You're puzzled, I know. But time isn't a luxury our friend here has, I'm afraid. Please follow me downstairs. There's something we can give her, if she's not too far gone.'

All Boyd could think was, *Lamb's not my friend*. She meant far more to him than that.

Agnes took Boyd and Lamb through a half-lit, denuded office, where partitions and chairs had been piled against the retaining wall like a bonfire, and wiring looms and torn lagging hung through broken ceiling tiles. Agnes's torch described the same moss from their Sile house, though here it was greyer, longer-established. He cradled Lamb's head as she followed the light beam, and fixated on the corners of each area, where the moss grew thickest. He took no comfort in the girl's low keening; he could still feel her heart pounding against his ribs.

'It's warmer downstairs,' Agnes said.

They came into a corridor lit by green emergency exit signs. The floor was pitted with heavy use, and the walls were furred with white mould. Boyd's wet shoes squeaked loudly. They entered a service lift, where Agnes pressed a button marked B2, sniffed the air, and hugged herself.

'She'll start melting our electrics if we don't get this dose in,' Agnes said. 'My word, I've not smelled it this strong in a long time.'

Boyd tightened his arms around Lamb. Agnes was right: she stank. The lift car descended for longer than felt comfortable. When the doors opened, Agnes raised a hand. 'Come in,' she said.

'I'm right here,' Boyd whispered to Lamb.

LAMB

The sub-basement was draped with sheets of patterned cloth. In another context, it could've been a festival market, stalls in rows between pillars, each individually hand-painted with great artistry. As they went through it, however, the right-angled corners transformed the space into a gentle maze. Fragrant smoke hugged the ceiling, where so many gathered mosses might have been clouds – thick and whorled, impenetrable. Agnes brought them into an area filled with cushions, mattresses and chunks of settee foam. At the heart of the space were three old television sets, arranged with their screens facing outwards, a kind of simulated campfire. Their power cables ran into the ceiling, braided like the trunk of a ficus. It was clear to Boyd that Agnes *did* live here. Just not what kind of life that might be.

She paused by a legless chaise longue. 'Can you place the girl down here for me?' she asked.

Boyd unzipped his jacket and loosened the sling and sat down himself, arranging Lamb on his knee. She was hyperalert, face turned out, eyes frantic. 'You're with me,' he reminded her. 'You're with me.'

'She's afraid,' Agnes said.

Boyd nodded. Lamb's withdrawal was disturbing; he didn't understand why she'd help him find the way here, then refuse to engage. Unless she'd done so despite her fear. He thought of all the times he'd tried to impress his mother, tried to win her affection or attention, and felt sad that he couldn't remove the same need for Lamb.

When he glanced up again, Agnes had gone. Boyd and Lamb sat in the quiet, in the darkness.

'Does she eat much?'

This new voice was stronger than Agnes's. A younger woman, late twenties at most, part-obscured by shadow. She was another near replica of Agnes, and so too his mother.

'You really can smell her, can't you?' added someone else.

A third woman, younger again, further away but illuminated by television static. While her face was less of a duplicate – perhaps it was even disfigured – the likeness, her poise, was consistent. 'Haven't you noticed?' she said.

Boyd, awkward but committed to protecting Lamb, stared into the girl's crown. The air was humid. His socks, still wet, itched. The utilitarian harshness of the building had all but vanished, replaced by these softer, more organic features. They could've been in the folds of a warmed-over fabric, or inside a body, some great otherworldly creature, being digested. He felt the pull of exhaustion.

'He's gone shy,' one of the women said.

'He's terribly thin,' said another.

'Hey, boy. Over here. Can you see? You're interesting, aren't you?'

Boyd raised his chin, but kept his eyes on Lamb. He was wary of holding her like a shield; he was aware he should be ashamed for that.

'Look at us,' one of them said. 'See us.'

He found some courage and looked. Five women circled him. They posed no obvious threat, but their walk was synchronised, practised. They might have all been sisters, any subtle differences cancelled out by obvious similarities. They wore a mix of clothes, vintage and modern, sporty and old-fashioned. He saw his mother, his grandmother, a line through all of them. With a rush – it was so obvious in context – he also saw *Lamb*. He saw Lamb and heard his mother, drunk and slurring, saying, 'Bad copies.'

And the smell was so strong.

Agnes broke from the circle to join Boyd and Lamb on the chaise longue.

'Why have you come here?' she asked him, more direct. 'They want to hear it from you.'

The women closed in to listen.

'Mum went missing,' Boyd admitted. 'She left a note. A picture, with the name of this building.'

Agnes thought about that. She said, 'We want to make the girl safe, if we can.'

'She's safe with me.'

'But are you safe with her?' Agnes opened her shawl and took from inside it a clear pen. She tapped its barrel. 'This is an injector, as for insulin. An emergency dose. You can keep holding her, if you like.'

Boyd hugged Lamb closer, but wavered. That he might give in was incredible to him. His trust of Agnes was hardly earned; at the same time, she was formidable, disarming. She seemed to know or accept who he was, which gave him vertigo.

'Tell me what it does first,' he said.

Agnes rubbed his shoulder. 'It's a stabiliser,' she said. 'It'll work quickly, with any luck, though we're worried she's quite far gone already. Have you noticed any effects?'

'Not really,' he said, thinking of the mould and the fabrics and the gulls and the fish and the smell and Leigh. 'Only the smell.'

Agnes nodded sympathetically. 'It'll be much better if you're honest with me, though. Do you feel all right in yourself? No headaches or sickness? Fever? Coughing?'

Boyd told her he was fine.

'See, it goes here,' and she tapped the top of her own arm. 'Pop, and done.'

Boyd said to Lamb, 'They want to make you better.'

Lamb gazed up at him.

'Do you promise?' he said to Agnes.

'On our sisters' lives,' she said.

So Boyd raised Lamb's arm and faced the other way. Another word from the past, flowing back to him: *suppressants*. He stole a glance. The surface tension of Lamb's skin; the pen's barrel clouding with blood.

Lamb, floppy, didn't appear to notice.

'All done,' Agnes said. She tilted Lamb's chin, wiped the girl's drool with her sleeve. 'Nice work, little one.' She touched Boyd's forehead and said, 'I can see she's got some on you, here. How do you feel? Honestly?'

'Lost,' Boyd said.

'That we can help with. But tell me, first, and don't fear silliness. Did you *see* anything? When you first noticed her smell?'

'See what?'

Agnes turned to the others. No one spoke. She came back to Boyd: 'If we know anything, it's that your mother won't have made it obvious. Did the girl know how to get here? Or was it all you?'

Boyd blew out his cheeks. 'I can't really—'

'Please, try. It's better for all of us.'

'I followed her directions, I think.'

'And what about memories? Have there been things you thought you hadn't remembered? Things you *shouldn't* be able to remember?'

He nodded.

'Where do they start?'

'I'm underwater. I'm drowning. I'm sick, and I'm—'

'When did she start to smell?'

'Maybe she's always... I don't know. In the van? Driving here. It got stronger outside.'

'All right. And, let's see – do you remember being here, at all? Not even *you*, not necessarily. The earth of the place. A perception, like déjà vu. In your chest, a tightening in your throat. You're uncomfortable, and you can't say why. You can't see what's happening, but you know it's all there, sliding beneath the ways you normally think, until, for a moment or less, it breaks in, as though a valve was opened and closed...' Agnes pinched her nose. 'Goodness, girls,' she said. 'She's honestly so strong, it's setting me off.'

Boyd stared at Lamb, whose eyes were locked to the television screens. 'I saw a bank of trees, and a car park,' Boyd conceded. 'And blank office buildings – these buildings. When we were outside, up there, I recognised the entranceway. I was sure I'd been here once. But I know that's not possible—'

'Good,' Agnes said, and turned again to the others. 'She's definitely doing it on purpose,' she told them.

Boyd was suddenly woozy. 'Lamb is?'

'Lamb? That's her name?'

Boyd sniffed. 'Yes.'

'Oh, I like it. Was that your idea?'

Boyd glanced down in shame. A flash of Lamb in Leigh's arms, that first morning, and Leigh's lost expression.

'Perhaps we should let Lamb rest,' Agnes said.

Boyd shook his head. 'I have to stay with her. That's the point.'

'The point? You do realise what she's given to bring you here?' Agnes drew a circle in the air, and the others gathered. 'Know her, girls. She's ours. She's one of us. Oh, this poor mite.'

Lamb was squirming in Boyd's lap. Not distressed, but listening.

'No,' Boyd said. 'She's staying with me.'

'Come now,' Agnes said. 'Don't let's squabble. We only need to know how long she's been changing.'

'I can't—'

Agnes shot him a steelier look. 'What about us? Do you remember *us*?'

Boyd nodded confusedly, because in some way he did. He saw them lined up. He saw them crawling and walking and feeding, and he saw Agnes. 'It's her?' he said.

'Let it open you,' Agnes said. 'They are your hereditary memories. It is your gift.'

Boyd fought to breathe. It was so obvious. Lamb's fumes, the smell of her hair, was unlocking him, unveiling nested memories, like black flowers unfurling. He called out, gripping the chaise longue. Everything contracted to a single image: rain on thick glass, and panic. He was pushing through foam, suffocating, towards a gaunt stranger's hands. He was caught in a soft leather cloth, wiped of vernix…

'Tell us about your grandmother,' Agnes said.

Who was her.

'She was—'

'Right here, yes. You feel her now. The girl – Lamb – she is showing you. You see her face in ours and in hers. Your grandmother passed herself to your mother, and so to you. But you're unlike us, in other ways. Because you have a father, don't you? A real father.'

Boyd shook his head. He thought he was going to pass out.

'Don't be pedantic!' Agnes cried, almost laughing. 'The girl is opening *us*, too! We can see you, all of us. We see your mother. You *had* a father. We can see him! Douglas! You're half your mother's and half your father's. You think you don't wear them in your skin? You think we can't tell, just from the shape of your lips?' Agnes stroked Lamb's hair. 'We're all in her, all of us. And she's in us.'

Boyd exhaled slowly. The women searched between themselves, then returned their attention to him. The youngest woman whispered too loudly, 'Is he really up to this?'

'It's what she wanted,' Agnes snapped. 'She knew exactly where to bring him.'

Boyd cradled Lamb. He was very weak.

'Do you see it, yet?' another woman asked.

Boyd saw the outline of something, yes.

Agnes touched his hand. 'We have a father,' she said. 'An unnatural father. And Lamb has shown us that your mother wanted you to meet him. It's him the girl has brought you to see.'

'Isn't it too much?' said the youngest woman. 'Shouldn't he rest, too?'

'No,' Boyd said. And Lamb shifted away from him, as if surprised by his bluntness. What was the point in waiting? He'd done so much of the work, moved through his grief, endured the labour of loss. He deserved to know why Maureen had gone right to the edge of abandoning him; deserved to know that she'd still had the best intentions for him, even as she'd deteriorated, and made her choice, and whether that choice was one of cowardice or resistance. Because his understanding of parenthood was sacrifice, and giving. It's what Maureen had tried to do after Dougie died. It was all Boyd had been trying to do for Lamb.

The ceiling felt lower as he accepted that being here fulfilled his mother's wishes, Lamb's wishes. And perhaps the women's wishes, also.

'I need to know who she was,' Boyd said. And now he didn't know if that meant Lamb, or his mother, or whether it mattered.

'Then stop denying yourself,' Agnes said.

Boyd inhaled Lamb's smell. Hypersense. Somewhere a pipe was leaking. His fingertips sparkled where they touched Lamb's skin. The richness of blood and honey on his tongue.

He exhaled. Agnes and the others regarded him with fresh pride. Lamb's warmth, and the light.

'All right,' Boyd said.

Agnes grinned. 'And leave the girl with us, just for now. Because, and I promise this, we love her as you do.'

'All right,' Boyd said.

9DH

The next room smelled of boiled cotton. Strips of grey fabric hung from rusting rails for bay curtains; there were yellowing infant cots and mouldering incubators; there were bins lined with perished tarpaulin. A stainless-steel operating table with stirrups. A run of bunk beds along the far wall, their sheets perfectly made, but their blankets moth-bitten.

At the heart of the room stood an enormous cylindrical pressure vessel. A man sat with his bare back against a glass panel in the tank's belly. His long white hair was tied up in a loose ponytail. Boyd could clearly see his spine and shoulder blades through his skin.

'Hinkley,' the older woman said. 'Fix up – we've a guest.'

The old man stood and turned. His face was younger than his sagging flanks suggested, though there was a fatigue in his movements, and his eyes were milky with cataracts. He placed a hand against the glass and squinted at Boyd. Somewhere in the ceiling a speaker crackled.

'Oh,' the man said. 'Agnes.'

'This is Hinkley,' Agnes told Boyd. 'Respectful enough, but please don't tell him the time, if he asks. We prefer that he doesn't know.'

'Okay,' Boyd said.

Agnes passed Boyd a fold-out plastic chair from a cabinet

by the tank. Inside were shelves of tinned foods and bottled water, a large canister marked *OX*. Boyd opened the chair and leaned over the back of it.

'And this is Boyd,' Agnes told Hinkley, 'who's here looking for his mother. He's brought one of us with him.'

Hinkley raised his eyebrows and grimaced. Sharp ribs, rotten teeth. '*Really*. And what would you like me to tell him?' he asked. His voice was reedy, edgeless.

'About us. Honestly and openly, in the manner of your testament.'

Hinkley nodded slowly. Boyd wiped his brow.

'May I dress first?' Hinkley said.

Agnes tutted. 'For his sake? Or yours?'

'Oh, for posterity,' Hinkley said, churlish. 'Part of me would sooner you played my tapes, except I don't recall the last time we had a visitor.'

'Ahh,' Agnes said, 'we don't want you forgetting any of the details, do we?'

Boyd watched as Hinkley pulled on a simple grey tunic. The man moved precisely, as if it was important for him to have things just so. When he was contented, he returned to the glass and said to Boyd, 'What was the name again?'

Boyd told him.

'I'm Randolph,' he said, nodding. 'Or I used to be. Did they make you feel welcome?'

Boyd shifted on his feet.

'Am I scaring you? You're young, aren't you?'

'I'm not scared,' Boyd said, and came round his chair to sit down.

'Gumption!' Hinkley croaked. 'I miss having some of that, too.' Then he pointed beyond Boyd, to Agnes. 'Perhaps the more pertinent question is, is *she* scaring you?'

'Do you ever come out of there?' Boyd asked.

Hinkley laughed hoarsely and looked to Agnes, who said

nothing. 'Oh, sometimes. If one of them is hurt…'

'But the rest of the time?'

'I stay quite still, thank you, and reminisce. One has to conserve one's energy.'

Boyd was heavy in the folding chair. It was too small and hard, and he couldn't stop his legs from bouncing. Hinkley, by comparison, was coiled, measured, squatting against the glass as though waiting to seize an opportunity.

'Agnes said you knew my nan,' Boyd said.

'Did she?'

'Did you?'

Hinkley leered. 'That rather depends, doesn't it? If that's who you tell me she was.'

Boyd didn't reply.

Without warning, Hinkley slapped the glass. 'Of course!' he cried. 'Of course you are! Boyd, will you describe your mother to me? Was she devious, too? Was she cunning?'

'I don't—'

Hinkley grimaced. 'My *God*, she's *on* you, isn't she? Agnes, Agnes – is this what I'm smelling through the filter? I'd know that stench anywhere. And, and… She's left him, hasn't she? This boy's mother? Did she let herself go too far? Did she fall to pieces, come the end?'

Agnes came closer to Boyd, who didn't answer.

'Don't be crass,' she told Hinkley.

Hinkley smiled. 'Sorry, Boyd,' he said. 'Except… you're not quite her, are you? Not quite. Which must mean she forked away from us. A *man*, was it? Oh, let me…' And Hinkley closed his eyes. 'A *natural* siring… This has so many implications, doesn't it? Gain of function… recombination… Where is she now, your mother?'

Boyd shook his head.

'Incredible,' Hinkley said. '*Incredible.*'

'You're meant to tell him,' Agnes replied, with a sharper tone.

Hinkley smiled quickly. 'Yes,' he said. 'Yes, of course.' Then, to Boyd, and more thoughtfully: 'You do deserve that.'

And after a few moments more, thick and slow, the room's air somehow textured by the tank's sickly light, the old man cleared his throat.

'Our work stemmed from that great speculative question – *what if?*' Hinkley started. 'But we weren't imagining our way through branching possibilities, unknowable second-order effects. We *did* it. Deliberately, iteratively.

'Of course, we met with resistance – just because one *can*, that doesn't mean one *should*. Yet I always felt our critics missed the simplicity of our project. We weren't interested in ethics, a technological debate. Only in science as art. Because isn't godcraft the height of human creativity? How can you apply fickle law or morality to that?'

'He's not sure now, mind,' Agnes said.

'No,' Hinkley snapped. 'But *context*, Agnes. Our first eight cycles had already produced groundbreaking results – cellular mutation, observable growth characteristics, and so on. Funding was found, the Ministry of Defence caught wind, a delegation from Porton Down arrived. What was secret became scrutinised. We went into sequence nine with the government's tacit backing, while accepting that our findings could now be adopted, paid for. Or swept away.

'Consider, then: our third sequence had established that a viable zygote could be generated in an adult chimpanzee, minus insemination. By sequence five, our chimps' uteri had stopped rejecting these zygotes; while sequences six and seven proved that splicing mammalian DNA with our proprietary plant-based genetic material could not only guarantee but *accelerate* the zygote's cleavage rate, using a process like photosynthesis. Which is to say, immaculate conception, happening on fast forward. Using plant matter and light.'

'Godcraft,' Agnes said quietly.

Hinkley nodded reverently. 'Our next step was human challenge trials – and finding a suitable candidate.'

Boyd fidgeted in the chair. He could tell Agnes was trying to get his attention.

'They called her 9DH,' she told him. 'She'd been knocked over by a lorry in central London. Twenty months in a coma. Acute retrograde amnesia. No family, no job – she hadn't even been in London long enough to make a friend.'

'But, with us,' Hinkley said, 'she'd make a full recovery. We'd care for her, and rehabilitate her—'

'And they just *let* you?' Boyd said, leaning forward.

Hinkley squinted at him. 'She was on the organ donor list. Legally, we could argue she'd volunteered to help us. Given Porton Down's involvement, we were confident in our assessment.'

'And she did help,' Agnes said.

'Yes,' Hinkley said, rubbing his jaw. 'At first.'

Boyd waited.

'Our protester friends became increasingly well-funded and organised,' Hinkley explained. 'But their inaccuracy, their noisiness, also gave our work solid cover. We were even collecting their slogans at one point, making games of it. Success felt inevitable.'

'Except,' Agnes said.

'9DH cottoned on,' Hinkley continued. 'Whenever we moved her between therapy suites, she could see the unrest on the plaza – the placards and crowds. We discussed it, of course, and agreed it was better to expose 9DH to brief, complicating stimulus than confine her indefinitely. In any case, we were all too distracted by her data, which was remarkable. Given our work with photosynthesis, for instance, we expected 9DH to exhibit acute photosensitivity – an aversion to ultraviolet radiation. Instead, she actively sought out the light, and drew strength from it.'

Boyd thought of Maureen and her sun cream, and their old bathroom. Lamb crawling and Lamb with teeth.

'So much so, in fact,' Hinkley went on, 'that when 9DH achieved auto-conception, the prenatal development was remarkable. Her first blastocyst became the equivalent of an eight-week-old embryo within hours. Not weeks – *hours*. She grew a recognisable infant in *less than a day*. I still remember it: "Behold, a virgin shall conceive!"'

'When was her baby born?' Boyd asked. He was standing up, now.

'She miscarried,' Hinkley said. 'There was a series of miscarriages. And with each one, her behaviour became more unpredictable. During routine checkups, she'd turn her back to us and agitate her wedding-ring finger madly. We measured spikes of acidity in her tank, wild increases in brain activity. She wouldn't eat, wouldn't respond to any standard stimuli. Fairly quickly, we came to the conclusion that certain memories – fragments of her old life – remained extant, were still active within her. And she was finding ways to expand these memories. As if 9DH *missed* somebody.'

'Herself,' Boyd said.

'Yes,' Agnes said. 'As you were, out there. As Lamb is.'

Boyd swallowed thickly. His eyes stung. He could still smell Lamb.

'After 9DH's fifth miscarriage,' Hinkley said, 'the tank's rubber seals came apart. We found a toxic, self-replicating spore on them, not unlike a moss. Something in 9DH's liver and pancreatic tissue. Our consulting psychiatrist suggested that precipitating stressors – anger and isolation – were triggers.'

'So, they decided to *treat* her,' Agnes said. 'Didn't you?'

'We changed our methodology,' Hinkley said, matter-of-factly. 'We introduced the outside world to 9DH's therapy. Television, film and music to occupy her, to sate her desire for the past, or even *overwrite* it...'

Hinkley trailed off, expecting a reaction, but Agnes stayed quiet, and Boyd followed suit.

'Exposure worked,' Hinkley said, his voice softer. '9DH's demeanour and aptitude improved. We introduced a regimen of immunosuppressants, which subdued the production of 9DH's "side-matter".'

'And then what?' Agnes said. She'd come closer to Boyd, as though standing with him in judgement. He thought she was about to put a hand on his shoulder, and realised he wanted her to. He could still smell Lamb's hair. Was the scent coming from Agnes, too? He brought his gaze back to Hinkley and steadied himself.

'I should say, as a matter of record,' Hinkley said, 'that I'm proud of what 9DH did. It's not to excuse anything – I've had time enough to pity myself. But all the same. First, it was her sleep. Deeper, longer, not at all. Seasonal... hormonal... tidal; we ruled out every factor. The tank was held at a steady temperature. Her feeds and medications were consistent, her serotonin, cortisol and adrenaline markers likewise. Despite her obvious *awareness*, it wasn't a period of depression, in clinical terms. Around then, I was presented with concerns about one of our research doctors, Tomasz, who occasionally smelled of alcohol, and who was filing incomplete reports. Surveillance revealed that Tomasz was staying with 9DH's therapy tank for much longer than it usually took to change her drip, take observations, replace a line, et cetera. And while he wasn't speaking to her—'

'They were talking,' Boyd said, cutting in. 'Tapping to each other.'

Agnes swivelled to him, eyes blazing.

Hinkley swallowed audibly. 'Sorry...?'

Boyd shook his head at how clear it all was. He'd spoken almost involuntarily; he was remembering what happened as fact; he was *seeing*, as he had been with Lamb and the women in the next room. A sensate calmness as images and sounds rolled to him in the fetch of black waves. He was in the tank, Tomasz peering in at him. He was 9DH, and spiteful. The same searing clarity. Careful taps on the glass—

'She had Tomasz change her sedative doses,' Hinkley said. 'Naturally, we had to let him go – his actions had jeopardised too much. Which was when 9DH's miscarriages ceased, and her body stopped responding to therapy, and 9DH began to – and I don't know how else to put it – smirk at us.'

Now Agnes touched Boyd's shoulder. The connection was instant. Not comfort, but solidarity.

'Tell him,' Agnes urged Hinkley.

'I was a scientist,' Hinkley said, 'and dutiful. I asked 9DH what she thought of the programmes we were showing her. She asked why I thought she'd stopped menstruating. I told her we wanted to ensure her comfort. She asked if I was happy – if I had a family. She'd lick her lips, savour my discomfort. Once, she asked, "Do you actually *know* what you've done?" And I can still picture her face. "I've been making bad copies," she told me. And she held her belly and said, "But not this one."'

Boyd sat back in his chair. Agnes knelt beside him.

'She was on course to reach full term in less than a month,' Hinkley said. 'No abnormalities in her placenta, hormone or blood protein levels, nor amniotic fluid; no other risk markers. As her pregnancy developed, the truth was clear: the infant was her exact genetic double. We were witnessing true parthenogenesis. A clone pregnancy, created in pure defiance, or revenge.

'We'd underestimated her. And we'd underestimated

Tomasz, and their allies in places we had not seen. And the very night she was due to give birth—'

'She escaped,' Boyd whispered, his heart soaring; and before Agnes could stop him, he was running at the tank.

'Boyd!' Agnes shouted.

Hinkley sprawled backwards, and in his pathetic expression, Boyd saw the man's insignificance. The black waves crashed over him; Boyd was 9DH again, watching the facility lights flash and burn out, and people in masks approaching the tank. He tasted panic but not his own. The heaviness of the baby inside her. Inside *him*. The tank breaking and the coldness of fresh air, and a man's face, a gaunt man, the man called Tomasz—

'Two squads,' Boyd told Hinkley. 'Five minutes. They came and arrested you the next morning.'

Hinkley, cowering, nodded. 'Officially, the protests had paid off, and our research was incinerated or requisitioned. But most of my colleagues were taken in by Porton Down. I entered solitary confinement for six weeks as the manhunt unfolded.'

'But they never found her,' Boyd said. 'Or Tomasz.'

Hinkley shook his head.

'So why are you here?' Boyd asked.

'You already know, Boyd,' Agnes said.

Hinkley crawled closer to the tank's glass. 'On my release,' he said, meeker, 'I returned to London. Professionally, I'd disappeared with the institute. But personally, having nothing was a kind of freedom. I concentrated on my fitness, and on my books. Then, Porton Down called out of the blue to say they'd located a person of interest living alone on a smallholding off the Medway Estuary. Feasibility studies for a fracking development had turned out a soil sample with unusual markers, which flagged our work. I was brought in to outline the implications of a former test subject living in the community, without suppressants. The big concern was that if 9DH's condition were to go unchecked, a period of destabilisation and potentially mass-effect deterioration would follow.'

'But this wasn't 9DH, was it?' Boyd said.

Hinkley pursed his lips. 'I was taken to Ascension Island, in the Pacific, where the subject was being held in confinement. A woman, mid-twenties, largely unresponsive to exterior life, the vagaries of modernity.'

Boyd looked at Agnes.

Hinkley nodded. 'Porton Down had worked with some of my ex-colleagues to conceal that not every miscarriage had been so; that a secondary stream of work had been taking place under my nose. Yet when she saw me, the woman's demeanour changed. She recognised me through memories inherited from 9DH. She saw me as a friend, and...' He gestured weakly to Agnes.

Agnes gave no response.

'We struck a deal, with reparations,' Hinkley said. 'In lieu of formal prosecution, I would continue to advise Porton Down, and Agnes would receive options for assisted living. Instead, however, she requested to come back here to live. Bright House was all she knew as home – was all she desired. The catch was that I would take 9DH's place in the sequencing tank. And Agnes would be free to leave at any time, with sensible precautions.'

Boyd was dumbstruck.

'It's true,' Agnes said.

Hinkley smiled sheepishly. 'For all she'd been given a new life, ushered to Kent by Porton Down, *I* still provided instant security. Agnes knew me, and here we exist together. A home to her, and her own four daughters, and to 9DH in their received memories. And I accept this, as I accept my hand in their fate. As I accept my own sentence.'

Boyd turned from the tank. The black waves had retreated, leaving only the impressions of his grandmother Joan, and Maureen, and Lamb, and Agnes beside him. Not subjects, nor candidates, nor data. His family.

'I'm done,' Boyd told Agnes. Because there had been a final gift, brought to him in the turmoil. The shock of future-sight: the white van beside a yellow garden gate, with a thickly flowering wisteria beyond it. 'I know where Lamb wants to go,' he said.

Walking away, he heard Hinkley say, as though in submission, 'I always thought about your grandmother, Boyd. Now I shall always think of you.'

DEW

Agnes took Boyd to one of the bunk beds in the corner.

'It must be a lot,' she said. 'Are you disappointed?'

Boyd looked back across the room. The tank's internal lights had dimmed, leaving Hinkley all but invisible. He wasn't sure what he was feeling. As he'd listened to the old man, he'd been conscious of his life taking on a new depth and breadth. Overwhelming awareness; his knowing given form. But over here, the black tide was a long way out, and he was drained. He was struggling to find Joan's face, to remember it, to hold it in his mind's eye for long enough. He wanted the right setting in which to place her – a memory distinct from their journey from coast to Cotswolds.

When Agnes stroked the back of his hand, he said, 'Where's Lamb?'

Because Lamb had to be his priority.

'With the girls, watching television,' Agnes said. 'I have to tell you, though: she doesn't have long. We can contain her, for a while, but she's very far along. And when we ask her what she wants, whether she understands what's coming, she only asks for you.'

Boyd studied the wall close by, the fine cracks in the concrete, the freshest mould like a dark frost, crystalline and delicate. He knew he should ask, 'What's coming?' but instead he said, 'Do you think she remembers everything Mum did? And Nan? Is that how it works?'

Agnes shook her head. 'No, not yet, and probably never with total recall. She's still her own person, too, don't forget. It's not always *on* – it's more of a tap, and one you have to open yourself. Like you, Lamb is learning her gifts. She's special, but there's so much room to grow. For me, for all of us here – my girls, that is – we've learned to see what we want to. We've made our own comfort – it's not as though we can live backwards. They're my daughters, and they're also my sisters. They are my daughters and my mother. I dare suppose I'm your aunt. Yet we're still our own people. And for that reason, the front door stays open, always. They can go, if that's what they need to do. Me, as well. But son, we don't matter. When that little girl in there looks at you, she doesn't need to remember. You're a big feeling to her, all your own. Part of her carried and nursed you, don't forget – and I think she's letting herself go because that way, she can show you. Your mum couldn't say it, she couldn't bring herself to explain, so she's been telling you another way.'

'Nan's house,' Boyd said. 'I saw it.'

Agnes smiled. 'If that's what was coming through, then yes. That's where Lamb wants to be.'

Where the circle might close.

'You could come with us,' he said. 'Nan's your mum, too.'

Agnes laughed, and not unkindly. 'Didn't that bastard in there say it best? Where else do we know? What else can there be? Your mum's had her own crack at life, by hook or by crook, and look where she ended up! Leaving you to come out here, all grubby-faced, her brave little soldier.'

Boyd sucked his teeth. Again, he glanced at the tank.

'I'm sorry,' Agnes said. 'That was unfair. I'm just saying I don't expect you to understand.'

'I think I wanted to kill him,' Boyd told her.

Agnes hesitated, then smirked. 'I can believe it. And I wouldn't have stopped you. His oxygen line goes in at the back, if that's any help. There'd be a poetry in it: a man playing God killed by His creation. But what would that make you? It'd be a rough way to go – you'd certainly hear it.'

Boyd knitted his hands together. Agnes was calling his bluff, just like his mother used to. Hinkley was only his grandfather by design – a figurehead, at best. And he was already being dealt with. He was pitiful.

Boyd let Agnes have a smug moment before he nodded and said, 'Would Nan know about you?'

'Honestly? I hope not.'

'I could tell her about you, if you like. When I get there.'

Agnes held up a hand. 'I have a picture of her in my mind. I can hear her voice.'

'She's called Joan. I guess she named herself that afterwards.'

Agnes frowned incredulously, then chuckled. Boyd stood up from the bed.

'That was the name of her first cat,' Agnes explained. 'Before the coma, I mean. Before her accident.' Agnes rubbed her wedding-ring finger. 'Together, we've worked out that she was married once, much as we don't remember the marriage. She was orphaned, and young, because we have always felt her loss. But we *remember* such few things from before. She harvested rosehips in the autumn, made syrup for the winter. Her home had crooked floorboards, white-washed and dreadfully loud. Young, probably a teenager, she stole a ginger tabby cat and called it Joanie. That's our sum of your nan before the lorry knocked her down. Before him, in there, and the tank. Before all of us. And you.'

'So don't you want to know who she is now?' he asked.

Agnes wiped her eyes and shook her head.

Boyd turned away, thinking of Red, and what used to be their home. Agnes linked his arm and walked him into the seating area. The blue light of the televisions strobed the walls. In partial silhouette, four heads visible over the back of a sofa.

The smallest head rose and rotated towards him.

Lamb smiled, and Boyd smiled back.

'We'll pack for her,' Agnes said. 'At least enough for you to get there.'

Boyd recognised the last few miles into Joan's village. It was the dry-stone walling that surfaced his strongest recollection – a holloway through yellowing birch trees, a stretch of road from which in late summer you sometimes saw shire horses grazing on red clover. The divide between past and present was thin, porous. Last time, he'd been a passenger in the hired Luton van as they moved Joan to her retirement flat, squashed between his mother and his grandmother, the axles groaning under the weight of all the teak and mahogany furniture in the back. Not long after she'd moved in, Boyd had spoken to her on the phone. 'Will you visit me, when you're old enough to drive?' she'd asked. 'When I can tell you so much?'

Now he was driving another van, with Lamb, Joan's granddaughter, beside him. She was weak, her face glowing with fever, but her fumes were still helping him see the way. Did she also remember the dry-stone walling, the flat, the smell of the old van, through Maureen? Did she feel the same melancholy at coming back?

'I know where the house is,' he told her. The yellow wooden gate. The roses and hydrangeas, the wisteria. Other flowers whose names his grandmother had tried and failed to teach him. When Lamb turned to him with lidded, watery eyes, he realised she felt the proximity of the cottage, the home where Maureen had grown up.

'Let's check Nan's flat first,' Boyd said, putting on a brave face.

Lamb slumped back, spent, before reaching behind to try and scratch whatever was happening inside her spine. Then she closed her eyes and lay across the bench.

Boyd, filled with three generations of memory, with lineage, trusted himself with the rest.

Boyd must have looked a state – the receptionist notice-ably flinched as he approached the desk. Lamb, though, the charming if drowsy-looking girl in his arms, gave Boyd easy passage. He could play the young parent or older brother, didn't matter which. He was prepared to exploit the fact that residents thrived on family visits, a kind of local currency.

Boyd gave his name. He tried to keep Lamb's face angled away, over his shoulder, so she couldn't poison anyone. The receptionist said she hadn't heard a peep from Joan in some days, had an inkling she might be on a coach holiday. This wasn't a care home, she was keen to stress – they had no real power to check. 'But I can call her flat directly, if you like?'

Boyd said they'd just go and knock; it wasn't a big deal. Joan had often told him how she left her front door unlocked in case she should receive a better offer. Lamb, limp, pushed her mouth into Boyd's shoulder. He felt her breath down his back. He could only hope his top was enough to filter her, stop her from contaminating the lobby.

'Little one poorly?' the receptionist asked.

'Tired,' he said.

The receptionist gave Boyd a door number and waved them on. The corridors smelled of diluted bleach and Parma violets. When Boyd tried the door and found it locked, Lamb simply held a hand over the keyhole until the barrel broke.

The flat was pristine and mostly empty. Boyd put Lamb

down; she shuffled over to the kitchenette, where she leaned against the fridge door. Boyd, for want of a way to process the place, to imagine Joan's days here, sat in the rocking chair opposite. The arched window overlooked a private car park and the corrugated side of a light industrial unit. Beyond a graveyard filled with oaks stood a church of wet limestone, crows perched along the apex of its roof. Beneath the window was a cabinet of miniature crystal glasses, a shelf of reference books on plants, wildflowers, native birds and fungi. Maybe the combination of these was enough to keep her going, he thought. But for a woman whose life had been long and infinitely complex, how could it be?

Lamb groaned. She'd fallen to her side and was rasping. Boyd lifted her onto Joan's chair, poured her a tumbler of water and pressed it to her lips. She drank it greedily, smiled at his efforts, but they both knew they were running out of time. What might come next, he could only base on Sile, on Maureen's deterioration. Nothing said this might go differently. Yet Lamb wasn't scared and wanted him to see that. Her acceptance was, on balance, the thing that hurt the most.

Boyd did a final sweep. On the kitchenette top was a sheaf of bills and assorted notes held down with a snow-globe. There were ragged discolorations on the fridge where long-stuck magnets had been removed. All the plates and cutlery were perfectly in place. A clean tea towel had been threaded through the oven handle. He had the impression the flat had been packed up, cleaned, treated. That Joan had moved on without wishing to leave a trace.

Crossing into Joan's bedroom felt as transgressive as entering Maureen's that morning back in Sile. He was Boyd the boy again, all too young, and by her dresser he unlocked a new memory through the faint smell of make-up. Joan was standing at the bathroom sink, removing her dentures to clean them. Boyd, rapt, was trying to remove his own teeth in mimicry, and Joan was chuckling at him.

He searched her wardrobes and drawers, all empty. Joan hadn't managed to conceal everything, however. Mould was creeping along the silicone sealant around the bath, and – as always – was starting up the tiles.

Boyd flushed the toilet and came back into the main room. Lamb had climbed onto the bed, so light she hadn't disturbed the sheets. So quiet he hadn't heard her moving. There was an envelope on the pillow beside her, unaddressed. Boyd opened it and shook out the contents. It was a photograph of Boyd sitting on Joan's knee, with Maureen beside them. His mother at her mother's shoulder, both women with half-smiles. It was too perfect to be truly candid, as though the photo had been taken to meet a purpose, not record a moment.

His grandmother and mother were close to identical, right down to the creases around their eyes. Their canniness and their mischief. He showed Lamb. She peeled herself from the sheets, leaving what looked like scorch marks in the cotton. He took her into his arms and held her against him until they were breathing together, the same. Then he stood up. This photograph he'd leave here. Lamb needed to go home.

Boyd parked the van right next to the yellow gate. His chest was still tight and his hand was tingling after wiping a grey film from the inside of the windscreen. The van was running badly – something had fallen off in the car park outside Joan's flat – and its gears kept slipping as he drove it round to the cottage. The bench seat fabric was sloughing away, exposing a brittle foam that left luminous crumbs on their clothes. None of the switches worked. When he scratched his shoulder, the stitching of his top disintegrated under his nails.

LAMB

Lamb was in and out of consciousness. Awake, she had the same few expressions, clearly intended to be reassuring – smiles and earnest glances, innocent blinking. Then a catatonic glaze would descend, and her eyes would roll back and close.

Boyd came round the van and opened Lamb's door. She lifted her arms so he could pick her up. She was bird-light. Her skin was hot and damp. He carried her frog-legged through the gate and up the path to the door. Heavy brambles had colonised the front garden, displacing the flower beds. He led with his shoulder to protect Lamb from its thorns, tucking her legs under his arms. He rang the bell, knocked, then tried to push open the door. It wouldn't budge. Either the fittings were seized, or there was something pressing on the other side. The curtains were closed and the lights were off.

He followed a partially sunken path around the house. The flagstones had too much give, as though the soil and sand beneath had been siphoned away. The side gate, newer than the fence but covered in green algae and already rotting, was locked. Boyd checked for passers-by, placed Lamb behind him, and kicked out a panel so he could reach through for the latch. Lamb, distressed, let out a long whine. Boyd rubbed his shin and picked her up. She stank. She clung to him.

With the latch open, Boyd shoved the gate. It swung past its natural stop and popped off its top hinge. The yard before them – only small, perhaps twelve feet square – was wild with dead grey moss and tall weeds. A broken, overgrown ramp into the roof revealed itself as the gable end of the house, which had partially collapsed, leaving broken stone and timber strewn on the flags. Boyd picked his way through the rubble. At the far side of the yard, beneath the fence, was an L-shaped raised bed. From its soil grew several thick, pale trunks, whose shared canopy was a wind-frayed, sun-faded sheet of blue tarpaulin. The trunks resembled mushroom stalks – they had the pallor, the ridged texture, but were otherwise much too thick.

Boyd inspected the one closest. Lamb keened and whistled. When he tried to put her down, even to turn her face to him, to calm her, she resisted. When he touched one of the stalks – tough and dry, not spongy or supple, more like bone – Lamb yelped as though in pain. He kissed her head to comfort her, and pictured something – a distant, distorted shape. He said to Lamb, 'Do you know what this is?' If she did, she didn't want to tell him. He inhaled Lamb's hair again. This time, it was clearer: a memory as a gift. Joan and Maureen had stood out here once, or many times. They'd buried something in these planters. Whatever this was had been growing here for a long time.

Boyd made his way to where the back door frame barely stood. The door was missing – blown out, most likely, and covered by the wall. The kitchen was flooded with stagnant water. He cupped Lamb's neck and stepped inside. The ceiling bowed above them, lines of water fanning out in the shape of bracken. Mould and grey moss webbed the walls and ceiling. On the table was an empty hessian sack with LIME printed on its side.

'Nan?' he said. His voice sounded too big for the space and made Lamb jump. He asked if she wanted to get down. She shook her head, her heart against his. As though pinched by an unseen hand, one corner of the room contracted. The shadows there shifted, warped, and fell back. The kitchen felt *full*.

'Is that you?' came a gentle voice, channelled through the beams and joists of the cottage.

Boyd didn't answer. He wasn't sure if the voice was inside him. He went on through the kitchen, the emptied living room, towards a gloomy hallway. The click-clack of tiles underfoot. A mass was wedged against the front door, solid gristle from edge to edge, sealing the frame. Up the staircase behind them, a new reminder, a jolt from his own past, or from Lamb's. Yes – he'd spent time sulking here, aged five or six, because he couldn't keep his grandmother's full attention. He touched a step. The gouges and stains were familiar. As a child, he'd traced these imperfections, conjured whole worlds from them. After being put to bed – Joan reading him a story as he settled in a nest of pillows – he used to sneak back out of his room, read in moonlight on the top step, while the adults laughed downstairs.

He went up. Lamb was perfectly still. The landing walls were spotlessly clean. A chairlift rail had been installed; the chair itself was still shrink-wrapped on the landing.

Joan was on the bed, bundled up in self-knitted blankets. Dried candlewax cascaded down the bedstand beside her. She wore a multicoloured knitted jumper, the hood up. Was it that Joan had waited, and he'd taken too long? He set Lamb down. He couldn't hear any breathing. The air was very dry. He came round the bed. Joan's face was sunken and grey, almost unrecognisable, but her expression was satisfied.

He sat on the bed. There was nothing useful to say. He understood, then, that the cardigan and blankets around her body were actually parts of her body, separating out. The arm furthest from him, Joan's left arm, was several feet long and connected to the far wall. Its skin had come away, while the muscle tissue had unravelled and blossomed like flowering ivy. Beyond the elbow – the exposed bone a single defining shape – her fascia had unwound into tendrils, which spiralled across the wall in a way that made Boyd believe they were holding it up. Her right arm, meanwhile, sagged away from her torso, dislocated at the shoulder, and dangled from the bed frame. This arm was heavier, thicker, than the other; it had been elongated from the elbow to the wrist, as if stretched by its own weight. At the end of it, Joan's hand had formed a lattice across the floorboards, seeping into the gaps between them. Boyd realised that their entry points matched the bracken-like patterns in the bowed ceiling below. Possibly his grandmother had even pushed the gable end of the cottage into the yard – one last act against the walls that had once contained her.

Boyd was more fascinated than perturbed. There was an artistry, a beauty, to Joan's distorted body. The way her legs had unspooled and woven themselves together. The way her ribs had opened out.

'Nan,' he said out loud. Lamb already knew. It wasn't a novelty for her; she had come from the same kind of death. With what must have been the last of her strength, she took Boyd's hand and led him round the bed. The absurdity of stepping over his grandmother's extruded arm. The pain of watching Lamb try to pat the mattress. 'Here?' he said. 'Are you sure?' Lamb nodded. He didn't want this to happen. She tugged his arm. He sat down but faced away, disbelieving. Low sun, hard light, held the room's dust. He kneaded his thighs. He didn't want to be alone again, not without her, but the circle was closing. Lamb was where she wanted to be.

He remembered that he still had his mother's penny in his sock. He took it out, rubbed it on his top.

'Boyd?' Lamb said. She'd never used his name before. He'd heard his mother, calling him to the table for small talk over breakfast, all those moments shared when Dougie was at work.

'Boyd,' Lamb said again. 'It doesn't hurt.'

He tried to smile at her, wiping his nose with the back of his hand. Then, wordlessly, he gave her the penny.

Lamb's eyes brightened. As she turned it, the coin fell from her hand onto her chest. She held one hand over it. 'Here,' she said, in return. And she extended her other frail hand towards the dresser. Three dusty mirrors in a mahogany frame, and three drawers. Echoes. He went to them. There was an envelope in the middle drawer, marked with an elegantly calligraphed *B*. Underneath it was a plastic document wallet. He brought them back to the bed. Lamb tried to speak. Her mouth worked slowly but formed no sounds, moistureless. A clock ticked in another room.

He opened the envelope first.

Dear Boyd,

I hope you can still recognise me. By now I've learned to control what my body is wont to do, but stubbornness alone cannot sustain it. Think of a mountain. You have summited, and now you are descending. Your breath is lengthening again, though your thighs are tired and it's getting cold, and soon you choose to rest, risk the dark. It's bitter there, with the sun the wrong side of you, behind, and you have to let the wind cut through you. It doesn't take so long for your body to notice, to divert blood to your essential organs, your heart and brain. This is why you lose your fingers and toes first. This is why, all things balanced, you don't seem to mind.

The same can be said of me. Beyond the pills, my regimen, I do begin to change. But I'm tiring, and I'm old enough to know I cannot hold the door forever.

What I want you to hold is tenderness. You and I both have friends in places we can't see and merry meet. Those people who once took care of me, who took care of your mother, have taken care of you, even from afar. An old friend – you met her! – told me how you ran away. She said you were stubborn, like I was. And do you know it made me proud? It told me you were probably coming.

I'm sorry we've missed each other. It would've been famous, to see you again as your own man, and in you our Reens. But in the absence of a smile, of the kind of love you can really, truly see, you should try to accept that I lay down gladly.

Would you trust me? I'm sure you've been asked so many times already. But this is not, for once, a blind leap, and you can doubtless see what I've become. If I've learned anything in my foreshortened life, this second life of mine, it's that to live honestly is to live well. And so I'll put this simply, much as I expect that you, my keen boy, will know by now:

I was stolen. I was changed. But I still remembered. And with good grace, I held to that, and got out.

I've also learned that not much that is good comes without pain. I gave birth to your mother on the darkest night of my life. We fought on, hiding from the sun, until she found her own tenderness, which was your father. And do you know that I saw your father for who he was? As he saw me, when he had forgiven me? Dougie, that boy, he gave your mother what I never could. Although, that's not quite the whole of it. Those two, they took each other on, and they both won.

My great regret is that I couldn't comfort your parents the way I wanted to – the way they deserved. Writing this, I tell myself that for both of them it was only the fear of being caught, or their fear catching up with them, that defeated them. Yes, what happened with your father's job untethered them. Stress got in through the cracks, they lost their way. And parenting was a strain! It is a strain. Neither of them was ready for the reality of you, to exit their own lives, as none of us truly are. But without her Dougie, without the strength they shared, momentary as her lapse was, your mother lost control of what mattered. And fear took them both.

But, Boyd, they were in love. Your father didn't want to do what he did. He was a proud man, felt he'd failed you both. He lacked the tools to articulate himself, and in the end blamed the wrong thing, took the wrong turn. Trust me that he was a simple man, and a decent one. So while he fathered you as he might have been fathered, which is to say with a frightened coldness, I know his heart was full with you. Can you remember the good of him? I hope you'll try. For I'll never forget the way he described you, that day you arrived. Or the way he told me about you watching him leaving the house of a morning.

Trust that your mother was kind, too. And trust that she was formidable. All of this, me, this life of ours, it was visited upon her. And she took that emptiness, and she filled it. Oh, Reens. What I couldn't teach, she learned herself. What I couldn't do, she did regardless. She adored you. I say if she is ashes now, then those ashes will glow with you.

Are you frightened? Breathe out. What you see here was only a vessel. I was happy, mostly. I'm happy to be writing this. And I know you won't find me alone. I know you've brought your sister, who can see. And so you've also brought my daughter back to me. Your sister carries Maureen, and me in turn. That is what motherhood means to us. That's how we meant it to be. And never forget that all of us are in you, too. Which is why I have no more need to be careful.

The folder I left with this letter contains the laboratory reports. It explains the what of me, much less the why. It tells you what they did. It tells you who your mother is. And it tells you who you are. Of course, you may not even need it. You may already know. You may, going on, getting older, begin to remember yourself.

You may choose not to.

There are never easy answers, Boyd. I loved your mother as best I could. Trust that she found her way, and that you will find yours.

Nanna x

Boyd folded the letter and dropped it between his shoes. Lamb seemed to be waiting for him, for his reaction; he lifted her into the nook between his legs and held her fists against his chest. Her eyes were half closed; she wasn't really there. But she was still clutching the coin.

He placed her back on the bed and stroked her hair. Her hand searched for and found the plastic wallet with the lab reports and pushed it onto his lap. 'There's no point,' he told her. But Lamb being Lamb, her mother's daughter or simply his mother, she insisted, snarling. Boyd opened it, read the first page twice. Mostly it was biomedical jargon that tried to quantify the kinds of things that resist all measurement.

'Lamb?' he said.

The girl was trying to prop herself up on one elbow. He could no longer ignore the sloping of her shoulders. One of her hands was beginning to peel, opening itself from the palm. The penny slipped down to her stomach. When he touched her, her skin was cooling, felt too elastic. Her other arm had become stuck to the sheets, and she tried, feebly, to pull it away. He put his hand over hers. She calmed, and so did he. A blackbird whistled cheerily in the yard. The coin glinted, and Boyd understood. He should be unafraid, forgiving of himself. He was half of his mother, half of his father, and immune to his sister Lamb, who was his mother and grandmother both. And, in a way, his daughter.

'Please,' he said, 'don't forget.'

Lamb's lips parted. She slurred, and a foam came through. Boyd wiped it away. She wasn't in pain – not that he could see. It was like all the times she'd settled against him in her sling, comforted, while he waited for her breath to deepen. Or the time he'd carried her back to Sile, the two of them in the night, when she was all that kept him warm.

Lamb's breath was shortening. Her face was turned to one side. He considered moving her closer to Joan, her aged twin. He didn't, because she was where she wanted to be. He shushed her, and her eyelids flickered. She rasped a word, urgent but well meant, like a friendly reminder, but he didn't catch it. She placed her one free hand on his arm and let it flow away, silken, the skin turning iridescent as he watched. Those same fingers found Joan's gnarled shoulder, then fell to Joan's breast for comfort. 'You're there,' Boyd told her. And Lamb drifted on. Her forearm bloomed against his hand with liquid warmth. Boyd held his breath as she changed, awe and gratefulness. His own skin turned lustrous, pulsing with light. As he watched, her blood vessels laced his wrist, held him. When the process slowed, the vessels released him again, opened mandala-like across the bedsheet. The rest of her was spreading out. He leaned over and kissed where he thought her forehead might be. The bed glistened silver with dew. The penny had gone.

Boyd took the letter and the laboratory report out to the landing, and sat down on the top step. For a moment he was younger again, and his parents were downstairs with Joan and Ted, all of them playing cards, and raucously, free with each other in a way they could be with nobody else. He was glad to remember.

He pushed the report back towards Joan's bedroom door. She and Lamb, the cottage, could dispose of it now. He pocketed Joan's letter and went through the house and into the back yard.

As he crossed towards the broken gate, the moss parted for him.

OLD ROADS

In the end, Boyd must have covered a hundred miles on foot, keeping to rural paths where he could, guided by road signs glimpsed over hedgerows, the odd time by covering his face with his collar and asking hikers or dog-walkers to point him towards the next town north. For most of it, he battled a kind of psychic fog, dense enough to render the surrounding countryside and weather a blur. Now and then, he fell out the other side, startled by a noise – a grouse, a chuntering horse, an anxious sheep – to find time had warped and slipped behind him. He'd be standing beside a fallow field, or halfway over a stile, or with both feet submerged in a bog. At least twice he saw a small figure in the distance, a young girl with an awkward gait, long arms made of grass and wildflowers, and called after her. She never turned.

Which was not to say Boyd went without peace. There was a power in enduring. He found relief in the quiet seconds after waking, when the pain of the ground, his wet back, his parched mouth, were displaced by cold. There was a kind of contentment in the warmth of an early sun, silvery slug trails on his trousers, in the fast spiders and beetles in his hair. It was there in frost, in blowing on his numb fingers, in the mist rising from the fields, from the lakes, from the streams. And it was there in silvery dew, where – to his mind – Lamb lived on. He didn't know what else to depend on.

Boyd came into Sile on the old roads he'd once walked to and from school. It was the middle of the day when he reached the roundabout, and the sun came down squarely; there were no shadows. He caught the profile of a raggedy fox in the distance, slinking towards the tree line beside the trunk road, low bellied. As he watched, its body flared and strobed with wild colours. Naturally, he thought of Red, on the pillar in their front room, and the purple moss; things he knew to be abstractions of Maureen, whose last act had been to send Lamb in the care of Red. To show him, to try and release him.

As the fox slipped away, the possibility lingered. Maybe it was Red, still patrolling. And just like that, as if he'd given himself permission, Boyd sat down where he was and put his hands into the cool shale, his legs straight out in front of him. After a few minutes there, he tore away the plastic bags he'd wrapped around his feet and pocketed some of the stones. Then he walked up the hill.

His first throw was useless – the stone pinged off a corrugated section of the landfill site's storage area. The second went higher, struck metal. The third curled towards the mound, out of sight.

'I fucking *knew* it was going to be you,' Leigh said, peering around the wall.

Boyd was limping. She came and brushed the chalk from his shoulder, his sleeve. They stared at each other. She'd shaved her head.

'Lice,' Leigh said. 'Where is she?'

'With Nan.'

'Where?'

'Safe.'

Leigh grinned. 'Obviously,' she said. 'How did you know I'd be here, anyway?'

He shrugged.

She took his hand and led him through.

Boyd ate four rounds of toast while they drank pineapple weed tea on the side-step of Leigh's van, which she'd clearly spent a good while cleaning. There were people in hi-vis overalls working the mound with earth-moving systems. Gaff still hadn't been back, Leigh explained. Seemed like true love, with this woman in Scarborough. To make a fast buck, Leigh had invited the local scrap and rag merchants on site to harvest the mound for a flat fee – most had already been up there a few days. When Boyd pointed out a squad of workers whose movements were more deliberate, precise, Leigh told him they were professional hard-drive hunters, using detecting gear and probes.

'I did think about taking after you,' Leigh added, 'and burning it all. But there'd be fuck-all cash in that, would there?'

Boyd shook his head.

'What else was there?' Leigh asked.

Boyd sipped his drink, turning the mug in his hands.

'Well?'

There was a lot for them to untangle, and he didn't know where to start.

'Does Gaff know you're doing this?' he asked. 'You've actually heard from him?'

Leigh pursed her lips. 'Only briefly. My first nights back here, I swore I heard him breathing through the doors. And I do keep dreaming about killing him, really doing it. But I can't hold a grudge.' She shoved him. 'Obviously.'

Boyd considered whether or not to mention Bright House, the letter, and the fact that he, Leigh and Lamb had apparently been protected from a distance by Joan's network. The grey-haired woman in the yellow anorak. In the end, he said nothing. He didn't want to settle for an apology, either – not yet. Leigh deserved more.

'Drink up, anyway,' Leigh said. 'There's something you need to see.'

They went down to the scruffy patch of land where Leigh had sown her mother's seeds. Leigh covered his eyes as they neared, her palms warm and dry. 'Ta-da!' she said, releasing him. A group of healthy seedlings stood proud in the soil, their stems and leaves a startling green. 'Not the worst start, is it?'

Boyd squatted in disbelief, a hand to the ground. It seemed impossible that anything could grow so well in such poisoned soil. He crawled to the seedlings and scented Lamb. Faint cucumber, turned earth, rust. She was part of him, now – they'd made a sacred promise. He touched a stem and sensed her roots.

ACKNOWLEDGEMENTS

It took a while to get here, but it was never a lonely road. Thanks to Oeil Jumratsilpa, Anne Charnock, Penny Reeve, Mark Griffiths, George Sandison and Anne Perry for their time and thoughts. Special thanks to James Smythe, Nina Allan and Chris Priest for all their support.

I'm massively grateful for the care and faith of everyone behind the scenes. Huge thanks to Dead Ink's Harriet Hirshman and Nathan Connolly, to editing dream team Gary Budden and Dan Coxon, and to Gus Brown, Tom Lloyd-Williams, Vanessa Kerr and my superstar agent Max Edwards at ACM UK.

Lastly, thanks to Luke Bird for the book's sublime cover art.

Love – always – to Suze, Albie and Felix.

About Dead Ink

Dead Ink is a publisher of bold new fiction based in Liverpool. We're an Arts Council England National Portfolio Organisation.

If you would like to keep up to date with what we're up to, check out our website and join our mailing list.

www.deadinkbooks.com | @deadinkbooks